BORDERLINES

The Literary Anthology of the University of Portsmouth

The School of Creative Arts, Film and Media

Volume II
2008

BORDERLINES
Volume II 2008

Staff
Faculty Advisor
Sam North

Editors
Poetry Editor
Freya Scott
Travel Editor
Aby Davis
Layout & MA Representative
Ryan Sirmons

A joint venture of:

The School of Creative Arts, Film and Media
The University of Portsmouth MA Creative Writing
The University of Portsmouth Creative Writing Society
The international writers journal – www.hackwriters.com

ISBN 978-1-4092-0494-7

All rights reserved. No part of this publication maybe reproduced, stored in a retrieval system, or transmitted, in any form or by any means, electronic, mechanical, photocopying, recording, or otherwise, without the prior permission of Borderlines, SCAFM, University of Portsmouth.
© 2008 University of Portsmouth
Wiltshire Building, Hampshire Terrace, Portsmouth PO1 2EG
First volume published 2007
Published by lulu.com

BORDERLINES

Table of contents

Short Stories & Poems

Andrew Williams As Good As Gold Ink	1
Calvin Hussey Eternal Darkness	6
Carolyn Hughes Sand Dollar	10
Liz Barlow Rolos In Bed	15
Tracey Leach Asleep Under a Purple-Spotted Duvet	16
Ria Floyd-Berry White Squares	18
Freya Scott Love Song	19
AR Marsh The Brown Fedora	21
Alison Habens The Magic of Marriage	23
Sam North Jennifer	26
Ryan Sirmons Dead Jim	35
Diana Bretherick Fragments	39
Emma Callan The Wasp	42
Linda Albert A Small Bird	43
Anona Evans The Wolf	44
Andrea Bowie The Bumbless Orange Bumble Bee	45
Beth Weaver Italian Girls & American Cokes	47
Dean Borok The Passion of Niño de Jesus	57
Lisa Timmerman Hidden	62
Linda Regan I Saw Nothing	65
Karen Clark The Virus	68
Liz Barlow Skeletons	70
Anita Sheard After the Night Train	71
Victor Manley A Drive in Winter	72
Rebecca Wass Tree	74

BORDERLINES

Chris Burden Little Red Bucket	75
Andrew Williams Club Pride	77
Calvin Hussey The Illusion Specialist	81

Travel

Caitlin McCallum Everything's Coming Up Crazy	82
Aby Davis Vikings On Buses	86
Rachel Kay Visit to a Karen Village	90
Tiffany Lee A Bite of the Apple	96
Brian Appleton	
Forty Days in a Heartland of Wilderness	98
Sounds of Siena at Dawn	100
John Edwards The Finnish Connection	101
Bryan Blake Marathon Preparation in Naples	106
Josephine Green The Long Way Home	112
Loree Westron Road to Reparation	119
Quentin Bates Astray in Iceland	127
Jane Anderson Bega Valley	133

More shorts & poems

Freya Scott Colour	139
Emma Callan Loss	150
Linda Albert A Fable	153
Tessa Foley An Apology to a Former Self	154
Tracey Leach Five Times to Market	156
Anita Sheard Death + Forgiveness	157
Nikesh Murali Girl from Ipanema	159
Freya Scott Watermelon for Breakfast	160
Victor Manley When We Were Younger	162
Dean Borok Ghostal Regions	167
Diana Bretherick The Muse of Camden	176
Andrew Williams Sunday at the Pictures	179

BORDERLINES

Elke Morice-Atkinson Electricity	182
Louise Matthewson Monsters of the Sky	186
Andrea Bowie Lose Your Words in a High Wind	188
Catherine Coles Headache	190
Ria Floyd-Berry Ode To A Piece of Cake	191
Russell Thomas Weekend	193
Olivia James Intelligence Can Be So Lacking	195
Steven Stemp The Love Taker	197
A R Marsh Mayme	202
Ina Albert The Letter In Behalf of Myself	205
Anita Sheard Unimaginable Choice	208
Liz Barlow Dear John (Letters to the Dead)	209

Excerpt from a novel

Ali Shaw Chapter One, Extract From a Life	210

Poems

Callam Graham The Hobgoblin	219
Jade Juilien Tulips	220

Contributors 222

BORDERLINES

Preface

The process of collecting, selecting, editing, and organizing over 70 short stories, poems and travel pieces was always going to be difficult and time-consuming. Add to that M.A. projects, dissertations and numerous part-time jobs, and the task seemed nearly impossible. However, for all the hard work, it was also an enjoyable process thanks to our support for one another and the GSOHs that made us bearable.

It was the first round of selection on a very wet day in March that we realised what a monumental task we had set ourselves. Myself, Aby, Victor, Ryan and Sam all were sitting drenched in Ryan's living room in Old Portsmouth reading and arguing over the merits of various stacks of fiction and poetry and it was a real taste of how difficult it is to winnow material and fight the good fight for text you like. Occasionally we would find a diamond that sprang from the pages and pounce on it. This is publishing democracy and it's tough, but it did show us that there really is a lot of talent out there and for that we thank you all for submitting.

So after gallons of coffee, litres of midnight oil, hours of arguments, friends disappointed and relatives forgotten, we present our final collection.

Unfortunately we could not include everything we wanted, for the very reason that the anthology would be twice the size it is now had we done so. But we thank everyone that contributed, and furthermore we hope you enjoy this new creative work that you hold in your hands.

My thanks go to the dedication of my co-editors Ryan Sirmons, Aby Davis. Ryan pulled many hours in a long cold Wiltshire room editing this. Thanks also to Sam North for setting up the project and to Kit Thomas who pulled it all together in the end.

Freya Scott
Co-editor May 2008

BORDERLINES
Andrew Williams
AS GOOD AS GOLD INK

'It's like this,' said Posh John. 'My Mother's old cleaner, Mrs Dalton, is moving into sheltered accommodation this week, she's eighty-nine God bless her, and I've taken it upon myself to ensure that she sells enough of her old knick-knacks to buy a decent television. I can't find Eddy Wright so I thought you could do the honours.'

Skinny Joey nodded, trying to look as if doing geezers like Posh John a favour happened every day.

Posh John gave Joey the address and told him: 'Go round there now, before Oxfam take the lot away for nothing. I'll see you in the pub later and let me know how you get on.' So Skinny Joey arranges a budget of five pounds from the thirty he is carrying, which encapsulates his entire fortune, and reckons he may spend only half of it if he is careful.

Mrs Dalton's house was a nicely appointed semi-detached; the door was answered by a tall middle-aged woman, dressed for a nightclub.

'Er, Mrs Dalton?'

'Don't be daft,' she said. 'You come to buy her stuff?'

Joey said, 'Yes, I...'

'Come on then,' she said, turning and walking through the hall into the front room. Pointing to a row of boxes lining the far wall she said, 'There you are - forty quid the lot.'

Joey spluttered so the woman said, 'Alright, alright, thirty-five then. Don't do your nut.'

'But I didn't come to take the lot,' said Joey. 'John just asked me to have a look and...'

'There's only a few boxes. Just bung them on your van and give us thirty.'

Joey looked at his feet and said, 'I don't have wheels. I just...'

'Flaming norah,' said the woman. 'What sort of businessman are you? I didn't think my son knew prats like you.'

Joey gaped at her. 'You're John's mum?'

She looked skywards. 'Give me strength.'

A fragile voice called out from the kitchen, echoing in its emptiness. 'Marge, you there?'

'Hold on, Ethel,' said John's mum. She turned to Joey. 'See if there's

BORDERLINES

anything you want, and don't bleeding pocket anything.'

Posh John's mum's accent, heavy make-up and surfeit of cheap jewellery provided a sharp contrast to her son's urbanity. Even so, he had to make himself look good and while she was away he prepared a lie. When she came back he said:

'There's been a bit of a misunderstanding here. You see I deal with antiques, and when John said there may be some items of interest to me...'

John's mum suddenly became more personable: 'Oh I see,' she said. 'Well, Ethel has been here a long time.' She went to one of the boxes and pulled out a chunky glass vase with a deeply engraved floral pattern. 'This is probably old. What do you think?'

Joey held the thing gingerly. 'This is probably from the seventies. It's kitsch, really.'

'Is that any good?'

'Well, the seventies wasn't really a good period for kitsch.'

'She's lived here for fifty years. There must be something that's older than that.'

'I'll have a look,' said Joey kneeling at a box.

'They lived in America before they came here, you know.'

Joey looked up. 'She's not American is she?'

'No. Her and Mr Dalton went there after the war. They lived in Hollywood; used to see the film stars walking about.'

'That's interesting.'

'Never know, you could find Marilyn Munroe's knickers in there.'

Joey looked up at her. She smiled and winked. Joey felt his cheeks colour so he turned back to the boxes.

'I've got the kettle on. Fancy one?'

'Oh, no thanks,' he replied.

'I mean tea,' she said.

'I...yes...no. Thank you.'

John's mum laughed and left the room.

Joey wiped his forehead with his sleeve and continued rummaging through the boxes. Now he didn't have to spend anything he could concentrate on making an impression on John's mum without her getting the wrong idea.

Looking around the room he could see the lingering signs of Mrs Dalton's long occupation. Oblongs of pristine wallpaper showed where pictures had hung for decades. There was a similar pattern on the carpet where the furniture had rested. The room exuded an atmosphere of loss.

BORDERLINES

A box of books piqued his interest and a brief rummage through romantic novels and spy thrillers turned up an autograph book. It was slightly larger than a cheque book and had 'Autographs' in gold lettering on its blue faux leather cover. A cursory look told him it was fairly old; the inscriptions were all in fountain pen. The autographs were hard to read but he made out Bing Crosby and Bob Hope on one page. On another, Barbara Stanwyck and Fred McMurray, and he soon realised that it contained the names of almost every major Hollywood star of the forties and fifties.

'See anything you like?'

The intrusion startled him and he dropped the book.

'Well, do you?' she said, hands on hips.

Joey looked down, his heart racing. The autograph book had landed closed on top of the box. 'I'd like to buy the books. They're all in good condition for their age...'

'Alright, love. That's thirty quid then.'

Joey's jaw dropped. 'Thirty? But I only want the one box.'

The woman's posture instantly changed to one of mannish aggression. She jutted out her chin and snarled, 'What sort of bloke are you? This is an old lady we're talking about here.'

So Joey paid thirty pounds for a box of old books which he abandoned at the corner of the road, minus one book of autographs.

A trip to the internet café told him that the autographs in his new purchase were the real thing and worth plenty. Marilyn Monroe's alone was going for three-hundred pounds. Admittedly it was a signed photo and buyers paid a premium for items, but the book could be considered an item in itself; it had to be worth thousands. His excitement was feverish and a celebration drink was in order, which placed him in a dilemma.

He was penniless and he had to be cagey about selling the book. If he sold it immediately on the manor Posh John would get wind of what had happened. Then, he would either be angry about poor old Mrs Dalton being taken for a ride or want a cut from the sale. Or worse, he'd tell his mum and she'd come after him. Joey reasoned that, on balance, the latter was the more probable outcome, forcing him to decide on the long route of searching out an autograph dealer in the West End.

Then Joey saw Tommy Graham outside the bookies. This man was renowned for his staunchness of character; he was a legend and his word was considered sacrosanct. Joey approached him and Tommy said, 'Yes son. What can I do you for?'

BORDERLINES

Joey hesitated for a second.

'Come on,' said Tommy. 'What is it?'

'I've got something.'

'Well come here and let's have a look.'

They went inside the bookies and stood leaning on the mantel in a corner, Tommy's broad back shielding them from unwanted attention.

Tommy looked at the autograph book, puzzled momentarily, and then his eyes flickered recognition. He began to scrutinize the pages, rubbing them between his fingers.

'Where did you get this?' he asked.

'I bought it from an old woman,' Joey answered.

'I'm not prying, Skinny. Like, was she a dealer?'

'No.'

'Were you finessed into buying this?'

'No way; she wanted me to take a load of boxes from her house and it was buried in one of them.'

Tommy slipped the book into his pocket. 'Come on then.'

They went to a shop. Tommy asked the woman at the counter for Mick and she went through to the back. Then she came back, followed by a big, bespectacled man with thinning hair slicked back. He nodded and they went through.

Mick looked through the book as if he was handling Green Shield Stamps.

'Very nice,' he said. 'What are you looking for?'

Tommy looked round at Joey who said, 'Two grand?'

'Two grand,' said Tommy.

'What?' said Mick. Tommy showed a poker face; Mick cleared his throat. 'I'll have talk to someone.'

Mick went upstairs and Tommy said, 'You sure it's worth that, Skinny?'

Joey nodded. 'Probably more.'

Mick soon came back. 'Alright, gents, I can offer you a grand take it or leave it.'

Tommy turned and nodded to Joey, who looked horrified.

'What's up?' asked Tommy.

Joey knew that by offering them a thousand for the book, Mick had just heard it was worth at least ten. He also knew that if he now told Tommy that the book wasn't compromised in some way he wouldn't believe him, because he'd played it that way up to now. 'It's okay,' he said.

BORDERLINES

'Alright,' said Mick. 'I'll take it to my pal's this evening. If he gives me the nod you can pick up the dough in the morning.'

Tommy said. 'Let us have a couple of hundred up front so I can take my commission.'

Mick looked pained. 'Tommy, if this book's snide...what can I say?'

Tommy personally guaranteed the loan so Mick coughed up. Tommy split the £200 with Joey and went to the pub. Skinny Joey savoured his drink as Tommy held court in over in his corner.

When Posh John came in Joey stood him a drink, asking, 'You want a chaser with that?'

'What did you do, find her life savings?'

Joey laughed. 'I couldn't, could I? Your mum was there.'

'Of course,' said John. 'She'd have beaten you to it.' He scanned the crowd as if looking for someone particular.

'It's funny that Mrs Dalton was your mum's cleaner,' said Joey.

Posh John turned to him: 'Is it?' he said.

'Don't get me wrong,' said Joey. 'I mean where she lived, it's quite posh for a cleaner.'

'Oh,' said John. 'I see what you mean. Well, when Mr D. got five years she was on her uppers. Mum helped her out.'

'Her old man was a villain? I didn't know that.'

'He was an accountant; got done for fraud. It was his first offence but he got so long because of the amounts involved. I was a kid when it happened.'

'That must've been hard for him. Jail,' said Joey.

'Nooo,' said John shaking his head. 'They loved him in there. He was the best forger going; copied the Governor's signature perfectly first time he saw it. They were queuing up for him.'

'Forger,' said Joey.

'Yeah,' said John. 'Look, I've go to push off. Thanks for the drink.'

Joey watched John thread his way across the pub and saw him brush past Tommy Graham. The big man turned and looked at Joey as if he'd felt his eyes. He raised his glass and winked.

BORDERLINES

Calvin Hussey
ETERNAL DARKNESS

Bread. Bread, milk. Bread, milk, cheese, er…Fucking Snickers! Err…Bread, milk, cheese, Snickers, eggs, newspaper… …rizlas… …er…lobster. Wait, what the fuck? Where'd lobster come from? Now I've forgotten everything, knew I should've made a list. Ever had one of those days where everything starts bad and then gets worse? Ever had one of those days where everything skips the "bad" and starts directly from the "worse"? This was one of those days.

I was dragged kicking and screaming into consciousness at 7.30 a.m., hung over, by the piercing, monotonic chime of the alarm clock I had no recollection of setting for such a ridiculous hour. After hauling myself from bed I paused, momentarily, to examine my reflection in the bathroom mirror. Short, black hair matted from the night before. Brown eyes: bloodshot. Face: pallid and weary. The usual morning routine commenced; had a shower, a shit, a shave, went to the kitchen to check the food situation. Nothing.

Yawning, I entered the living room, falling into a couch next to the three-piece containing the comatose shell of my roommate Stu.

"Stu," I called in a shrill voice, slapping him once round the face. "Stuey!"

"Fckuff," he muttered back, turning, burying himself deeper within the sofa cushions.

"Heavy night last night?" I asked, amused by his dishevelled appearance. "Don't suppose you got any fags left?"

"Nnngh." Stu muttered, his face still buried deep within the sofa. He pointed towards his back pocket, tapping it. I reached into it pulling out a baggy containing a diminutive amount of cannabis.

"Got no Rizlas though," he yawned, turning to face me.

"S'alright," I sighed, "Got to go to Tesco anyway. No food."

"Get us a Snickers while you're there," he replied, tossing me fifty pence.

As I got up to leave, Bartisé, our French housemate, stormed past me, furiously waving a coffee stained document above his head.

"Stuart!" he screamed, "Vous aves le cerveau d'un sandwich au fromage."

"Speak English," Stu replied.

BORDERLINES

"Si vous étiez deux fois plus intelligent, vous seriez encore stupide!" He stormed off, slamming the door behind him.

"Well, voulelez-vous un fuck the fuck off Frenchy," Stu screamed back in frustration.

We didn't much like Bartisé. After just a month of moving in he'd labelled himself as a yuppie, killjoy, snob. Not part of the team. Anyway, deciding to escape any further potential conflict I left for the shop, which brings me to where I started...

Returning from Tesco's, having substituted what I was supposed to buy with a bunch of random crap, I discover that I've lost my bus pass. Now I've got to leave early and walk to the university. So much for having the morning off.

Walking through the front door, I can see Stu dancing foolishly around the living room to Killa Kela, whilst playing Gamecube with a wireless controller.

"Haven't you got anything more productive to do?"

He shrugs, sits down. "Got my Snickers?"

"Yeah, lost my bus pass though."

"Well that's a bastard," he raises an eyebrow, "Rizla's?"

"Fuck!" I scream in a vexed frustration, and then sigh, "I can't anyway, I've got uni." I throw him the Snickers. "Where's Bartisé?"

"Cheers. Dunno, fucked off."

"Good."

"You going to that party in town tonight?"

"After last night? You've gotta be kiddin'. Whose is it anyway?"

"Some art fag, I dunno. You've got to come anyway, I've already sorted your party prescription."

Stu flicks me a baggy. I examine its content carefully. Two pills. Blue. Covered with minute speckles. Three quid each. 'Dolphins' apparently.

"Well, what d'ya say?" He asks.

I pause for a second, considering the contents of the bag once. After a second I look back at Stu. Smile casually. "Party time."

I arrive at campus approximately fifteen minutes late. A note left on the studio door reveals that the afternoon lecture has been cancelled. I sigh at the wasted time, stroll around examining the breasts of passing females, and get nagged by some lecturer about some deadline I don't know about. I'm glad when the flaky old cock finally gets out of my face. I walk around

BORDERLINES

some more, bum a cigarette off some repulsive girl that I know wants me, grab a coke from the cafeteria and get my arse home in time for The Simpsons.

After The Simpsons I huddle in the sofa and power-nap off the remainder of my hangover until it's time to party.

When I get to the party everybody is already wasted. Stu is walking around spouting some nonsense about cannabis being the cure to global warming. One particularly wasted moron is throwing up in a fish tank occupied by fish. The pills I've swallowed have started to take effect. I feel different, altered, and synthetically happy. I walk around in a daze; laughing at conversations I'm not listening to, drinking out of bottles I didn't open, professing my love to people I don't know, or don't like. I rub my thighs in anticipation…

…I look at my watch. How long have I been here? Where's Stu? Who cares? My throat's dry and my jaw tightens manically. My vision is blurred and I'm starting to feel dizzy. I stumble between sweaty torsos in search of a bathroom. Behind me I can hear Stu shouting, incoherently, about the relationship between Ronald McDonald and Hitler. As I peer over my shoulder to spot Stu I feel something hard slam against my chest, liquid splashing at my feet. In front of me stands a beer-drenched, muscle bound, drunken brute. He grabs my throat.

"Watch what you're fucking doing!" The blood rushes to my head.

"Man, I'm just, man, I'm just, man," I almost swallow my tongue.

"What the fuck you say to me?"

"No man, I'm just…Man I didn't say anything, just chill out, mate," I begin to plead.

"I'm not your mate, you fucking waster!" he screams back.

The following minutes fly by, whilst almost completely grinding to a halt. Five fingers make a fist. The fist, ever approaching, closer and closer, gaining force. I blink. Collision. Blood erupts from my nose. I fall to the ground. Everything fades into darkness.

I open my eyes and am greeted by an intense throbbing that spreads across my face. I pull myself up and put my hand to my nose. Broken. The party is far different from the last time I was conscious. Bodies lie across sofas and floors; barely alive, yet far from dead. Stu is nowhere to be seen. I navigate around the bodies and head towards the front door. I take a

BORDERLINES

moment to examine my appearance in a vanity mirror hanging besides the door. Dry blood surrounds my mouth. My lips quiver from whatever poisons the ecstasy was cut with. As I stare at my reflection I think back to the studious kid at the back of the class. I think of the kid who joined the choir, book club, debate team, and the kid who finished top of his class. As I examine my reflection in the mirror I think, "Who are you?"

Outside the rain falls with an icy harshness. It is the dark hour of the morning. Shadows, created by the headlights of passing cars, occasionally form across my face.

Before I left the house I had scrounged what I could for the long, lonely walk home; a half empty bottle of cola, some fruit Chew-its and a couple Xanax tablets that I'd swiped from the medicine cabinet. I neck the Xanax with a swig from the cola bottle and discard the rest. I no longer recognise my reflection and feel like the ethereal reverberation of a total stranger. I have no soul.

The Xanax take effect, supplying a haze of clarity. I can feel individual raindrops as they fall and drench my skin. I no longer recognise my surroundings, yet feel that I am reaching my final destination. I am oblivious to time; however, in the sky, birds begin to sing their morning tune. My eyelids begin to feel heavy and I start to take little naps as I'm walking…

Waking, I fumble for a sticky, melted chew-it. Eyes closed – opened. I notice that I've adverted into the middle of the road and that I'm beginning to choke on the Chew-it. I head off to the left. Eyes closed – opened. A blinding light draws ever closer. Closed – opened. The trucks headlights reflect in the whites of my eyes, its brakes screaming, struggling to stop. Eyes closed.

Eternal Darkness.

BORDERLINES

Carolyn Hughes
SAND DOLLAR

Alex was bored. He was perching listlessly on a log in the middle of the wide sandy shoreline, gazing idly out at the dramatic Pacific breakers crashing on to the rocks, and at the mist rolling in towards the shore. He half-heartedly watched the gulls paddling in the wet sand, looking for worms, and the cormorants diving for fish from the rocky island some way out to sea. Apart from the birds, the beach was deserted—no surfers, no walkers, no dogs. Here he was, alone at the far-west frontier of the American continent. As far as Alex was concerned he was at the end of the world.

His parents had, as usual, chosen the remote, west coast of Vancouver Island for their long winter vacation. The flight from London, the ferry crossing and the long drive from Nanaimo had taken a mind-numbingly tedious two days. Right now his parents were pursuing their usual vacation objectives—to read, to rest and to imbibe. They aimed for total relaxation and zero hassle. They would provide a meal of some sort three times a day, but otherwise their son was expected to fend for himself and find his own amusement. It didn't occur to them that this might be difficult for a boy whose principal enthusiasms were playing his guitar and gaming on his computer.

Bored with the view and the birds, Alex plugged his headphones into his ears and the Arctic Monkeys' strident music filled his head. He longed for his own guitar—without it there was nothing to do here. But of course his parents hadn't heard when he asked if he could bring it.

He became absorbed in the music, his eyes closed, and took no account of anything outside his head. But after a while he became aware of a peripheral sound insinuating its way into his brain. He opened his eyes and looked around. A flock of gulls had taken to the air—were they screeching? He wasn't sure. His eyes followed the flock as it headed out to sea, and then, as he looked, he thought he saw something—someone?—in the waves, rising up from the falling breakers, and then disappearing as the next wave rose. Alex ripped off his headphones, leapt up and ran down to the water's edge, scouring the turbulent surf for a sign of life. He stood there for several minutes, his trainers getting repeatedly soaked from the waves lapping on to the beach, straining his eyes to see what he

BORDERLINES

thought was there. But it seemed there was nothing. Disappointed at being deprived of some—any—excitement, Alex turned and began to trudge back to the cabin.

Then, just as he reached the scrubby vegetation that marked the boundary between the cabins and the beach, he heard the sound again, and he turned back to face the sea. The seagulls had now all gone from the sand, their feeding over, and there were no cormorants out to sea. The mist was low, and Alex struggled to find the shape that he thought had appeared again in the waves, and did indeed seem to come towards him with the tumbling breakers. But when the waves broke on the beach, there was no shape or figure—whatever it was had disappeared into the mist.

Baffled, Alex went again to sit on his log to watch and wait. He plugged in the headphones and listened to the music again, staring intently at the rollers, mesmerised by the music in his ears and by the mystery of the ocean.

A tap on Alex's shoulder startled him. Looking round, he saw a girl standing just behind him, brown-skinned, dark-haired, round-faced, with black, slightly slanting eyes. Water dripped from her long straight hair and from the fringes of her clothes. Alex was astonished and yet not surprised to see her there. They regarded each other for a short while and then she spoke, in a language he thought he didn't know, but which he somehow understood.

'Boy,' she said, 'You alone?'

He nodded. 'Yeah,' he said. 'Just me. Me, the sand, and the sea.'

'Why you just sit here, Boy?' she said.

'Nothing to do,' he replied.

'What you want to do, Boy?' she asked.

'Play my guitar,' he said, gloomily. 'Do stuff on my computer.'

'Guitar? Computer?' she said. 'What are they?' This was surprising.

'Guitar—you know—play music? Rock? Arctic Monkeys?'

The girl shook her head. 'This is "rock",' she said, gesturing at the black, barnacle-encrusted outcrops that fringed the shore and studded the waves.

Alex wondered where this girl had been living, that she hadn't heard of the Arctic Monkeys.

'And "computer"?' she said.

'You know,' he said, 'The Internet, e-mail.' She shook her head again. 'Tomb Raider'? he tried. 'Age of Empires?' She shrugged, uncomprehending.

BORDERLINES

Alex lost heart in the conversation, thinking she was pretty enough but obviously dumb, and began to replace the headphones in his ears. But the girl knelt in front of him, and took his hands in hers before the headphones could make it to his head. He felt a peculiar sort of warmth spreading from her cool, wet hands and did not resist.

'I do not understand your things, Boy,' she said. 'But I do know mine. I can show you. Here is not "just sand and sea"!'

Alex looked into the girl's dark eyes, and found himself drawn in. 'OK,' he said, smiling, 'show me', perhaps hoping for some exciting adolescent discovery.

'Come,' she said, and gestured him to follow her.

She took his hand and they walked together along the beach, smiling at each other but not speaking. Shortly she stopped and, bending down, picked up one end of a long tapering tube, almost translucent and perhaps three metres long, with a large bulbous float at the other end.

'Kelp,' she said and, raising it high in the air, she whirled it around and around her head like a lasso, and then lashed it down on the smooth, wet sand with a crack like a whip. She skipped and danced with her seaweed whip and Alex didn't know whether to find her performance childlike or sexy. But then she offered the kelp to Alex, who also whirled and whipped with it, and was curious at the plant's strength and suppleness.

While he played, the girl ran on to a small tidal pool and, wading in to the rocky pond, began gently to turn stones and to delve into the sand. Then shortly she stood up and called to Alex.

'Boy! Come and see!' Clinging to the walls of the pool was a profusion of anemones, brilliant green, red and pink, their graceful tentacles waving in the gentle ripple of the pool.

'Touch!' the girl said, and Alex gently let a single finger graze the delicate tentacles of a huge bright green anemone. The sensation made him quickly remove his finger—it was somehow sticky and tingly. The girl laughed.

'Anemone wants to eat you!' she said.

'Eat me! You mean it's an animal?' said Alex. She nodded and Alex laughed too, pleased that this hitherto solemn girl had some sense of humour.

Then both of them spotted an orange-coloured five-rayed starfish nestling in the sand. The girl gestured Alex to touch again—and he let his fingers rub against the rough knobbly surface. He was amazed at the

BORDERLINES

colour and elegance of these creatures—no-one had ever shown him such miracles before!

But now the girl was scrabbling about in the sand around the edges of the rock pool—she appeared to be searching for something, digging in the wet sand with her fingers, discarding bits of shell and stone as she went. And then she found what she was looking for and held it up in triumph.

'Sand dollar!' she said, smiling happily, and Alex went to look. She placed a roundish shell-like object into the palm of his hand.

'Sand dollar,' she said again. It looked like a piece of exquisite native art—pale grey with a five-petal flower etched in dots into its surface—and yet its eccentric and imperfect roundness somehow proved it was not man-made.

'Was animal,' she said.

'Really?' said Alex, turning it over in his hand, finding that hard to believe.

She nodded. 'Yes, spiny animal.'

Then she took his hand and gently closed his fingers over the improbable skeleton. 'Keep it,' she said. 'To remember.' And Alex nodded, putting the sand dollar into the deep front pocket of his baggy jeans.

Entranced by all these discoveries, Alex ran on ahead to the next tidal pool, while the girl danced on the wet sand, whirling and pirouetting at the very edge of the waves. He made his own, amazing, discovery—a magical, if a little unprepossessing, purple starfish with, he counted, twenty arms. He touched it lightly—it was soft rather than rough—and he turned to show the girl. At that very moment a huge breaker crashed on to the shore and the girl was no longer dancing on the sand.

For a few moments Alex panicked, believing her drowned, and ran to the water's edge, his eyes yet again searching the pounding waves. In his fear, he began to cry, taking no account of the water lapping round his feet. But soon he found he was calm again, as if he knew that somehow the girl could not drown.

He turned back to the rock pool and the twenty-armed starfish. He touched it again gently, stroking its soft flesh and wondered why he had never seen one before. It seemed to him that he had been living in a cocoon of ignorance, when there were so many weird and exquisite things in the world that he knew nothing about. At length, he stood up and looked out at the waves again. He felt in his pocket for the sand dollar, and smiled. The girl was safe, he knew that—she had gone back home.

Back at the cabin, his parents were at the window with their binoculars trained out to sea. 'Did you see the seals,' they asked, 'breaking the waves?'

'No.' Alex shook his head. 'But I met a girl,' he said.

'Really, Alex?' said his mother. 'We've been watching the seals for nearly an hour. We saw you get up from your log and walk along the beach, looking into the rock pools. But you were quite alone.'

Alex shrugged and took out the sand dollar. He held it out to show them.

'But she gave me this,' he said.

Liz Barlow
ROLOS IN BED

I don't see my grandmother much.
She never liked my tongue –
complained that
I was spoiled
(but fed me those
Rolos in bed).

This time, she lay asleep
in cold white cloths
with a clipboard
by her feet.

The woman next to her
had days to go
and a cave of skin
for an armpit.

Her swollen feet hung
from the bed
like a baby's.

The nurses did everything
to make her feel comfortable.
But I wasn't comfortable.

Her distant relatives
talked amongst themselves.
They brought teddies,
plastic flowers,
patted her head.
She fought wars for them.

My grandmother wakes.
I hold my rotten tongue.

Tracey Leach
ASLEEP UNDER A PURPLE-SPOTTED DUVET

That sound seems so desperate,
Of grasping
And reaching,
Of groping
And needing,
Of air moving quickly
And jumping beside me.

That sound could be hopeful,
Of living
And seeing,
Of wanting
And being,
Of waves crashing heavily
But you safely watching.

That sound is surrounding -
Before me,
Beside me,
Without me,
Within me,
Your ribcage a carcass
On a treasure filled island.

That sound can be frightening -
Of time passing,
Skin growing,
Bones breaking,
Dreams cracking,
Of boats to the sunset
Sunk by cancerous cells.

BORDERLINES

That sound is not stopping,
Not changing
And deepening,
Not heightening
Or lightening,
Like the bee passing easily
Each year to each flower.

That sound is not just yours,
It's not mine
And not theirs,
It everyone's,
Yet no one's;
It's the sound of you breathing
Until the world makes you end.

Ria Floyd-Berry
WHITE SQUARES

White squares and balloons in bed
All jumbled up together and printed in your head,
Picked at scabs and bits of fluff
Sellotaped along the walls
To the inside of your mind.

Black dots and cotton buds
Sprayed recklessly over the lawn,
Tiny little insects lie
And crawl about behind your eye;

A badly fitted jigsaw puzzle
That probably cost about a tenner
With layers of a second meaning
And ideas of a different world
Keep presence in your thoughts.

Fairies that can fly about
Red pens that can ink them out,
Bumble-bees with wings of silk
Honey that is made of milk
All these interrupt your day
And cause a catastrophic sum,
Patchwork mirrors and prison walls
And beauty can arrange them all.

Freya Scott
LOVE SONG

He pulled away her face,
Plaster white, to hang on a wall
And worship.
He took from her hands
The rubber gloves that encased her fingers,
Tiny, thin pockets of air
That perfectly remembered the shape of her bones.
He undressed her, thread by thread,
And wound them into a ball,
A satin green ball that he turned in the light;
The shade of her eyes, he said.

She waited.
Long days she stood at the open window
And watched him build, ever greater,
His monument to love and beauty.

"It is not finished," he said,
The day he borrowed her shadow
To hang in dark folds
Across the archways of his temple.

"It is not quite ready," the day after that,
As he tugged out her hair
For a white-blonde cloud.

"It is nearly done," he said,
When she had next to nothing left.
She held her laughter in her fist,
No smile to expel it with
(He was exacting in his tastes;
He left what did not fit).

BORDERLINES

But one day, finally,
It was complete.

He stood and admired,
From every possible angle,
The perfect shape of love.

He turned to her, his muse,
But he was met with silence;
The window was empty.

He stood with his tower of beauty,
That could not touch or love.
Could not be the very thing
He wanted a replica of.

Her beauty was in fault,
At such length he realised.

Outside he heard her laughter
Drift across the green, open sky.

BORDERLINES

A R Marsh
THE BROWN FEDORA

Every Monday morning for eighteen years Randall Parker took the weekend receipts from the State Theatre and deposited them in the First Fidelity bank. Every Monday morning for eighteen years he dreamed about sandy beaches, exotic Far Eastern cities, the lure of Paris and the hills of Provence. Every Monday morning for eighteen years he sat in the parking lot of First Fidelity waiting for the bank to open. Across the street was the Broad National Bank.

Randall Parker was 64 years old, single and had been a bookkeeper for the town's only theatre for eighteen years. He lived in the same insignificant little house where he grew up. He never married, never traveled. Once a year he went to New York City and visited the Museum of Natural History. He always meant to stay the whole week and visit more museums but the noise, the crowds, the chaotic atmosphere of the big city frightened him and he routinely cut short his visit after two days.

Randall had no friends, no family, no outside interests except the movies. He saw every movie ever shown at the State Theatre for the past eighteen years. He knew them all. Every star, every director, every producer. He knew which were nominated for Academy awards, who won, who lost, and when.

He ate most of his meals at the Olympic Diner and ate the special every night except Friday. Friday's special was always some kind of fried fish. He hated fish. On Fridays he had meatloaf and read travel magazines while he ate.

He thought about this Monday morning for a long time. He had carefully examined the comings and goings for weeks and timed the procedure time and again. The Broad National opened its door exactly fourteen minutes after the doors to his own bank, First Fidelity, opened. That gave him time to make his deposit, return to his car, leave the receipt, pick up his simple disguise, walk across the street and rob the Broad National. He rehearsed it over and over - sure he had the perfect alibi. He was across the street making a deposit. He pictured the blue waters of the Mediterranean and smelled the vineyards of Italy.

Randall made his deposit, walked quickly to his car, took out a pair of sunglasses and his father's old brown fedora. He strode across the street

BORDERLINES

and as he approached the Broad National the doors burst open and a hooded man raced down the short flight of stairs and crashed into him. Cash flew; a gun fell and a man, stunned by his encounter with Randall, slipped to the ground unconscious.

The paper headlined, "Local Man Thwarts Bank Robbery."

Randall still makes his deposit every Monday. He's a bit of a celebrity now and every one in town knows about the man in the brown fedora who caught the bank robber. The Broad National, ever grateful, rewarded him with a trip to New York City.

BORDERLINES

Alison Habens
THE MAGIC OF MARRIAGE

"Not tonight, love," said Nick. "There's a match on TV." The problem was, 'not tonight' had turned into 'not this week', then 'not this month' and would soon be 'not this year'!

Cindy was starting to despair of ever having a normal married life again. She'd tried everything she could think of to rouse her husband's interest. She'd tempted him with steak and red wine; oysters and champagne on his birthday; massaging, lap dancing, flirting with other men in front of him; everything she could think of to inspire a manly response. As she lay in bed and listened to him snoring, she thought there must be a healthier way to restore his libido.

"Fancy taking the dog for a walk?" she asked him, after work one day. Maybe a run on the common would bring back Nick's natural bounce.

"I'm worn out," he said, collapsing on the sofa. "Can't one of the kids do it?"

At the weekend, she suggested they go kite flying on the hill, hoping that the wind might blow their cobwebs off. They used to do it years ago, and she hadn't forgotten the thrill of his arms around her as they struggled together against the pull of a stiff breeze.

"I've got to wash the car," Nick replied. "The only parking space left yesterday was under a tree, and it's covered in…"

But Cindy had left the room. Crashing around in the kitchen, she decided to leave him in peace for a while. Their relationship was fine as it was. He worked hard, loved the kids, never raised a hand to her in anger. That was more than some women had.

So Cindy tried not to feel there was something missing; but she looked at the other mums on the school run and wondered if they'd had 'it' last night; and she looked at everybody in the supermarket and wondered if you could tell, from what was in their trolleys, whether they were sexually satisfied?

Barely registering what she was doing, Cindy bought a set of frilly underwear, trimmed with pink lace and pearls, and took it home in a carrier bag along with the bread and milk.

She put it on, after the kids had gone to bed on Saturday night. Downstairs, the frustrated housewife paused, shivering in the hallway

BORDERLINES

outside the living-room door. Nick was watching a James Bond movie; blasts of music and gunfire came from the room. Cindy tiptoed inside.

Sitting on the sofa, Nick was entranced with the television; he didn't notice his wife come in. On TV one of Bond's babes had just entered; a tall, blonde model in a tight black swimsuit.

Cindy looked down at her own body, and fled before Nick could look up and compare the two. She stuffed the new underwear at the back of a drawer, climbed into bed and cried.

She couldn't help blurting out the problem to her friend Cathy, as they stood outside the school gates on Monday, waiting for the bell to ring.

"Nick's gone off me," she whispered. "I don't know what to do."

Cathy smiled mysteriously. "I may have just the thing," she replied.

Next morning, Cathy pressed a magazine article into Cindy's hand.

"Magic spells," she said, "potions for your marriage problems."

There it was: how to restore your husband's sex drive. Normally, Cindy would have laughed, but she was desperate enough now to give it a try.

"It says I need to collect his toenail clippings."

"Sounds simple enough," Cathy replied.

But it was harder than it sounded. Nick always cut his in the bath, and let the water drain the horny half-moons away. Cindy had to get them first. She checked the plughole every time he bathed and found nothing but hair. That was for a spell against baldness and her husband didn't have a problem with that.

Cindy was dying for a toenail as well as a screw, now. Everything else was in place; the wax candles, the photograph of him, the magic words. She was just waiting for the vital ingredient.

On Sunday afternoon, Cindy couldn't hold on any longer. The children were playing football in the park. Nick had spent the morning fixing a dripping tap in the downstairs bathroom and was now relaxing on the sofa with a newspaper.

His wife appeared with a bowl of warm water, a sponge and some scissors.

"Darling," she said, laying the equipment out in front of him, "I'm going to give you a pedicure."

"Oh," Nick shrugged behind the sports page, "okay then."

Cindy unlaced his shoes, and peeled off his socks. As she suspected, he hadn't cut his toenails for some time. There would easily be enough to make the spell work.

She started to wash his feet, trickling the soapy water between his

BORDERLINES

toes, scrubbing the hard heels, stroking his insteps with her rounded sponge.

At first Nick giggled, but when it stopped tickling he sighed.

"That feels nice."

She soaked his feet in the bowl of deep water, carefully trimming off hoary yellow claws to reveal soft pink skin underneath. Cindy made a neat pile of ten toenail clippings, but she no longer needed them for witchcraft.

While Songs of Praise gasped silently from the TV, one thing led to another on Nick and Cindy's sofa that Sunday afternoon. They were sitting at the altar of marriage, till the kids came home for tea.

BORDERLINES

Sam North
JENNIFER

Jennifer was particular from the word go. In fact, Jennifer wouldn't use the word 'go'; go would be too short for her. She hated using short words when long words would do. She liked long explanations as to why she was always late. Lengthy expositions on why her problems were a lot greater than yours ever could be and even longer pauses between words as she 'considered', from her extensive lexicon, the exact appropriate word that would describe her suffering; and she did so agonise over her suffering.

Jennifer had dating difficulties. Anyone who had taken the risk of dating her would regret it from the very first time they ever went to Bean Around the Corner or any other coffee shop that wasn't Starbucks. (She, of course, would not frequent Starbucks because they oppressed coffee pickers somewhere – she was never specific about where.)

Her coffee had to be Americano, the cup had to be porcelain, half filled with coffee and half with hot water, but making sure there was room for milk, which had to be 2%, but not fully skimmed and certainly never half & half. Then it had to be brown sugar and stirred with a wooden stick because she'd read that plastic spoons heat up and leach carcinogens.

Then, assuming there would be a chair (she'd leave, abandoning the coffee if there wasn't), she'd sit and stare at the coffee mug rather than talk to you until the coffee was the exact right temperature and then she'd drink it really fast in case it got too cool. Then she'd immediately need to pee. The washroom would always be too dirty by her standards, so she'd feel compelled to clean it first and negotiate with the baristas for bleach to assist her in this. Mostly they would be only too obliging as they hated having to clean the toilets anyway and customers were always mistreating them. This would take, oh, around an hour, or so.

Jennifer was always complaining to 'friends' that her dates would abandon her in coffee shops before they ever got to say a word – go figure.

If you saw Jennifer walking down the street or at a party you would be stunned. I have seen men instantly dump whomever they have arrived with and cut in and cut out whoever she was talking to at the time. She was striking and tall, never went out without her black hat jauntily placed on one side of her long blonde hair which just brushed her shoulders. She

BORDERLINES

had slim, elegant legs that were usually encased in something very tight from Zara and to look at her, see her move, if you didn't know her, you'd fall in love.

Her best friend Louise has suggested to me (and others) that perhaps she had bonded with her Barbie just too tightly when she was young and that could account for her rather self-obsessed behaviour.

Of course living up to Jennifer's standards was hard. She had a list and if you didn't have the qualities she required, clearly defined and well known amongst her friends, you wouldn't stand a chance.

Even Brad Pitt wouldn't have made it to the list, especially Brad Pitt, as she didn't like married men, or men with beards, or day old growth or men shorter than her, or men with perfect teeth and polished shoes. She was especially circumspect of men who paid too much attention to their grooming.

I was not on her list. I am not even sure how we met, or how she had my phone number, or why she considered me her 'friend', but the odd party invite would come along and I would go and mock her catering arrangements. She preferred dry food as then it wouldn't make a mess. I liked to watch her anguished eyes as she followed people's plates around the room just waiting for them to drop food on her teak floor, or spill wine on her white sofas.

She called me out of the blue late one Wednesday night. I was about to go to bed. I hadn't heard from her in about five months. I'd not even thought about her much except to try and warn someone about her when he called to ask what she was like. I seemed to remember it was Rob, a journalist I'd met at an Italian coffeehouse in town. I am not sure of my exact words, but it ran along the lines of 'he'd be better off throwing himself under a truck'. He just laughed, he was pretty confident he'd 'get her into bed'. Clearly he did not know Jennifer well. Louise has assured me that Jennifer did sleep with the occasional date, according to legend. But no person any of her friends actually knew. I think she favoured people from out of town.

'Look, I am sorry to call you out of the blue like this,' she was saying, 'I don't want to inconvenience you Sam, but I need your assistance.'

Other people might have just said 'Help me,' but not Jennifer.

'Hi Jen, what do you want?'

'I need you to help me to remove Rob.'

'Rob?'

BORDERLINES

'Yes Rob, he's a friend of yours. He said he was.'
'Rob Mellor?'
'Rob Mellor, the third, actually. His father owns quite a lot of downtown.'

That's the kind of thing that made it onto her list. Owning downtown, calling yourself 'The Third'. Having been to a good school, being a member of the tennis club and possessing great teeth. But no trust fund babies; she liked men who had careers. 'Trust fund babies have no focus, they always do stupid things and you always end up mothering them,' she would say. Not that she knew. Mothering didn't seem to be one of her natural skills.

'If he's drunk, if he's being rude or obnoxious….' I began, but she cut me off. 'I need you now, Sam. He's heavy. I need your help and I know I haven't been a good friend, but I am a friend and I need your help now.'

I sighed. There's a code in friendship. You shouldn't have to beg people to help you if you are a 'friend'. Besides it would take a strong personality to say no to such a request and no one ever said I had a strong personality before.

'I'll be there in –' I checked my watch. 'Twenty minutes.'
'Thank you.' She abruptly disconnected.

It was cold and damp. I would have walked, but given the urgency, I took the bus. Jennifer lived virtually opposite me, across the Burrard inlet. I lived in an old house, on Kit's Point; she lived in a high rise. She lived on the 4th floor because she hated to climb if the elevator ever packed up, or there was a fire. She was mortally afraid of fires. The family home had burned down one night whilst her parents were at the theatre. I believe the family fortune was based almost entirely on the insurance payout after they sued the family of the baby sitter who smoked. But I can't be sure any of that is true. Her father had bought the apartment for her and although it was two bedrooms, she lived alone in pristine hygienic splendour.

Naturally the elevator was out of order. I walked up, noting that even in expensive apartment blocks kids had scrawled graffiti on the walls.

She answered me on the second buzz.
'Who is it?'
'Who else did you invite?'
She opened the door and pulled me in. 'Don't take off your shoes.'

She was dressed in old jeans and some scrappy sweater. This was not

BORDERLINES

the girl I knew, but all the better for it. I knew she was naked under the sweater and for some reason this excited me. (I had long ago given up on expecting anything other than 'friendship' from Jennifer).

'So where is he?'

She sat on the floor with the white pages trying to find an address. 'I want the sheets burned, where would I find someone who does that?'

I looked at her and saw she was much more distressed than I had thought. What had Rob done? I immediately thought of him raping her in some drunken stupor and that naturally burning the sheets would be part of some cleansing ritual. But then he was still here, which was strange.

Jennifer looked distracted and distant. 'He's in the bedroom. You'll have to wrap him in the sheets.'

'Is he stoned?'

She didn't answer. I went into the bedroom.

Rob lay there on the bed naked. He looked drained, his face was bluish, he was not a well guy. 'Rob?' I asked cautiously.

I looked more closely and it was plain after a moment's consideration that he was dead. His body was so pale I felt I should look for tell-tale vampire marks on his neck. I looked back towards the open door.

'Jennifer? You do know he is dead . . . right?'

Jennifer said nothing for a moment, probably thinking hard about the appropriate thing to say. 'He swallowed something. Of course he's dead.'

'Aren't you suppose to call an ambulance or the police?'

'He's dead, Sam. He's dead and I want him out of here.'

I left the bedroom for a moment. She was still staring at the phone book.

'Jennifer, when a person dies there are certain things you have to do.'

'Not in my home. Not here. Not with me. He swallowed something and he's dead, Sam. I want him to die somewhere else. You understand? He did not die here.'

I looked at her and frowned. Talk about putting a friend in an awkward situation. 'Jennifer, you have to report it, by law. You didn't kill him.'

'I reported it to you. You have to help me.'

Would it be any use in me asking her why I had to do anything at all?

'He was your friend,' she added.

'He was your lover.'

'I did not have sex with that freak. You understand. I didn't have sex with him, we barely kissed.'

BORDERLINES

'He died naked in your bed, Jen. You don't have to pretend to be Mother Theresa with me.'

'I'll pay you. I know you need money. A thousand dollars.'

'A thousand?' I was surprised.

'Two thousand then,' she said, misinterpreting my remark. 'But I want him gone now.'

I let a silence fall between us. Two grand was two months' rent. Useful. Of course I had to help, but wouldn't this make me accessory to murder? If it was a murder. Of course it was an accident. Rob swallowed something.

'Then we have to burn the sheets,' she added snapping the phone book shut.

I went back to the bedroom.

'When did he die?'

'About two hours ago.'

'Two hours?'

'I was in the bathroom. He was dead when I came out.'

That figured.

I looked at Rob more carefully. Now that I thought about it, his clenched hands, and his distorted neck indicated that this man died in pain. I tried forcing open his mouth but couldn't get much movement: rigor mortis was setting in. I moved the side table lamp and looked down his throat. Amazing white teeth the guy had and there, at the back of his throat, along with some vomit, a chunk of aluminium foil. I knew what that was. A wrap. You see these things being handed around at parties. But the assumption is that you unwrap a wrap to smoke it or swallow whatever it was (and I didn't want to think about what really was in there.) I tried to surmise on how it had lodged in his throat. Had Rob begun sucking on it, waiting to surprise her with whatever he had in there? Had he been bored, endlessly waiting for Jennifer to come out of the bathroom, then fallen asleep and the wrap had somehow had lodged in the back of his throat? Nasty way to go. A stupid accident.

'He choked to death, Jen. You didn't hear anything?'

Jennifer was looking for an old blanket in the cupboard, something she could burn without missing it too much.

'This one – it's got paint on it.' She looked at me. 'Wrap him up, Sam. Don't forget the pillowcases.'

Rob rolled up pretty well. I hadn't noticed how short he was out of his heeled boots. Jennifer rolled the blue rug around him and taped up the

BORDERLINES

edges with masking tape. I watched her make sure it was secure and had neat edges. She didn't want any part of Rob to flop out. I couldn't but help think that she had done this sort of thing before.

'The Bridge is too bright,' she mused, 'is there anywhere else we can dump him?'

'You want to dump him? What about his parents? They'll miss him. He had a girlfriend, too – Grace somebody.'

'Grace Haffley?'

'Mmm.'

'Well, he was with me. She's not going to miss him now, is she.'

She thought for a moment, screwing up her eyes to think.

'Spanish Banks. The tide will take him.'

'It's pretty public and the police patrol that area.'

'It's winter, it's dark, the cops are in the doughnut shops. I just want him gone and disconnected from me. That's all I care about.' She pointed at a box. 'Everything he touched is in there, plus his boots.'

I looked at the box and back at Jennifer, then sighed, 'OK.'

We carried him down the stairs to the basement. We didn't meet anyone and she dropped him twice as we negotiated the bends, but finally with effort we got him into the Jeep. No one appeared. No one surprised us, nothing happened. I drove us to Spanish Banks out by Point Grey. The tide was coming in, and it was windy, so that meant waves. Jennifer never said a word the entire time. This event was already over as far as she seemed concerned. We parked as close to the beach as we could get and I switched the lights off. There were no other cars around and I could see the usual ships moored out in the bay their lights twinkling in the black night.

'We need to be quick, they patrol quite regularly.'

I dragged Rob to the beach and Jennifer followed carrying his clothes.

'What are you doing Jennifer?'

'I read that when people commit suicide they take their clothes off and wade into the ocean. Unwrap him. I'll his leave clothes here.'

'We have to put his trousers on and his sweater. It's more realistic.' I said.

'I don't want to touch him.'

'Jen, help me dress him. OK?'

I felt her staring at me with annoyance, but couldn't see her too well in the darkness. 'OK?' I repeated. 'I need your help.'

BORDERLINES

We unwrapped him and although she didn't want to touch him, she helped me pull his pants on. This is not an easy task on a cold beach with the freezing water swirling around. Jennifer was staring at his sweater with obvious disgust.

'My god, it's acrylic.'

I shook my head. This was no time for aesthetics.

'Give me his wallet.'

'Why?'

'Because it will look more natural if it is in his pants.'

'There's a hundred dollars in it.'

'All the better. Where's his phone? Get me that too.'

'Wait, I have to delete my number.'

Eventually after some difficulty with negotiating the cell database, she brought the wallet and phone to me from the box, along with his boots. 'I deleted your number too.'

I looked at her. Either she watched CSI very closely or she had definitely done this before. We put the boots on, but my hands were so cold I couldn't tie the laces and left them loose. I think I may have put the boots on the wrong feet. It was impossible to see in the dark.

As Jennifer huddled in the blue blanket and sheets, I waded out to sea. The problem with Spanish Banks is that you have to wade quite a way to get a body launched so it won't come back at you. He sank a little, but not much.

The cop car arrived about two minutes later. I was still out in the water transfixed by his headlights. Jennifer shouted to warn me and then (she confessed later) actually pissed herself and started crying.

The cop shone his flashlights on her and then at me out in the water. I waved to him, calling loudly.

'Officer? You'd better see this, there's a man in the water.'

I could sense that he didn't want to wade out into the cold ocean.

'You know you can't park out here after sunset,' he was saying.

I was wading back towards him. 'I was trying to call the police, but my signal's dead. There's a guy floating in the water. I was trying to pull him in but he's heavy'.

He shone the strong car searchlight across the water and finally picked out Rob floating there, rising and falling with the waves.

'Shit,' was all he said. 'I'll have to call the Coast Guard.'

BORDERLINES

'You want to help me get him in?' I started back out into the ocean, trying to look as co-operative as a body dumper could in the circumstances. 'Lucky we stopped. She was feeling sick and my headlights just caught him as I turned.'

The cop waded in after me. 'Fuck, this water's cold.'

'Sorry, the guy's dead, but I had to look.'

The cop was still cursing his luck. 'No, you did right. Damn this water's cold.'

'Is he dead?' Jennifer was calling from the shore in her most innocent little girl lost voice.

We reached Rob and the cop shone his flashlight at him and swore again.

'Yeah, he's dead. Get floaters out here all the time.'

This floater was taking on water, but I was sort of glad to hear it. Suddenly there was this great surge that rolled over the both of us. The cop dropped his flashlight, I was bowled over and found I was swallowing seawater in a moment of panic and the cop was struggling himself.

'Dammit'. Both of us were swearing and coughing up seawater when we surfaced and of Rob, there was not a sign.

Naturally we looked a bit longer, but neither one of us was keen to get pneumonia and we eventually called it quits and headed back to the shore.

Jennifer was sitting in her Jeep looking miserable and expecting the worst. The cop looked frozen and not really in the kind of shape to do this kind of thing. He took our names when he could finally hold his pen again. Then seeing as both Jennifer and myself were turning blue with the cold told us to go home. 'And next time neck in the park or something,' he added.

I ended up sleeping over at Jennifer's that night. She was too scared to sleep alone and since there was only one bed, I was obliged to share it. Of course we had to make the bed and she had to soak in the bathroom, but she did let me take a warm shower first, seeing as I didn't have any dry clothes. Sometime later in the early hours of the morning I found that she wanted comforting. Only then did she finally settle. Curiously I spent the rest of the night wide awake thinking about Rob on his way to Hawaii.

Six weeks later, after no contact from her at all, she arrives at my office to tell me she is pregnant and thinking of killing herself.

As far as she is concerned I am the guilty party. I think about Rob, but

BORDERLINES

then remember she said she only kissed him. Now, of course, I wondered if that was true.

We went over to the Bean Around the World and talked about it as she warmed her hands on her Americano. Somehow, I am not sure why, duty I suppose; that, and knowing that she was Catholic, I asked her to marry me. She looked at me with horror, then back at her coffee and then at me again. After what seemed like an hour, during which time she was probably weighing in her mind the right kind of polite but adroit and balanced response to my sudden, but hardly unexpected question, she suddenly sighed, looked at me again with searching eyes and said: 'Yes, I suppose so.'

I can't remember what I felt. Duty has no feeling, perhaps. I think I heard the sound of a heavy stone drop a hundred feet into a well but I can't be sure.

They found Rob, or what was left him, the day we had our engagement party at her apartment. The cop from the beach came around to tell us. He seemed happy to see us and stayed for one drink when he realised we were "gettin' engaged an' all." It was a lucky thing Rob had such good dentistry, he told us. It was all that was left of him, those white shining crowned teeth.

I know Jennifer was glad Rob had washed up at last. Now his family would know where he was and realise why he hadn't called in a while. His girlfriend, Grace, was at our party and Jennifer was very particular in making sure she hugged and comforted her a lot once the cop had gone away.

'Poor Rob, what a terrible thing to have happened,' she repeated more than once, for everyone's benefit. She did not of course explain why the cop had come to her place to tell her about it, seeing as Grace was supposed to be the girlfriend.

Grace, who hadn't especially missed Rob, but had been slightly miffed that Rob hadn't called her, suddenly realised that he had meant something to her after all. She was happier to share this sudden blow with someone so caring as Jennifer.

Jennifer, particular as always, wouldn't have wanted it any other way.

BORDERLINES

Ryan Simmons
DEAD JIM

Behind me I pulled a sled of mail and letters, strapped atop of which was Dead Jim Wells. The storm coming off Lake Superior was forcing chards of ice across the great American plains of the Dakota Territories and into my eyes. I was crying, but it was the strength of the wind that caused the tears, not Dead Jim.

Jim had died yesterday, the day after we had pulled the canoe into Saint Ignace and left it there for the overland route to Sault Ste Marie. We had learned in town that the St Mary's River, the normal way to reach the city perched on the further northern reaches of the state, had begun to freeze over. I think Jim had expected that.

The day after we left, the snow had begun to dust the trees. The grey-white birch trees stood out against the sky, their bare branches scratching the low grey clouds. If it had been a lithograph, the only thing that would be missing was a red horse-drawn sled. I would love a red horse-drawn sled right now.

"We have two days to get to the Sault, or the storms of Gitchee Gumee will trap us out here," Jim had said in his infrequently used whiskey-scented voice the day before. I had nodded, walking next to him as I tried to pick up the art of snowshoe walking.

Jim died two hours later. We never walked after sundown, so we had stopped as the sun was getting lower to set up our tent and collect wood for the fire. I was setting up the fire the way Jim had taught me, by placing the smallest kindling in the middle and setting the large sticks against each other "like a western Injun tepee," while Jim sat on the edge of the sled and put back some whiskey.

"Tom, I'm tired," he said. He'd never said anything relating to how he was feeling in the past three weeks, but I didn't look up from what I was doing until I heard a gasp.

The flask was lying in the snow emptying its yellow-brown contents; a light steam was rising off the stain. He always kept the whiskey warm inside his coat, by his chest. He was pitched forward over his knees, his right arm grasping his chest.

"Jim?" I pulled him up. His eyes were wide and bulging, the yellowed whites looked as if a finger was behind them pressing them to

BORDERLINES

jump out of his sockets. His pupils had no focus. His breath rattled, and his body fell limp. His eyes looked at nothing, though they reflected everything. Soon he was dead.

For nearly 200 miles of canoeing across the shores of Lake Huron, to the rough soldier and trader town of Michilimackinac on the island, and to the winter-beset wilderness of Michigan's Upper Peninsula, Jim had been my friend. I was never convinced he liked me – I was fresh from university in Connecticut and was in Michigan escaping the grey-black clutches of life as a banker. He had to teach me how to build a fire and walk in snowshoes. Yet we had shared whiskey and paddled a mail-laden canoe through the Lake and a number of small towns delivering their last news and mail before spring. But now we were in the middle of . . . God knew where I was.

I had a degree in finance and economics from Yale University; the piece of parchment proving this was tied with a string in my father's house. There was no course in wilderness survival. What I knew was only that we were roughly on the Mackinac Trail to the Sault, that I would remain in that frontier town for the entire winter, and that a dead man was lying on his mail sled, which I supposed was now mine. He was the only man I knew who could make the voyage to get me to the town I was supposed to live in for the winter.

There was no chance of digging him a grave, as I neither had a shovel nor would I be able to penetrate the frozen ground. If I just left him frozen alongside the trail, I fancied he would thaw with the spring and become carrion for any number of wild beasts.

I sat around the fire across from the sled and Dead Jim. I was upset that the last of the whiskey had drained into the snow. I was certain that I wouldn't take it anyhow, given that it had last touched a dead man's lips. I might have gotten desperate enough, though.

I chewed on some smoked fish leftover from our last catch before we left St Ignace. I was fairly certain we were closer to the Sault than St Ignace, and so I determined we would keep heading along the path. Eventually I would have to hit the coast of the peninsula. Maybe even a cottage where a trapper had holed up for the winter.

I had to take Dead Jim with me the next morning. I finished my fish and strapped his frozen corpse to the top of the mail sled with the leather straps on his jacket. He was covering the mail, and I thought of a "Dear So-and-So" letter written by some East Coast wife to her frontier husband that was now covered by Dead Jim. The writer would be horrified and

BORDERLINES

need to be revived with smelling salts if ever she learned of this.

I slept restlessly enough. I had no problem realising when the early morning light came up, and quickly broke down camp and harnessed myself up in the sled.

As if exulting over Jim's death, the harpies of wind had intensified over the night. They came screaming out of the west, unleashed across the vastness of the Great Lake Gitchee Gumee – Superior, as the people in Detroit called it – bringing with them their frozen pellets of snow that stuck in my beard and burrowed into the fur pelt coats I had heaped upon me that made me a walking wigwam. They managed to claw through all that fur. After all, animals the pelts came from were smart enough to sleep during this time of year – why should their coats stop the winter wind?

I had little time – maybe five hours – to march before nightfall. Jim had said that the storm would be only getting worse, and in typical Jim fashion he hadn't told me how far we had left to the Sault. I only had my assumption.

"Where the hell are we, Dead Jim? Huh? I see plenty of snow – should I turn right at the next snowbank? No, how about the one after that? Or do I keep going straight? Dead Jim?"

I discovered that Dead Jim was, in many ways, as conversational as Alive Jim.

Together we went up and down the snowdrifts, crunching the piles of snow with my catgut snowshoes that I had been introduced to three days before. I saw nothing but snow, talked only to Dead Jim, and never got a reply. The only problem with him being dead and mute was that I was afraid I might be obliged to answer for him. This was tempered by my greater fear of dying out here buried in a pile of snow, ending my illustrious life as a spring breakfast for an obscenely hungry bear coming out of hibernation. I idly thought of the bear mixing our bodies together, bones atop bones. Dead Jim would at least be whiskey-flavoured. A drunk bear. Dead Jim didn't laugh at that joke.

The sun got lower again and I saw no town. The wind was too strong to make a fire. I shivered under my coat, recalling the times I had stood dripping in the natatorium at Yale waiting for my next lap in the pool, shaking but withstanding it because I was tough. But these shivers weren't the shivers of a boy in swim trunks, and I felt them biting into me like little furious insects of cold, crawling over and surveying my body. I tried hiding under the sled, but the snow kept building up around me.

"Jim, you're dead. I need your coats," I said to his back.

BORDERLINES

Dead Jim was frozen dead. I wrestled him off the sled and flung him into the snow. He landed on his back. His arms and legs, which had been a concave curve down over the mail sled, were now a concave curve up, as if someone had knocked him really hard in the stomach and sent him flying torso-first to a wall. His eyes were opened, frozen in the moment of the shock of that hit. I remembered closing them last night.

I started to tug at his jackets, but the arms were outstretched and frozen solid. I needed the coat. I put my foot on his chest, and began pushing his left arm down, trying to move it, but he held steady, in that same knocked-out position. Snow was beginning to cover what his eyelids couldn't. I thanked God. I didn't want him to see me shatter his arm.

It was a horrible snap, and I fell on top of the arm into the snow. My breath grazed over Dead Jim dusted face.

"Oh God, Jim," I whispered. I was crying, but this time it wasn't because of the cold of the storm.

BORDERLINES

Diana Bretherick
FRAGMENTS

Catalogue numbers 53-59.
Diary entries extracted from rudimentary
computer storage device prior to predicted
extinction level event circa 2008.

April 20th
Tsunami, it's such a beautiful word – almost inviting. When you say it, it flows around your mouth like a really good wine. It sounds calm, peaceful, even harmonious. Unless, of course, it forms a small part of the end of the world - then it becomes rather more alarming. I say small part because apparently we're also looking at the equivalent of a nuclear winter. So even if you're lucky enough not to drown you will still be frozen solid.

I was in the precinct the other day and a man started to rave about impending doom and so on. Everyone just ignored him. Does that make him mad or us, I wonder? I was there, I heard him, but like everyone else, I didn't listen. Perhaps we should have, but how do you prepare for the end of the world? Repent? Will God swat a comet out of the sky? I don't think so. If only I had become a Jehovah's Witness. They've closed their doors now. I could have ridden it to hell with the rest of them…

Perhaps I should explain. There is a large comet heading right for us. They've been calling it an 'NEO' – Near Earth Object – except that now it's going to be rather nearer than was, at first, anticipated. You couldn't even say that we didn't see it coming. You can't miss the bloody thing – it's huge and it's been up there for months. Actually, you can't help but admire it in a twisted kind of way. It's beautiful though it doesn't look real – as if it's been stuck onto the sky with glue. There it hangs like a malevolent jewel, almost as if it's laughing at us. Maybe it is.

This then, is my end of the world blog. I'm not sure who's going to be left to read it - intelligent cockroaches maybe, who knows? But someone might and that's good enough for me.

May 15th
Once we had a huge comet heading right for our planet – and now we have two. The governments of the world, in their wisdom, got together

BORDERLINES

and sent a missile up in order to destroy it, Bruce Willis-style. Unfortunately due to ...well let's just say a certain level of incompetence – rather than bombing it into bite size chunks which would burn up on contact with the Earth's atmosphere, they merely managed to divide it into two lethal fragments. It was bad before – but now it's worse. Bruce Willis must be laughing himself silly.

Ironically the predicted date of impact is Friday 13th June. Unlucky for some.

May 17th
Nobody seems to know how to act. Should we still go to work? Should we abandon ourselves to an orgy of unbridled hedonism? Everyone seems to be carrying on as normal, except of course it's a different kind of normal. We look at each other in a new way, as if we're trying to find some kind of an answer. We're denying our fate. Can you blame us?

May 26th
Apparently there's been some looting in Waitrose – in Waitrose! Nothing signifies the break down of law and order more than members of the middle classes helping themselves to extra virgin olive oil and sun-dried tomatoes. Elsewhere they're rioting in the streets but here the anarchy, though present, is quieter. People have stopped going to work and I've noticed the couple next door are having more sex than usual but other than that, life is, on the surface anyway, much the same.

May 31st
There's no water and no electricity now and if you haven't got food already you're going to go hungry. It's getting increasingly grim out there. Some people are wandering the streets as if in a daze. Others are begging for food. Everything just disintegrated ... seemingly almost overnight.

No one seems to know exactly what's going to happen or whether or not there are any measures we can take to protect ourselves. For a government who used to be so fond of issuing edicts about how we shouldn't do this or that in case we harmed ourselves, they have become alarmingly silent. Before the TV went off for the last time there was an interview on the news with a government minister. He was being asked about where it would hit and what would happen. He just kept saying he didn't know. The interviewer wouldn't leave it there.

"Is there anything you do know, minister?" he was asked.

BORDERLINES

There was an agonising close up of his fat sweaty face, wide eyed and terrified. He just shook his head. When politicians stop lying you know that the game is up. I think it was around then that it really started to hit home. In less than a month I'm going to die.

Fuck. I don't normally swear but – Fuck!

June 5th
Less than a week left. For a while regret almost overwhelmed me – all the things I haven't done or said – but now I've accepted it and it's come as a relief.

A lot of people have gone now. I'm not sure where. I've started to think about that myself. But the question is – where should I go? – high ground, low ground, underground? Which is best? There's been very little guidance. Once it became clear that both fragments were going to hit, everything started to shut down. We've given up. There's no chance of a Hollywood ending. The certainty of our end is terrifying.

June 12th
Hours to go now and I've made a decision. There's a hill outside the city. That's where I'm heading. I've no idea if it will offer any protection but if I'm going to witness the end of the world then I might as well have a good view. The worst thing was leaving my cat. I've had her since she was a kitten. Saying goodbye was hard. I gave her some of her favourite food. And then I picked up her up to cuddle her….but she wriggled free and went off through the cat flap. And I realised I'd never see her again.

It's time to go. Nothing left to stay for. As I look around my little flat it doesn't seem like home anymore. I feel somehow rootless, abandoned. I'm used to a solitary life. I'm self contained, always have been. But in the last few weeks I've felt more alone than I've ever done.

I don't know who will read this, if anyone. I suppose I should say something momentous about looking after the planet but I don't really have the heart. You can't possibly be worse than us, whoever you are. All I hope is that this disaster will bring a fresh start and maybe we, or you, will do better this time. I suspect however, that you'll make as big a mess of it as before. But then I'm a born pessimist and with what I've got to look forward to – maybe it's just as well.

Emma Callan
THE WASP

Hair is the first thing I see, I imagine.
An angry meteor of razored hair,
Menacingly crisp
- number one in length.

I always know when to expect you.
Languid, lazy,
Sharp and spit-quick
Always humming, always screaming to
Summer's hot intrusive tune.

Ominous. You are the ugliest symptom of the
Creeping heat. A pest?
You demand a stronger title. More
Words. Predator, Investigator, Dive-bomber,
Schizophrenic.
Not enough? Too many?

Maybe I should stick to sounds.
A violating drill, a shrill-kill drone deep
Deep. Deeper.
A single syllable striped knock at my window.
A golden charcoal blot of buzz on my
Picture perfect August day.

BORDERLINES *Poetry*

Linda Albert
A SMALL BIRD

He flutters there;
trapped.
I swallow around twigs,
try to ignore the nest
mistakenly built
in my belly,
the planet's extra revolutions,
my limbs becoming lakes,
the helpless beaks,
the frozen sky.

My husband waits
for brain surgery
while all I can do
with my dizziness,
with the somersaults,
with the frantic bird,
is to hold as still as possible,
eyes fixed on the horizon,
and pray not to fall.

Anona Evans
THE WOLF

Amongst dark trees monsters in the shadows await,
'Danger' chimes the howls at midnight,
Hollow emptiness of fresh skulls
Cracking beneath gnashing teeth.

Thirsty for blood and famished for bones
Hear the crunching paws and scrapping claws
Moving slowly, silently,
Silver backs reflected in the moonlit sky.

Don't look outside, hide away;
Ignore the tap, tap tapping at the glass,
The mist of hot breath swimming across
Crawl behind closed doors.

Silence your beating heart, stifle the cries
 Lock up your bones.

Andrea Bowie
THE BUMBLESS ORANGE BUMBLE BEE

Imagine if you will,
What it is to be,
A harmless buzzing, bumbling bee.
But for some bees
To bumble is supplementary,
For example The Bumbless,
Orange Bumble Bee.

Orange he is,
But a bee he still be.
Never he does bumble,
And why you shall see.
For a bee who bumbles,
Can make only honey.
Stripes on his back,
Yellow and black,
Not so for The Bumbless,
Orange Bumble Bee.

Amongst the colonies
He was easy to see,
Scorned by his fellows
For not being yellow,
Stung by their mockery,
He bumbled solitary
For a year and a day.
Bumbling he bumbled all day long,
But when he got back,
He mumbled a half hearted 'bumble' –
The beekeeper had moved to Norfolk.
His hive was gone.

So The Bumbless Orange Bumble Bee,
Worked himself into an utter tizz-wuzz.

BORDERLINES

He tizzed and wuzzed until he started to buzz
"Buzz Buzz," buzzed the bee, "I'll bumble no more!"
Buzzing invigorated, he formed a plan.
If I can't make honey, I'll get into jam,

But the Robertson's men, they laughed,
They scoffed at his plan;
Whoever heard of a bee making jam?
But this time the mockery stung not at all,
For as he buzzed and not bumbled,
He finally saw –

He was a bee blessed by his unusual shade,
For an orange bee, of course, makes marmalade.

BORDERLINES

Beth Weaver
ITALIAN GIRLS AND AMERICAN COKES

D anny heard Maria's laugh just as he was lifting a forkful of meatloaf to his mouth, that husky little-girl-woman laugh he remembered so well. His fork froze in mid-air.
"What's wrong? Is the meatloaf mushy to you? Mine tastes like something from a baby food jar—nothing like what's in the picture." Matilda Matheson picked up a plastic-encased picture of a steaming serving of meatloaf, along with mashed potatoes, gravy and peas and rubbed her thumb over the greasiness of it, then frowned as she dropped it. "I knew we shouldn't have come here, knew we should've gone to that new Chinese place, even if they do serve unrecognizable meats. Damn shame your restaurant isn't still open. Now that was the place to go— Daniel, what is it? Daniel!" She stared at her son, exasperated.

Danny could smell Maria's perfume—L'Air du Temps—that he had given her when they'd first begun dating. He remembered dabbing it on the hollow of her throat. He shook himself. He couldn't possibly have smelled her perfume, the air being so thick with grease. Maybe it hadn't been her laugh at all, but the tinkling of silverware. He continued to eat, forcing himself to calm down. But a few minutes later—just after the waitress served dessert—he heard it again. Maria—and only Maria's— laugh.

"Are you choking?" Matilda demanded. Her face loomed before her son's, red pushing through the thick foundation that choked every pore of her skin.

"I thought I heard . . . heard . . . Maria." His voice was hoarse.

The pool of coffee in the old woman's cup quivered as she clutched it. "Maria?"

Danny raised himself from the orange vinyl booth and looked around until he spotted her on the far side of the room. She was sitting with friends they'd known together in the restaurant business. Her hand was cradled around a tall glass filled with dark liquid. She was swirling it, staring at the ice. He settled himself back into the seat with a squeaky thud, his face as pale as a boiled egg. "It's her all right, with the Kelly's."

"Well!" Matilda threw down her napkin. "I've lost my appetite. How 'bout you?"

BORDERLINES

It had been five years since Danny had seen his ex-wife. The coconut cream pie might as well have been shaving cream, choking him to where he could barely swallow. "I wonder if maybe I should—should—"

"Say hello?" She blinked at him through glasses that magnified her eyes. "Daniel, you're not serious?"

He picked up his fork and began mashing the back of the prongs into the pie crust, making little roads. "Hell no. Shoot the bitch. Point blank."

Neither one of them felt like sticking around, so they got up to leave. As Matilda's motorized wheelchair disappeared into the Ladies' Room, Danny walked over to the cigarette machine to get a pack of Marlboros since his mother was running low. He didn't feel like stopping at the store on the way home; all he wanted to do was climb the hell out of those stiff church clothes, fall onto the old sofa back in his room and watch a game on TV. He yanked at the tie strangling his throat, and then plunked some coins into the machine.

The machine didn't respond, just sat there mutely with its contents brilliantly displayed through the thick glass. He had a sudden urge to kick it, but jammed his hand back into his pocket instead and plunked even more coins down its steel throat. As the soft pack of cigarettes fell to the bottom, he saw Maria coming toward the Ladies' room. She saw him at the same time and stopped like a frightened bird a few feet away. Her hair was shorter than he'd ever seen it, with little wisps sticking out like fluffy bits of down. She was thinner, too—impossibly thin. He felt his insides stiffen and then turn to liquid as hot streaks of color rose to his cheeks.

Just as their eyes began to lock, Matilda's motorized wheelchair rolled out of the Ladies' Room and Maria vanished.

On the ride home, Danny's hands were shaking so much he could barely keep them steady on the wheel. He sat upright, his head scraping the sagging foam ceiling while his eyes remained riveted to the dotted yellow line—running stitches of giant golden thread piercing the gray asphalt.

"Time certainly hasn't done her any favors," Matilda clucked as she blew off the smoke from her cigarette.

"D'ya mind rolling down your window?" he asked. She was always blowing smoke in his face and never realizing it. When she didn't respond, he pushed her window button on his control panel.

"Skinny as a wet ferret," Matilda said as she blew off more smoke. "She always reminded me of one with her squashed face and long neck. And those eyes that were always searching for their next meal."

BORDERLINES

"'The ferret often eats prairie dogs and lives in their burrows.' World Book Encyclopedia, if I recall." His eyebrow rose. "I wrote a report about ferrets in the fourth grade. Remember? I wanted you and Dad to get me one."

The old woman smiled faintly. "You always had an amazing memory. I used to tell your father that with a memory like that you might very well become President of the United States."

"What the hell was she doing ordering a Coke?" He whipped around a pickup truck with PVC pipes hanging out its tail like long, limp cigarettes.

"Lord knows how far you might've gone if she hadn't come along. And you always making fun of me for saying you could've been President of the—"

"—She hated American Cokes! All because of high fructose corn syrup. High fructose!" He slammed his foot on the brake as he saw a cop and realized he'd better not run the light. "Said it made it taste oily; nothing like real sugar."

"—Slow down, son!"

He eased his foot on the brake. "Sorry. Are you all right?"

Two streams of smoke poured from the woman's nostrils.

Danny rolled down his window as far as it could go as Maria continued to loom in his mind. "Only in Italy could you get a real Coke with real sugar. That's what gives it a crisp, clear bite. Real sugar. She used to tell me that all freakin' time. American Cokes weren't worth the corn syrup they were—"

"—I put a lot of money into that restaurant. I believed in you, son. And you worked so hard!" Matilda's rising voice startled him.

He blinked at the blotches of red on her cheeks and realized she'd been talking away, working herself into a sweat. As he thought about her words, his eyes narrowed. "Sixty hours a week, Mother. Sometimes more."

"It was just beginning to get off the ground." She sucked hard on her cigarette. "Everybody was so disappointed when it closed. It was back to fast food and feeding troughs."

"You really believed in me? That I could make a go of it?" His eyes stayed on the road, yet his voice carried a note of urgency.

"Of course. You're a Matheson. From a long line of achievers."

"Well, you certainly were there for me throughout the whole ordeal." The hard lines creasing his face softened. "I don't know how I would've survived without you. Sometimes I feel like I'm nothing but a ball and chain. A curse to you."

She reached over and patted his shoulder. "You're nothing of the kind. If anyone's a ball and chain, it's me with my bum hip. Very few sons would take care of their old crippled mother the way you do. If you were an Eskimo, you'd put me out on the snow, a nice lunch for the polar bears."

"Come on, I hardly do anything."

"That's not true. I'd be lost without you. I'd be forced to rely on strangers and you never know who you can trust these days. Besides, when your new ristorante opens you'll be rolling in money the likes of which she's never seen." She fell silent for a moment, blowing smoke. "So much of my savings went down the drain when Maria's folded."

"I know. That's why I'm not sure if you want to risk backing me again."

"Well, it won't be called Maria's this time, will it?"

"Hell no."

"Well!" she snorted. "What's the risk?"

Danny could feel the tension rise in his shoulders; the back of his neck grow hot. His hands rose from the steering wheel and shook. "I could kill her; I swear I could for what she did to me. How could I function—how could anybody function after the hell she put me through?"

"Put your hands back on the wheel before you get us killed," Matilda said evenly. "Stop a moment up at Wilber's Drugs if you don't mind. I'm suffering from indigestion."

"But we're nearly home. I'm sure we have some TUMS in the—"

"—You can pick up some nice apricot brandy while we're there. I know how much you love apricot brandy."

"Mother, it's Sunday. You've never bought liquor on Sunday."

"Nobody seems to care about that any more. The whole world's going to hell if you ask me. But you get something else you like. My treat."

He winced at the way she spoke to him when she wanted a favor, as if he were still ten. He parked in front of the drugstore and suggested that he dash in while leaving her in the van with the air conditioner on, but she wouldn't hear of it. She'd heard on the news that very morning about a couple camping in the Ocala National Forest who had slept in their car on account of the snakes and mosquitoes, no doubt, and were found dead the next morning. They'd left their air conditioner on all night and died of asphyxiation.

BORDERLINES

He tried to explain to her that she wasn't going to die sitting in an air conditioned van for five minutes, but she wanted to look at the brooches she'd seen advertised in the paper, anyway. That was, of course, if the TUMS worked immediately. So he unloaded her motorized wheelchair and helped scoop her heavy body—soft as rising dough—into it.

Once inside, Danny headed straight for the medicine aisle and picked up a packet of TUMS. Matilda aimed her motorized wheelchair toward the jewelry counter where she got caught up looking at the new line of sculpted dog brooches with faux jewels for eyes. She selected a gold sheep dog with ruby eyes, a silver Schnauzer with onyx eyes, and a white porcelain collie with a jeweled collar.

Quite a line had formed by then (everybody in the small town now finished with their noonday meal and also browsing), so Matilda told her son to get a couple of PayDays for himself, since he hadn't chosen a treat, while he waited in line with her brooches and TUMS and the five dollar bill she pulled out of her purse, after her fingers struggled for a wild uncomfortable moment to open the tight metal clasps.

Danny usually didn't mind lines. But today he found himself shifting impatiently in his loafers. They were miserable shoes, ill-fitting and stiff as wood—not the usual decent quality he found at the Salvation Army.

Every time the front bell jangled he craned his neck to see who'd come in. After seeing Maria in the diner he figured she might show up anywhere. He clenched the PayDays. Why was she back in town?

"Great sermon Reverend Daniels gave today about the importance of family," Matilda remarked after they were finally in the van again. She began talking about the sermon, stretching out her words the way she did when she concurred with something the reverend—whom Danny suspected she had a crush on even though he was thirty years her junior—had said. As she spoke, she popped open the overhead mirror and used the sharp point of her lacquered fingernail to fumble with something stuck between her front teeth. Food was always getting stuck there as one tooth slightly overlapped the other and she was forever popping open mirrors and picking at her teeth.

Danny had always found it to be an odd, distasteful habit for a woman who had been married to a district attorney.

He had given her every advantage—materially speaking—until a heart attack took his life while dining on his favorite meal—thick, aged, raw filet mignon, seared two minutes on each side over a hot charcoal grill and served with freshly grated horseradish. When he keeled over at the dining

BORDERLINES

room table, Matilda thought at first that it was the horseradish giving him a fit of indigestion, as she herself couldn't touch the stuff. But by the time the ambulance arrived he was officially pronounced dead. Danny remembered how he'd felt when he'd heard the news—his secret relief, followed by guilt toward the man he'd always let down in one way or another.

The unfortunate timing of his death occurred six months after Danny had gotten married and moved into a place of his own and two months after Matilda had undergone her second surgery for a hip condition she'd been born with called congenital dislocation. The socket of her hip bone was too shallow and had caused her all sorts of trouble in recent years, especially when she put on a sizeable amount of weight. She had just ordered—but had yet to receive—a motorized wheelchair at the time of her husband's death. At least that's what she told Danny when he and Maria came to stay with her for a while. She said she'd given up hope of ever walking again.

Danny had convinced her to have two more surgeries over the next four years, but he, too, finally lost hope that his mother would walk again. Maria and his ristorante were old history now and it was just Danny and his mother. In a selfish way, it was her vulnerabilities that gave him a feeling of importance, a feeling that maybe someday he might actually get back on his feet.

As he helped his mother take her blood pressure pills at bedtime, doling them out and then standing beside her while she struggled to get them down, she remarked, "There's a nice piece of property downtown for sale. John Stewart told me about it at church. Might be just the spot we're looking for. He said I should make an offer right away, before it's snatched up."

"Oh?" He took the water glass from her and set it down, his stomach muscles tightening in that familiar way they did whenever they talked about a new ristorante. He wanted to open a new place, alright. Spent most of his time drawing up plans. But whenever they got beyond the planning stages something inside of him froze up and he found one reason or another to back out.

"It's pricey, but after looking over your latest plans, I think you've finally got something that'll really fly. Never felt that way about the first place."

"How can you say that? You used to rave over the Roti de Veau á la Creme."

BORDERLINES

"Best veal I ever had," she admitted. "But the portions were too large—too American if you will—and you didn't spend enough time arranging the food on the plates."

He stared at her, surprised.

"It's an art as you well know."

"Of course I know. I spent half my life arranging the food."

"It's difficult, I think, to arrange food properly when you have overcooked spears of lifeless asparagus and broccoli that's lost its vibrancy."

"That was only when the plates sat under the lights too long —"

"And to be honest, the food sometimes looked—well—thrown on the plates."

"Mother, that's a terrible insult."

"I'm sorry," she sighed. "But once my veal was barely hanging onto the plate when it was plopped before me."

"And who was it that happened to have plopped it before you?"

They both stared at each other and said after a beat, "Maria."

Danny began to pace. "I busted my ass during those years. And for what—a fuckin' slut?"

"Daniel, watch your language."

"I'd go in at nine-thirty every morning and come home at one o'clock the following morning. Everything in between was a blur of steamy pots, stirring spoons, and floors so slippery you could slide a mile because of all the grease. That was the kitchen.

"Out in the dining area, in the beautifully recreated European cityscape, among the candlelight and the fresh-cut flowers, was my wife—advertising herself as the main course. I'd see that look in her eye when she'd talk to certain guys—that look of fire."

Mrs. Matheson's owl-like eyes snapped wide. "Remember the night I found a hundred dollar bill on her? She swore it was a tip."

"I'm sure it was." Danny's eyes glowered.

"Screamed like a banshee when I tried to take it from her. Oh, she was something. But," she grabbed his hand and squeezed it hard, "she's your past."

"Then why the hell is she back in town?"

"It is disconcerting, but no matter—"

"She sure is thin—someone else must've dumped her."

"It doesn't matter—she doesn't matter. Some people are simply born mean and you can't let them defeat you. You're a Matheson, from good stock. I'll hand-pick the hired help myself for our new venture. Nothing will slip by me this time. John said I should make an offer at once, that it's too good a deal to stay on the market long."

"We'll talk in the morning, after you've rested."

"You've got to concentrate on making this next ristorante a real success. That's how you show people like Maria they can't ruin you."

"You're right. She didn't realize who she was reckoning with. We'll look at that land first thing in the morning," he said as he punched her pillows into shape.

"Don't forget to leave the door ajar and the hall light on," she reminded him as he helped her remove her support hose. "Darn it!" she exclaimed as her big toe snagged the end of the reinforced toe. "There was a time I could keep a pair of stockings for months. Now everything is junk."

As Danny went to fetch the toenail clippers and then clipped the thick, yellowed nail, he wondered what Coke with real sugar tasted like, if it really did have a clear, crisp bite. He used to tease Maria for never touching an American Coke.

"I'm grateful son, my eyes aren't what they used to be," Matilda thanked Danny as he stared at her absently.

She insisted, however, on unbuttoning her blouse even though she'd always had trouble with the buttonholes on this particular shirt. She breathed laboriously as she concentrated on the task. Then, digging out her nightgown from underneath her pillow where she kept it, she waited for Danny to turn the other way before she pulled off her blouse and then slipped it on.

"My eyes aren't what they used to be," she repeated a moment later, "and I might have to get up in the middle of the night."

"I won't forget to leave the hall light on," he reassured her as he did every night. He considered it part of their bedtime ritual.

"You forgot to leave the toilet lid down the other night and I nearly fell in!" she snorted.

"I'm sorry."

"Well . . ." Her voice trailed off as she concentrated on tying the bow of her nightgown. "I don't see the purpose of this silly bow, do you? Might as well cut it off."

He knew better than to fetch the scissors. He'd started to cut off the bow one night and she'd gotten mad. So he let the subject drop.

"Is my water glass next to the sink?"

BORDERLINES

"I'll check as soon as I leave."

"Make sure you do. I can't very well be using the faucet with my hands, now can I?"

"Of course not," he said evenly. His mother always got snappish before she surrendered herself to the night.

She gave a quick glance toward the nightstand to make sure her cigarettes were there, along with a lighter. Following her eyes, he commented, "I really don't think you should be smoking in bed, Mom."

She waved him off. "Been doing it since I was eighteen. If I was going to get cancer I would've gotten it by now."

He rocked his heel in his stiff shoe. "It's just that you might set the bed on fire, or something."

"Nonsense. I could use a puff right now, in fact."

He sighed as she placed a cigarette in her mouth and fumbled with the lighter until the cigarette glowed. She took a few puffs before snubbing it out. Then, turning to him, she gripped his hands. "I can't imagine some stranger tucking me in every night, can you?" Her eyes, tenderly regarding his, were the faded, washed out color of coffee stains. Yet the pupils were clear and coal black.

"G'night, Mother."

She gripped his hands a moment longer before she slid into the warmth of the sheets he had washed for her earlier that day. "G'night, son."

After Matilda had drifted off to sleep, Danny closed all the doors and windows except for his own and then turned on the attic fan. Its roar filled the house as it sucked in air from every nook and cranny. He lay upon his bed, stripped down to his boxers and watched his curtains dance frenetically in their rattling frames as the wind tore through them. The energy of the chopping, whirling blades and the hungry wind filled him with a sense that his racing heart wasn't the only thing thrashing wildly in vain.

He didn't understand why he felt this way every night, teetering at the edge of a cliff. Yet even more so tonight, with Maria's face looming in his mind, her delicate fingers gripping the American Coke.

That Coke. That damn Coke. Why had she ordered it?

Or had she ordered iced coffee? No, it couldn't have been. She'd always drank coffee with pure cream. Not milk, but pure cream. And this liquid had been dark brown. Dr. Pepper? Couldn't have been . . . it had fructose, too. Diet something maybe? She didn't drink diet drinks. Hated Tab. Hell, did they even make that anymore?

    Laughing, she coaxed him into the cooler where the cakes, donuts and pies were kept and showed him the coconut cream pie she had accidentally dropped while cutting a slice for a customer.
    It lay in a lopsided heap in its pan with deep cracks splitting it into several pieces.
    "It's all ours," she whispered in the dim light of their hideaway. Her eyes were bewitched.
    "You sure you didn't drop it on purpose?"
    "No silly! Not that I haven't been tempted. Because I happen to know that coconut pie is your favorite."
    "Oh, you do, do you?"
    "Taste this—pure cream" she murmured as she dipped her fingers into the topping and brought the sweet confection to his lips.
    Danny bolted upright in his bed, breathing hard. Beads of sweat had formed on his upper lip, even though the air was cool. A tear streamed down his cheek as he remembered that longago summer with sudden clarity—the taste of the whipped cream, the taste of Maria. The tear left a cold trail on his cheek as he realized that was the moment he'd started to hate her—the moment he tasted the rich cream. How could anyone so beautiful, so chaste choose him? A movement caught his eye and he gave a start. "Maria? Is that you?" He waited for a tense moment and then realized it was nothing but the curtains dancing wildly in the coal black room.

BORDERLINES

Dean Borok
THE PASSION OF NIÑO DE JESUS

*Niño de Jesus Benitez has escaped from the mental
hospital on Ward's Island and made his way to
Hell's Kitchen on the West Side of Manhattan, where he goes
to the object of all his dreams and desires:
a garishly-painted fuchsia forklift truck parked in a vacant lot.*

Niño de Jesus had frequently marveled at the fuchsia forklift on his way to work and one day, when the proprietor had left the gate unlocked, he snuck in for a closer look. Climbing up the ladder on the side and peering into the control booth, he noticed that they had left the key in the ignition. After all, one might reason, who would steal such a monster? Only a crazy man!

From that day forward the machine became a constant landmark of his scattered emotional terrain. The idea of it would pop up when he was riding the subway into town from his rented room in Corona, when he was eating beans and rice in the shared kitchen of his boarding house, when he was watching Mexican gangster movies showing smartly tailored guys with mustaches smattering each other into fragments with machine guns.

The average person is distracted by thoughts of sex every eight seconds. Niño de Jesus Benitez, however, had found the ideal vehicle of transferal for all his earthly animal tendencies. He had not the slightest interest in any form of human contact and was a fanatical Catholic fundamentalist sober or drunk. The fuchsia forklift took over all his waking thoughts and dreams. He changed his commute so that he could pass it twice each day, crossing himself and uttering a devotional prayer on his way to and from his job as (what else?) a forklift operator.

The fuchsia forklift came to have a deleterious effect on his job performance at the industrial bakery where he worked. His previously close relationship with the dependable little yellow forklift that he drove became strained, the same way a man might devalue his plain but faithful wife after becoming infatuated with a younger, lovelier woman.

BORDERLINES

He began treating her with contempt and insouciance, letting her battery water run low and forgetting to recharge her when he went on break or ended his shift. Sometimes, out of spite for not being fuchsia, he intentionally banged her against concrete surfaces, damaging her fiberglass body and exposing her insides. Occasionally he would drive her around without first raising her fork, causing sparks to fly as the prongs scraped painfully across the reinforced cement floor.

The yellow forklift, named Teresa since its last driver had painted his child's name on it, sadly deteriorated from her previously spunky self and now dripped tears of hydraulic fluid as she dragged herself forlornly about the premises. Eventually the loading dock foreman, Bolivar Marticorena, took notice and stepped in to champion her cause.

"It's a crime the way you abuse this machine," he said.

"Why don't you go to hell!" retorted Niño de Jesus with the defensive indignation of somebody who knows perfectly well he is being justly accused.

Whether Bolivar was right or wrong was beside the point. Niño de Jesus knew the Mexican foreman had it in for him because he was from Ecuador. Besides, he knew Bolivar's hideous secret, that he was a demon from the depths of hell who had ascended into the world by way of a stairway behind the furnace in the sub-basement of the factory, a filthy, hellish place where the slops from the drainage system fell into the city's sewer system.

Niño de Jesus sometimes went down there because the foul odor kept others away, and he could get some peace and quiet while he sipped from a pint bottle of Ronrico to steady his nerves. As the old saying goes, once you get past the smell you've got it licked, and Niño de Jesus passed many agreeable solitary moments there, alone except for the occasional water bug or rodent. That is, until the day when he heard whistling, chuckling voices coming from behind the giant hundred year-old furnace in a dark corner.

The furnace towered like a steel mountain behind a blackened lagoon of a cesspool of shiny sewage and putrefied rat carcasses. Intrigued, he squeezed into the narrow passage separating the furnace from the wall until he had gotten behind it. There was a solid green door. He tried the handle, but it was locked.

The voices behind the door went silent when they heard somebody trying the handle. There was total silence for several seconds, then suddenly a terrifying chorus of howls and screams startled and

BORDERLINES

frightened Niño de Jesus. Panicked, he tried to scramble back through the narrow passage from which he had come, but in his haste he snagged part of his clothing on a piece of metal protruding from the furnace.

Unable to move, he heard the voices come right up behind him, mocking him and threatening him in unknown languages of gibberish. Disembodied faces spun around in the air, laughing and menacing as Niño de Jesus, soaked in sweat and praying to Jesus for salvation from these infernal spirits who now laughingly taunted and threatened him with destruction and the loss of his immortal soul.

He passed out, hanging there like a marionette in this dark, stinking subterranean pit of filth and demons for an immeasurable period of time. Once he woke up to find giant water bugs crawling all over his clothing and body, sucking the salt perspiration. At the end of the short passage, rats stuck their heads in curiously, wondering how long it would take for him to die so they could begin eating him. Passing out again, he retreated into a dream state of delirium.

At length he was discovered by the old man, Tato, whose job in the factory it was to search out and kill bugs and rodents, for which purpose he carried with him a little tin first-aid case that he called his "maleta de muerte," stuffed as it was with the traps and poisons that were his instruments of destruction. He would assemble all the little dead critters he had collected during his shift in a white bakery bag and show them to his boss as proof of his indispensability to the company.

His manager, a hardened man of fifty, might very well be biting into a sandwich at the time of such an exhibition, where a glance into the bag would transport him into another little unique dimension of hell, one of water bugs stuck to glue traps, their shells and wings in disarray, many still alive with antennae furiously thrashing about; maggot-ridden corpses of mice stuck to traps with blood flowing out of their mouths and laying in their own droppings.

"Muy bueno," the manager would tell the old man as he chewed his sandwich. And he meant it. Tato, with his small body and unabashed enthusiasm for squeezing into dark corners of the factory, flashlight in hand, performed an invaluable function. The manager, although repelled by this little menagerie of loathsome filth, was nevertheless heartened by the knowledge that none of these animals would contaminate the food product or, even more horribly, intrude their pointy little heads during a factory tour.

"You're doing a fine job," he would compliment the little man in fluent, though heavily anglo-inflected Spanish. "Get out there and kill some more!" The old man, elated by this encouragement, would recommence with renewed ardor.

Tato found Niño de Jesus Benitez suspended in the narrow passage behind the furnace, his clothes tangled in the machinery, and helped cut him free with a box cutter. After he had cut him loose, he cautioned Niño de Jesus in barely comprehensible Spanish, "Never go there. There are bad things."

This episode had a major impact on Niño de Jesus' mind, and he started going down to the sub-basement on a regular basis, not to nip the bottle but to monitor the activity behind the furnace. In the silence, punctuated only by the gurgling and plopping of the rancid, filthy factory waste water flowing through the drainage pipe into the slop sink, he could make out the sounds coming from the green door at the end of the narrow passage, the infernal whistling and chuckling of rats mixed with human voices shrilly screaming and the shouts and pleadings of tortured souls being impaled on spikes, branded with red-hot pokers, having their eyes gouged out.

This was the work of the Jews, he decided, who ascended a staircase leading from the pit of hell to emerge in modern New York. He formulated a clear picture of this diabolical intrusion of demons and determined that the bakery was a mere front for the methodical infiltration of Jew-demons into the world, a hellish Fifth Column organized to deliver humanity into the embrace of Satan.

Armed with this knowledge, Niño de Jesus Benitez came to develop a clear understanding of the events of September 11, which, though having occurred many years before, were still the major preoccupation of New York society. He came to realize that the buildings' collapse, while precipitated by the airplanes having collided into them, actually resulted from fissures in the earth's crust caused by the Jews burrowing underneath them and weakening their foundations.

Niño de Jesus could distinguish over the roar of the furnace and the rushing flop of sewage the barely audible moans and pleas of priests stripped naked and chained to posts, bleeding and sweating, their pathetic moans and pleas for mercy and salvation drowned out by the hellish baritone laughter of monstrous leather-clad lesbians wearing huge dildos who flagellated them unmercifully with barbed wire cat o' nine tail whips.

BORDERLINES

He decided to alert a priest, Father Guzman, a saintly man who ministered to the unfortunate Central American undocumented aliens out of St. Anthony's Parish in Corona. Father Guzman listened sympathetically to Niño de Jesus' description of the events taking place behind the green door and wrote him a referral for psychiatric counselling, which Niño de Jesus immediately tore up after leaving the priest's office.

"If they think they're going to get me, they're crazy!"

BORDERLINES

Lisa Timmerman
HIDDEN

*S*tories. *I used to think they were a part of this world, of reality. Now I realize that they are only a means of making you feel better or worse about yourself and of justifying the love or hatred you feel for your life and the world. I'm so scared. Scared that someday I might find out that human happiness depends on living lies and never confessing the truth. But if there are lies, will there be a future?*

I have decided to hate my father again. After the fight I sit in my old room for a while, on my bed and watch his cat play with its latest victim. I realize I feel exactly the same way I felt when I was six, twelve or fifteen years old. How adult can you get when you never say goodbye to the past?

Dusk has arrived early today, the sun has vanished behind some grey clouds and the air that fills the room through the half-open window smells of rain. It reflects my downcast mind. I'm still hearing his voice in my head, shouting at me with contempt. And the way he looked at me ... it wasn't him, those eyes weren't his.

From early on in my life I heard everyone describing him as brave and selfless, because he put his own life at risk during the war to help others. Even mum refers to it a lot, telling me how much I'm like him and how important it is to be a good person.

I am sick of hearing it. I remind myself of his past so often, but it's of no use. I can not help but think that she needs it as an excuse to stay with him, the thought of loneliness has always scared her.

My mother has sent me on a errand to the attic. Walking up the stairs, I feel observed, expected. Stop it, I tell myself, you're getting paranoid. I quickly climb up the last steps and open the door, but the feeling gets more intense. I stare about the room. It is bright up here . . . surprisingly. It is not frightening, but there's something murky despite the light. I move to the middle of the room where all the boxes are standing, covered in dust and spider webs.

I start opening a few cartons to look inside for what she wanted. It isn't there. I look through more boxes but eventually realize that I won't be successful; I will have to disappoint her once again.

BORDERLINES

What I find instead is a lot of old stuff from the Third Reich. I lift the carton and put it down to my right to get access to the last one. Again it's just old stuff from the war and, underneath, some photos of him and Mum. I take them out and look at them. How did they manage to look so happy?

Tears well up in my eyes so I quickly turn to the next photo, and start to shudder. It's a photograph of a Jew being forced to dig his own grave. Five SS men are standing behind him, laughing.

The picture was probably taken by my father or one of his companions in the resistance movement. I begin to wonder how much cruelty they must have seen. Can this make me feel something for him again? Something other than hate? I take a closer look at the sadistic faces of the SS men. What went on in their minds that they could enjoy those things?

When I'm back in my room, the whole world has changed, and I feel like I should never have gone upstairs. Suddenly things are much clearer . . . and yet still confusing. I look out the window again: it's started to rain.

The cat has disappeared from the room but its play-thing remains. Are all humans just like cats and mice? I don't want to hurt others but I also don't want to be trapped and pushed around. But then there doesn't seem to be any place in between the two, even if everyone does try to believe that.

He could not fool me.

Will I dare to tell him? Will I dare to tell her, or does she already know? Was that why she sent me up there, so I could finally learn the truth?

There was one man in the picture was not showing his face to the camera. Maybe he knew they were being photographed. Might there be a chance he wasn't enjoying what he and the others were doing?

I feel like I am hoping too much again. Trying to make myself believe that some of them were not that bad, that they acted only with the fear or shock caused by everything that was going on. At first the man just seemed strangely familiar to me, even though I only saw his shape. Then I noticed the chain he was wearing.

I kept looking at the photo for a long time. Staring, feeling nothing. I could not move, could not put it back. All the time trying to convince myself it was not my father's chain. The chain I was wearing.

I've worried about her for a good reason, but now, surprisingly, I actually worry about him. Why did he do it? I need his answer. Or maybe I need to accept that he would never let me find it. Did he ever think, even for a second, that it might haunt him later on? Did he not think someone mind find out?

He lied even though he was so eager to tell about his past, but nobody was interested, nobody wanted to hear. He told a fairy-tale that made everyone smile, gave everyone hope, made everyone believe humans can be good and decent and selfless. He became the hero figure in our little village, useful to mention whenever you were in conflict with someone.

This feels so different from anything I've felt before, I think. I won't forgive him. The hope he gave me years ago can't justify anything. Would I not be happier living a lie for the rest of my life? I know it's too late, but I try to think of my mother and how pleased she looks whenever he tells those lies about his past, but it doesn't help.

I rip off the chain he used to wear. The cross falls down on my foot and I pick it up. I don't know how long I've been wearing it. He gave it to me when he still liked me, told me he wore it "during those bleak times".

I will not forget this, and what's more, I'll tell whoever can bear the truth. Or perhaps this disillusionment will fade away before it can make me act, and I'll be like all those people I despise – repressing the past in order to focus on the future, even if there really isn't one.

BORDERLINES

Linda Regan
I SAW NOTHING

Most nights Albert was distracted from his television or radio because of the outbursts of fighting in the grounds below. The revving of bikes as gangs arrived followed by raised voices, the sound of glass breaking, then agonizing screams and angry shouting, and now, more frequently, the sound of a gun being fired. But then this was Peckham; this is what happened here.

He had lived on this estate, man and boy, for sixty-six years. He'd seen them all come and go: the teddy boys, the mods and rockers, the punk era; there was always something. But never guns - guns were new, and they bothered him. It brought back the nightmares he'd experienced after the war ended. Until recently Elsie was there to comfort him, but now he was a widower after fifty-three years of marriage. He would turn the television up and try and pretend it wasn't happening. There was no one to talk to about it. Everyone he knew on this block had either died or moved away, so he kept to himself, only venturing out on his weekly visit to the post office for his pension and to collect the meagre bits of groceries he'd need for the week.

The fighting seemed to always happen under his first floor balcony, or by the lift. Not that the lift worked; it had been out of order for a long time now. No engineer would come to this block. Recently, one had been mugged and beaten badly enough to need stitches, all for the theft of his screwdriver. The screwdriver was later found driven into the eye of a fourteen-year-old boy.

This particular night the fighting was even worse which made Albert more nervous. He was watching East Enders, one of his weekly highlights. But the usual raised voices, revved bikes, sounds of glass smashing or crowbars breaking into a skull and the screaming that followed sounded different. Albert turned the television down and nervously listened. The voices weren't familiar, and there were more of them. There must be a new gang on the estate.

Then he heard a shot, followed by the usual silence . . . then another shot rang out, followed by the screaming. Another shot followed that, and then another, another and another. Albert did not count. He was shaking, and holding his photo of Elsie. Then it stopped.

BORDERLINES

There was silence.

The silence continued. Someone else on the estate must have heard.

He crept to the front door. He had a chain fixed, so he felt safe enough to open it slightly.

He saw the teenager. He was crawling along the passage on the first floor, his light hand covering his side, where dark blood was fast dripping through his shaking fingers. He caught Albert staring at him and stretched his blood-soaked hand toward him, his face twisted in pain as he tried to speak, to beg even, for Albert to save his life.

That look on his frightened face touched Albert deeply; he had seen that look when he was a young, frightened soldier.

He released the chain to help the boy.

That's when he saw the other youth: older, darker, walking purposely toward the injured boy, gripping a large gleaming knife in his hand.

The younger tried to stand to defend himself. Albert watched, horror struck, as the older teenager (could he really be that young?) yanked the younger by his hair, sliced it across the young neck, opening the carotid artery. A rush of blood shot out, landing on Albert's only remaining pair of trousers and his checked wool slippers.

The young body slumped. Blood flowed along the passage and over the edge of the balcony. Albert went to shut his door, but the murderer had seen him. Their eyes held each other, one in terror, the other venom.

Albert slammed the door and latched the chain.

The police were surprisingly quick on the scene, and the blood at Albert's front door led to him being questioned. He was trying to wash the blood off his slippers when they knocked. He found it terrifying being taken down to the station, questioned and then shown pictures to identify the murderer.

He said he didn't recognise the culprit, even though the image of the man, the knife and those eyes were stamped on his memory.

He was grateful when they drove him home, even in a police car; he felt too shaken to take the bus.

It was the next morning. He was scraping charcoal off his toast; he had burned the last two slices of his loaf, and he wouldn't be going out for any more until the end of the week, even if he did have the money.

He thought it was the police again when the doorbell rang. He opened it without the chain.

Those same murdering eyes stared at him.

BORDERLINES

He tried to shut the door. The foot in it prevented him. Albert felt his saliva dry in his mouth. 'Th..th.. they asked me, sh..showed me your picture,' he said trying to control his stuttering. 'I s..said I never saw your face. I n...never gave you up. Leave me alone. Please.'

A hand came up from the youth's side. It held a revolver, the pack pointing at Albert's face.

His heartbeat doubled and his voice rose and then broke as he begged. 'Please, I never told.' His hand tried to protect his face but was knocked aside as the cold steel of the gun pushed into his wrinkled temple.

He started to cry. 'I..I..s..said I didn't know nothing, didn't recognise you . . . please trust me. I saw nothing.'

'That was your mistake, Old Man.' The cock of the safety catch made Albert gasp. His body shook pathetically.

'Y'see, I don't trust no one,' the youth said.

The estate heard another gunshot that afternoon.

BORDERLINES

Karen Clark
THE VIRUS

Daddy came home with a virus. At first I didn't notice anything wrong, but soon he wasn't like Daddy at all. He shouted and stayed in bed longer than was decent. Mother said he caught it in the war, probably in the trenches because they were rat infested and riddled with disease. She said Churchill had a lot to answer for, but Daddy had done his duty and we should be proud of him. I did try, though it's hard to be proud of someone who isn't very nice. What's more, I was forbidden to mention Daddy's illness to a single living soul. Secrets aren't easy to keep when you're a kid, are they?

For a long time I blamed Mother for Daddy not getting any better. If she hadn't saddled him with another baby he could have rested more. My new brother Billy was a squawking little sod. Some nights he even woke me. His pitiful cries seeped through the bedroom wall. Obviously he disturbed Daddy too. He would yell, "Get that brat out of here, Rose, and give me some bloody peace." Then I'd hear Mother move down the stairs.

Once I crept to the kitchen for a glass of water. Peeping through the crack of the sitting room door I saw her quite clearly. The moon was full and low and shone through the window, bathing her in a blue light. She was sitting on the old wooden rocker. Her breasts were bare and tears sparkled like jewels upon her face. She pushed a dark teat into my brother's open mouth and he became quiet. I remember thinking Daddy would be fine if it wasn't for them. Of course now I wish I hadn't indulged in such un-Christian thoughts.

It wasn't all bad living with daddy and his virus. When the pain didn't pester him he was lovely. Some days were nearly perfect. On those days, especially in autumn, he and I would crunch across the frozen earth wrapped up like Eskimos and go nutting for cobs. Or, in the fragile warmth of a Spring sun, I'd pick bluebells and primroses while he spun stories about the good old days. These are my best memories. As long as he took regular nips of medicine he was almost all right. When he wasn't sick he'd bounce Billy in his arms and make him laugh, and Mother would smile and so would I.

She didn't really smile much anymore. Before Daddy came home she smiled a lot, even though she worked all the hours God sent keeping our

BORDERLINES

grocery shop afloat. It wasn't a cushy job, what with the rationing and coupons and shortages, but she said it was for our future. She continued working as Daddy was, according to Grandma, "fit for nothing."

Daddy started disappearing for hours. He'd return so exhausted he could hardly stand or string two words together. I hated when that happened. A shadow of hopelessness would cloud Mothers' eyes.

I'd hold my breath and silently pray Daddy would take himself of to bed. He never did, though. He'd start accusing Mother of all sorts of things, from carrying on with Wally the butcher to hiding his money, and she'd say, "Money, Jack? What money would that be with you forever dipping your hand in the till?"

Then they'd have a terrible ding-dong, forgetting I was there to hear words I shouldn't hear at my age. When I couldn't bear it any longer I'd squirrel me and Billy away and hide. Those perfect days I treasured grew fewer and fewer as the virus manoeuvred a stranglehold on him.

One rainy January morning Daddy took a turn for the worse. The doctor was sent for. I recall asking Mother, "What's wrong with Daddy?" I didn't mean his illness. I was twelve now and, being an expert at reading between the lines, knew more than I should have.

Mother said, "Probably a touch of flu, Kathleen, nothing to fret about. I expect Doctor Ferguson will give him a tonic," but I guessed that was a lie, same as the hundreds I'd heard before. No-one else's Daddy had come home with the virus, not even Johnny Morgan's, and he'd been on the beach somewhere in France and shot in the leg. He'd been plucked out of the icy water half dead by the crew on a fishing boat from Portsmouth. Plenty weren't so lucky, Johnny said. Plenty ended up in Davy Jones's locker.

"I don't think Doctor Ferguson can do anything for Daddy," I sighed. "I think Daddy has had too much medicine." If I close my eyes I can still see the sadness etched deep upon my mothers' face. For a minute she didn't move a muscle. We stared at one another as if we were strangers. She pulled me roughly towards her and hugged me tight and I breathed in her Californian Poppy scent.

"Kathleen," she said in a wobbly voice, "when this is over I promise things will be different," and we clung together and sobbed our hearts out, for ourselves as well as for Daddy.

And that's the trouble with war. Men don't always die quick and clean in battle. Some make it home safe in body but not in soul. Some can't leave the horror behind. In the end I suppose Daddy was killed by a virus. Only this particular strain was called vodka.

BORDERLINES *Poetry*

Liz Barlow
SKELETONS

The blue hours
where the world lies
unconscious.

Bad smells.

Funerals.
   Can't we celebrate death
like Mexicans?
   And dance with skeletons
like props on the street.

Home, where my roots are set,
   underneath the pond,
   and beneath the graves
   of my cats.

Men with boring haircuts.

Boys that want
tits and arse
  and us silly girls
who fall for it.

Death. All those names
that will be carried in wreaths,
   like 'MUM' and 'DAD,'
and my own.

Throwing up my obsessions
and sinking back
  inside the bed.

Anita Sheard
AFTER THE NIGHT TRAIN

I've rented my chair
Two-fifty a cup
I'm watching the world go by
People rushing and running
Trains going and coming
No hankies or fond goodbyes.

It's seven o'clock
And all is well
As far as the eye can see.
It's bustling and hustling
On Paddington station
It's time at work to be.

So here I wait
An hour to go –
I feel like the eponymous bear
With marmalade sarnies his only fare
And a label to anyone to care.

Victor Manley
A DRIVE IN WINTER

The winter sun
Lights the tops of winter branches,
Climbing in red or gold
From chalky soil against cobbled walls.

Icy yellow, bright white orange
Silhouettes the crowned hillside
Where the evergreens perch high.

Tentative mists
Press fingers
Across the landscape,
Rolling careful veils
To hold the horizon in.

But on, on,
Past stately iron pylons,
Great follies of high steel,
That approach out of the mist
To balance the moon
For a moment on their wires,
Before folding themselves in fog again
And wrapping up close in gloom.

While white geese and swans
Kick legs against the ice
That reaches in from the banks
Like a slow, creeping vice.

Look there, at the smoke
That rises behind an old sandstone wall,
And above, a fat winter sun sets unseen;
But its glow still fires beyond trees.

BORDERLINES

I wonder what people trample the frost there?
Blow against sore fingers
And drag branches towards icicled flame.
A man and his son perhaps?
While a greying dog snuffles
At dead rabbit holes and the crunch of tired leaves.

Perhaps the boy is thinking
And remembers the spring,
When his father smoked the holes
And a dozen grey rabbits ran
Towards the cover of trees.
But now it is quiet
And the crackle of flames
Is all that's alive.

The sun appears for a moment
As the land falls and slips away,
Starting a mist edged forest fire
Before disappearing again
Behind a thousand skeletal arms,
An army of sleeping trees
Waiting to rise up
With the warmth of spring.

Moments slip
And suddenly now that the sun has passed
Night's freeze approaches,
And we hurry towards the strokes of midnight
Where slow chaos breeds.

Rebecca Wass
TREE

Inspired by a collection of words

He stands by himself in his forest, ferny feet firmly fixed to the floor.
Leaves in his skull, and dirt in his toes, deep wounds all over his corpse.
His wrinkles are deep, a sign of time,
And wet weather
In his outdoor home.
His face is that of a failure,
A drooping mouth
 Etched in cedar skin.
His eyes are dull,
Creased with age,
His arms have grown
Weak and thin.
No birds lay their eggs in his tender arms
He has no leafy protection for their young
And so he stands by himself in the forest
And waits for winter to come.

BORDERLINES

Chris Burden
LITTLE RED BUCKET

I never take trains anywhere. I think they're over-priced and more complicated than they really need to be. So, naturally, when I had to get to Cardiff from Portsmouth, being a non-driver, I was not happy that rail travel was my only option. Three and a half hours on the same train? I was definitely going to need something to distract me. Well, thank God for John Barrowman's autobiography. Yes, I know how that sounds but just trust me on this. Go and buy it now. Wait - actually, finish reading this first.

I realise that trains do have their positives. For example, J. K. Rowling got her idea for Harry Potter while she was on a train and look how well that worked out for her! Lucky bitch! So, I'm on this never-ending train journey, hoping that inspiration will strike me and I'll create the next world phenomenon.

It didn't happen. Not that I'm bitter. It just seems a bit unfair. I realise that by now you're wondering why this is called "Little Red Bucket". So far I've just rambled on about trains, J. K. Rowling and John Barrowman. So where does the little red bucket come in? I'm getting to it, really. Patience is a virtue. So I'm reading Mr Barrowman's autobiography (actually laughing out loud, drawing some strange looks from the other passengers like I was some freak, thank you very much) and I figure that I should maybe actually look out the window at some point to work out where I might be. All I see is fields. Typical England.

But in this one field I see a little red bucket, there all by itself. It was the answer to all my prayers: it was inspiration! So I start thinking up all these little stories about this little red bucket. Why was it there? Who put it there? Was it deliberate? Is it lost? Is it searching for its spade? Is it travelling the countryside of England trying to find its place in this crazy world?

I created a character for this bucket. It was very "Mighty Boosh"-esque and spoke in very posh English, crying out for its spade: "Oh spade, where art thou? Why dost thou desert me so?" Also, I've recently just re-watched "Shakespeare In Love," so I could be slightly influenced.

You might not believe me, but the bucket was actually crying so at this point I'd like to point out that buckets actually cry in a frequency that is

BORDERLINES

out of the range of human hearing. So there. It's over a week later when I finally have the time to actually sit and start writing my story about the little red bucket. I had already created my character and I'd decided that I was going to make it quite random and funny. So I sit with my laptop in front of me, "Skins" on in the background (how could I not watch it? The new series starts tomorrow and I needed to catch up) and I try to make my little red bucket come to life.

I couldn't. And trust me, I tried. I tried it as a story, as a poem, then as a story again, and I just couldn't make it work. Everything I wrote was utter crap. An absolute load of…well, you get the picture. So then I started to ramble, just unloading all the rubbish that was in my head. And here it is. That's what you're reading right now.

It's got the random-ness that I was originally going for and I've explained my little red bucket character. And who knows what I could write about next? I bet the suspense is killing you. I could unearth some eternal wisdom that could change your life. I could. I do feel sorry for that little red bucket though. I realise that it isn't real but now that I've created a character for it it's become alive in my mind. Imagine searching the countryside looking for your spade, your soul mate, the one you're supposed to spend the rest of your life with, creating sand castles together.

How fast do you think a bucket can move? It doesn't have legs! So now not only is it lonely but its also disabled. This bucket has had the hardest life ever. It draws a tear to my eye, really, it does. Imagine the bucket's childhood; that bucket was clearly picked on in school. Kids can be so cruel, especially when they're baby-buckets. You don't believe me? Just check online, the Internet has everything. All I ask is that when you're out and about, going about your business, you think of that little red bucket. And if you happen to meet a little red spade, tell him to search the English countryside for a little red bucket that sounds like it's auditioning for a role in "Romeo and Juliet." Remember: save a bucket, save a spade.

BORDERLINES

Andrew Williams
CLUB PRIDE

Business was slow. A few punters had trickled through but I was down for the night. Still, it was only Tuesday; tomorrow the weekend would begin.

I leaned on the rail and looked down at the dancers. A big club like this couldn't build any atmosphere when it was half full. The dancers looked like religious maniacs vying for attention at Hyde Park Corner but their energy was dissipated in the open spaces.

Then I saw Lynsey wandering about and stood erect. Her hair was piled high and she wore a mini skirt and knee high boots, a combination that sent tingles radiating through me, especially around my boxers. There was a little history between us. A week or so ago I saw her home because she got separated from her friend. She invited me in for coffee; well, the coffee stayed in the kitchen and we got off on her settee. When I got my hand down her knickers she stopped me on the grounds of it being a first date but I was intrigued - she was shaven down there. I wouldn't say it was a preference of mine but I can appreciate a job when it's well done and it was as smooth as marble. I had to respect her for that as well as her chasteness.

Modestly assuming she was on her way up to see me I arranged myself on the sofa ready to receive her. Instead, Tris appeared at the top of the stairs, sunken eyed, face drawn. He came over and flopped next to me.

'Oh man,' he groaned. 'I've had a bad day; give me two.'

I fished in my pocket for two bags and waited until he put the money down before making the switch. Before I even pocketed the twenty he had the bag opened and a large mound of powder on the back of his hand. He licked it up like a lizard then washed it down with my drink before lying back, moaning like a sick bear. This was usual behaviour, but tonight it felt odd. I was still trying for alluring and Tris looked like something unnatural had been done to him. If Lynsey were to appear now . . . well. After a minute, though, he snapped up in the seat and began rubbing his hands together: 'Nice one, Doc,' he said, his eyes gleaming like beacons as he grinned.

'Okay. Mind how you go.'

'Yeah,' he said. Then: 'Wait. I've got a bone to pick with you: the bags.'

BORDERLINES

'The bags?'

'These ones,' he said waving the bag of gear in front of me.

'Oh,' I said. 'Look Tris, you get a full gram of gear each time. Just go and weigh one if you don't believe it.'

'No, no,' Tris said. 'I don't mean that. These bags aren't recyclable.'

I shrugged: 'So what? I've got the bags covered, don't worry about them.'

He shook his head and looked at me with judgemental eyes. 'It's everyone's duty to recycle, Doc. We've got to save the world, man. These things are harming the environment.'

'Okay. Just bring them to me when you've finished with them. I'll recycle them.'

'Can't be done,' he said, shaking his head. 'I've checked.'

'Well, I'll just…burn them.'

He gaped for a few moments then his eyes narrowed before a smile cracked his face: 'Oh, man,' he said, slapping his thigh. 'You had me going there, Doc.'

I smiled out of politeness. He stood up and pointed at me: 'You're a card, man.'

'Okay,' I said. 'Take care. You know where I am if you need me.'

'Oh yeah,' he said sitting back down. 'I'm going on holiday.'

'Good,' I said looking over at the stairs.

'Yeah, I'm going away for five weeks.'

'That is great.'

'Three of us are flying to New Zealand, down on the South Island. There's this uninhabited island in a middle of a lake that's one of the last unspoiled places left on earth. Well, my mate's brother went over last year and met this geezer who took him there and that's what we're going to do. Go to the last unspoiled place on earth.'

I tried hard to listen but couldn't help looking out for Lynsey. Tris took this to mean that I was bored with his story and so became more animated, injecting urgency into his voice.

'I know what you're thinking, Doc. How can this guy take us onto an unspoiled island without us damaging the environment?'

'You'll take off your shoes?'

He shook his head: 'He's taking us over by helicopter. Yeah, swoops down low so we can see everything, man. The petrol only lasts half an hour so we have to go back a couple of times to refuel but he's giving us a discount because my mate's brother recommended him. It's a shame too,

BORDERLINES

though; he used to take you over at night, let off a few flares so you could see and everything. Everyone used to go up tripping off their nuts. But one time, just before my mate's brother went, a flare hit a tree. Whoosh! The tree caught on fire, man! Apparently they could see little animals running away and jumping into the sea; bad karma.'

'It sounds great. I wish I was going myself,' I said getting up.

'Yeah, I'll tell you all about it when I get back.'

As he left I darted to the rail and a quick look found Lynsey down at the side bar. I was in no mood to play a waiting game so decided to make the first move. Then, as I prepared to go I got butterflies; all these weeks sitting up here taking my pick of the desperate junkies who wanted gear had left me a bit rusty when it came to the smooth talk.

The answer was in my pocket; I got a bag and made a small mound on my hand, licked it up and gagged when I found my drink empty. I cursed Tris as the noxious powder seared my throat. I felt nauseous for a minute until the gear began to alter my system; my engine started to purr.

Vroom-vroom: Slide into first and head for the stairs. Yow! Suddenly I feel good. Slip into second; going down. Vroom-vroom: Oh my word, I'm up into third: Lynsey, Lynsey, this ante meridian, let me come and inspect your Brazilian. Vroom-vroom: Jammed up into four I hit the dance-floor. Let's cruise down the yellow brick road where fragments of shifting white light and amorphous blobs of colour show the way.

My radar is set on Lynsey but here are a circle of people, clapping and whooping. I join them and see that they are watching a couple who are dancing dirty. They're grooving to the vibrations of my engine and I start whooping and clapping too until I realise the dancers are Lynsey and Tris.

Reverse, reverse: Oh no, my engine stalls. I leave it at the side of the road and skulk to the bar along nightmare alley. Watch out for broken bottles, rusty hypodermics and giant rats masturbating over mounds of dog-shit.

At the bar I order two large rums. The first doesn't touch the sides but the second takes two swallows to die. I order two more which are able to be sipped. Pretty soon the alcohol has sedated my embarrassment, calmed the jangle of my nerves and I'm able to survey the damage to my ego. Hmm, a little scratch on the paintwork but nothing serious and no one actually saw the accident, did they?

Then: I was clapped hard on the back. I slammed down my drink and wheeled round: 'Tris! What the fuck do you want.'

Beads of sweat decorating his face, he pressed something into my hand saying: 'Sort it, Doc.' Lynsey giggled behind him: 'Come on.' They went back to the floor and I looked in my hand: Two empty plastic-bags.

Hot rivers of anger shot through my veins and it took a conscious effort not to go after him and…and what? I'm not a violent man; but he was out of line there. I'd be within my rights to give him a beating, though.

I turned and hunched over my drink. The doormen flashed into my mind; I felt the two-way radio in my pocket. The realization that I was capable of the order pierced my mind like a falling stone hitting water sending ripples of cold energy through me. Suddenly, a corner of my heart seemed illuminated: Envy and Vengeance were setting up home by Pride's longstanding castle. They built the type of stick and straw shack that could not withstand a blast of love or a few kind words, but although Pride looked down disdainfully at his brothers from the battlements, I knew he was wounded and would make room for two little pigs if need be.

I took my drink upstairs, two-way radio throbbing in my pocket.

BORDERLINES*Poetry*

Calvin Hussey
THE ILLUSION SPECIALIST

I can still hear the discontent resonate in the air as my time comes to take the stage,

The night's entertainment has been weak at best, leaving the crowd vexed, restless and crazed.
They grumble and hiss at the word "illusionist," and pass me off as another sequined, self loving lunatic,
But I'm no parlour trick pushing magician, nor narcissist who simply likes to watch himself exist, I'm the illusion specialist.
They're deluded into the knowledge that it's all just an act, but the illusion serves to confuse them as a matter of fact,
It's all just entertainment, just an act crafted to deceive them into believing they're safe in their seats, while I seemingly defy logic and bend reality, they fail to see that I'm merely a thief,
They sit and stare in disbelief at conjured on-stage antics, they'd panic if they knew of their treasured possessions that I remove,
But they don't have a clue, and besides the thief could be anyone, my countless crimes will leave no proof,
So I continue to mystify and remove their belongings and target post-show victims for untying of thong strings.
My final act is the illusion of the perfect man, false personas crafted to impress each victim begin my sordid plan, their naivety astounds me so I say whatever I can,
To deceive them into a state of undress and fondle breasts, as I remove the necklace from every neck,
And before anyone has time to suspect, or connect events, or inspect the absent valuables I've colleted, I make an exit, undetected in a way I have used many times before,
It is just another part of the act, a spectacle of deception, it's all just a matter of smoke and mirrors.

BORDERLINES *Travel*

Caitlin McCallum
EVERYTHING'S COMING UP CRAZY

Roommate Available 1/1/08 (flexible) to Open Yes Rental type Apartment Bedrooms Two, Available 1 Bathrooms - Parking Doorman High speed internet Smoker OK Pets OK Elevator Cable Laundry in bldg Air conditioning Utilities included Credit app. reqd Broker fee none

Arriving in Los Angeles as a starry eyed transplant from the Midwest, I had compiled a list of things to do and see that were quintessential California activities. Most were beach, art and nightlife scene oriented, but I had one pressing issue that needed to be addressed: finding a place to live.

Homelessness was an option, but I put aside my affection for free soup and dumpster diving chic for shelter and a roommate or three. After consulting the few present and former Los Angelinians I knew, the website Westside Rentals came out the unanimous victor over Craigslist. The cited reason boiled down to perceived legitimacy and sanity of potential roommates.

After charging $60 on my credit card for 3 months worth of web searching, my quest and subsequent adventures began. I found little legitimacy and definite insanity. Here are some highlights:

"Hi. I'm calling about the room for rent on Westside Rentals." A man in Middle Eastern accent: "Yes, I am Hugo. I am manager. What do you want?"

"Oh, I just moved here and am curious about the room for rent with one roommate and a private bathroom." My cheeks are hot, Hugo does not seem terribly friendly.

"You move in at beginning of next month. Right now I have two ladies in apartment, but soon just one lady as roommate was not granted green card and so she no stay in my building. Or in America (It seems this fact just dawned on Hugo). So I help find replacement."

"Oh. I'm sorry. Well, I'm interested in checking the place out. It's a room and bathroom right?"

I hear Hugo hesitate (RED FLAG #1), "Yes, but I use bathroom sometimes, but only when I stay in living room (RED FLAG #2). I bought

BORDERLINES

new shower head. I am manager and need to be there sometimes. It's my couch that I lent to Leyna and Pushpa, the ladies."

Am I being punked? "I'm sorry, but you stay in the living room?" Maybe Hugo is friendlier than first suspected.

Hugo is growing impatient, "Yes, yes. That's what I say. I am gay. Don't worry (RED FLAG #3). I go out to club at night. Gay clubs. Where I dress up. You know? Like woman. So I get ready at building I manage and where you will live? (RED FLAG #4) I don't want my neighbors seeing me dressed up. You know? Like woman (RED FLAG #5)."

I want to tell Hugo that I'm pretty confident that his neighbors are aware he is a Looney Tune cross dresser, but instead, like Yankee Doodle, he gives me one last feather to put in my cap.

"I also use kitchen to make sandwiches. I lent refrigerator too. I clean up. I make one for you too."(RED FLAG #6)

I feel high, is this really happening? Isn't it the landlord's job to supply basic appliances? I have an image of Hugo in fishnet stockings with his gut hanging out between his much too tight catholic school girl skirt and mesh tank top, smearing sauce on a gyro and he raises it to his coral lip-sticked mouth only to get onions caught in his beard.

"So how about you come tonight? I am getting ready there tonight. You can meet Pushpa before she is deported."

I hang up. How could anyone replace Pushpa?

The timer on my phone reads 6 min 34 seconds. I have a new perspective on time and realize this roommate searching may not be as easy as first led to believe. I have another option saved on my searches. This listing only offers an e-mail and no phone number. I type up a brief inquiry expressing my interest and expect no response. How could I when the following is at stake: a Spanish-style house in Brentwood, complete with movie viewing room and tennis courts with a private wing with balcony and pool for the too-good-to-be-believed price of $400 month.

To my surprise, I received an email the next day from the lister, a Miss Melanie Joy. She gave me the address and said to stop by anytime and someone should be home. I scribbled the street down and dashed out the door. I approached the house and had an eerie feeling, although nothing was out of the ordinary. A few overgrown bushes and weeds littered the lawn, but otherwise the property was immaculate.

I rang the doorbell and a woman who had to be in her mid eighties who came up to my knees answered the door. "Yes. I like you," she grabs my hand and is laughing hysterically saying how pretty I am and other

BORDERLINES

nonsense. I like old people and so I am not bothered by her obvious senility . . . and I also like that she likes me purely based on my looks. Another person, resembling Cousin It, sat silently watching some reality TV program with crazed brides (are there any sane ones?).

"Hi, I'm looking for Melanie. I'm here to see the house."

Cousin It looks up, "I like weddings. Do you like weddings?" Fuck.

I glance around for a glass menagerie. This is not a good sign and even after speaking, I'm unable to differentiate this person's gender. Before I can voice my opinion, Melanie Joy appears in all her sweat pant, matted-hair-angrily-pulled-into-a-scrunchie, Tweetey-Bird-size 3 XXL-t-shirt glory.

"I'm Melanie Joy. That's my sister Lauren Grace. Ignore her. And that's our great aunt Burma. Ignore her, too. Let me show you the place."

As I attempt to conceal my glee over getting gender confirmation of Cousin It, I observe Melanie Joy: an expressionless fat canvas. She leads me though the enormous house and proceeds to tell me a number of troubling tidbits: how her parents died in 2004 and she has a trust fund and that she decorated the house herself and that she has a son but never sees him and her ex-husband lives in San Bernardino and doesn't pay child support because he works for the government and that I seem very young, that she has not eaten dinner, that she had a long day at work, that I have to do a credit check if I want to live here, that she hasn't voted since McGovern was President, but the attorney who handles all the money is screening her calls so it might take a while (I'm impressed such an insane person can differentiate between screening a call and missing one). The entire time great aunt Burma (why no middle name?) is clutching my hand and ever so slightly drooling.

I slowly backed out and was checking every potential escape route. She has never depended on the kindness of strangers, nor do I think that it was ever an option. I took note of the plethora of pills hanging in the cabinets and haphazardly laying on end tables like paddles in a frat house and immediately texted the multi-syllable prescriptions to my friend Matthew who is going to pharmacy school. Less than five minutes later I had a response: bi-polar, manic depression, dementia, foot fungi and an extremely concerned friend who demanded to speak to me about this potentially lethal cocktail. The rest I blocked out.

As I was shown to the foyer and soon out of the beautiful home that I would never walk though again, Melanie Joy shows me the living room, "Sometimes my step-brother stops by and kind of sets up a fort, but we haven't seen him for about six weeks. Oh, and do you have a steady income? I don't work, so it doesn't bother me so long as you have money. We have a trust fund."

I want to remind Melanie Joy that she told me that she had a long day at work, but I don't as I'm afraid she might knife me. I pry Burma's clammy death grip from my hand. "I like you, you stay," she tells me, dabbing the drool with her nightgown.

"Not in your wildest dreams," I think as I step into the cool southern California evening air and not into my most frightening nightmares. Soup kitchens are looking brighter by the minute as my stomach growls and I begin dialing Matthew.

"Matt, stop, stop, stop. I am not taking those pills and you are not going to believe what I just saw."

BORDERLINES*Travel*

Aby Davis
VIKINGS ON BUSES

Landed:
We arrived, sleep deprived. The spooky darkness below the plane was Iceland. A small island poised above masses of red hot rock, straddling the North American plate.

Loaded with suits and briefcases, IcelandAir came safely into land, and we touched ground. Two nosy kids on a gap year, wanting to see something new.

A bus took us and some business men into Reyjkavik. A man got off when we did, took one look at our hostel and got back on the bus. We stood outside on crunchy cold ground and waited. The night assistant shuffled grumpily to the door in slippers, gave us a key, and shuffled back to bed.

2am: There is something unbearably beautiful about seeing the Northern Lights for the first time. Standing outside in our pyjamas, ice snapping under our stupidly bare feet. I climbed onto a picnic table and tilted my head parallel to the sky. A few school students stood nearby, their teacher explaining the beauty away with science.

Space was painted with turquoise wisps and bright blue flames that shifted and danced with an unfelt wind. Like a twisted rainbow. My own breath visualised in the air, it was absolutely freezing but I wanted to stand there and stare. And stare. And stare.

We only went to bed when we realised we couldn't feel our toes.

Monday:
I am in love with this city. Reykjavik is young, the buildings are ugly and corrugated. The streets are heated from underneath and the air tastes incredible. My lungs have never felt so clean. I imagine this is how a snow man must feel.

Seeing as its almost Christmas, every window holds little towers of candles alight and making the cold seem friendlier.

We sipped coffee in coffee shops with handpainted mugs, and someone's art glued to the tables. There are a few locals sitting in sofas on their apples. They wear scarves and hats like the ones my mum used to knit.

We came prepared for the prices. We soon realise you can't buy a pint for less than five pounds, and takeaway fish and chips cost seven. Bonus

BORDERLINES

Pig is our favourite supermarket, they sell sheep faces in bags next to the wafer thin ham, and Tesco baked beans in the can section.

When it gets dark at just after lunch time, we find the mountains over the river and we shout into the wind. We shout and laugh until our faces go red with cold. Climbing the bus home we sit next to man who looks like a Viking.

Wednesday:
Some Australian girls in our room tell us they made snow angels in the hills. We all drink hot chocolate and talk about Neighbours. They've already been to tourist hot spot the Blue Lagoon, and we all shriek in delighted horror when they tell us they saw some people having sex in it.

The Alaskan Ranger in our shared kitchen pours Vodka in his hot chocolate, and announces its awesome. We later learn that he says this a lot.

Thursday:
10am: Its still dark outside and we've overslept. We only wake up when the Spanish cleaner comes clip clopping in his high heels and does some dusting. When the door clicks shut five minutes latet we emerge, breathless with suppressed laughter.

The weather is still windy and wet, we've booked to go horse riding Viking style over volcanic fields. Some American business women are taking a day off work, and the bus driver picks them up from their lavish hotel. When we all dress in luminous waterproofs and hard hats, they moan about smudging their make up and ruffling their business haircuts. All I can see as we ride over the blackened ground are flashes of orange through the weather. My horse plods clumsily and I am uncomfortably cold. But the women shout interesting facts about icelandic trees to us through the wind. I am distracted from the jolting of my body and forgive them their previous vanities. When its over, I leave my horse with a kiss and a promise to visit again. My arse hurts.

Lunchtime: We open a packet of crisps and look at some geysirs. The earth spits egg scented water sky scraper high every two minutes. The biggest geysir hasn't woken up for ten years, we wish it would so we can be the first to welcome it back. A few other sightseers are scattered around the sight, but we can't really see anyone through the drizzle and steam. It looks like the kind of land dinosaurs were born into.

Dinnertime: The tour driver drops us off at a garden centre. We wander around politely while he shows us some bananas and a gift shop. We get

BORDERLINES

back in the bus, feel rude, and go back inside again where the other tourists are buying novelty key rings and post cards. We go to a toilet with Eve written on the door, and dream of going home to a cuppa soup.

Sunday:
After a few days of ambling around Rejkjavik looking for somewhere to try the local delicacy of rotten shark, the Alaskan Ranger offers to take us out on a road trip. We ignore the wisdom of our parents and say yes to a stranger. Everytime he pulls over for a toilet break, we hysterically expect him to come back with an axe and murderous grin. His grin however, remains amiably pleased with everything he sees. We share nutella sandwiches for lunch and he is overwhelmed by our generosity. He pulls over so we can all stare at a house built into a cliff face.

"Neat!" he smiles.

A spring trickles out of a rock, he gets out and fills his flask.

"Will you taste that? Its awesome!"

We see waterfalls, beaches with black sand, and stop in villages with twenty residents. The Alaskan Ranger says hello to everyone he sees and we address him loudly by name in case people think he's our dad. He says he's an expert at glacier climbing. So when we find one hidden behind some rocks, we all slide on it in trainers.

"Its about five feet thick!" he says gleefully when we tell him we can see fast flowing water underneath. When we get off, we see a broken bit and its actually about the thickness of a bible. We don't tell the Ranger as he's too busy smiling at a sunset.

On the way back, he stops the car and we all get out to look at a majestic mountain dusted with snow that could be cloud. It is the purest thing I've ever seen. The music breezing out of the car matches the moment perfectly, and we ask ourselves the age old question,

"Why is it so beautiful?" The words of the singer drift out quietly, "I'd do just about anything if I could just catch your eye..."

Monday:
Rejkavik's best CD shop 10 Tonar is also a prominent record label. They give you free espressos as you sit on the old sofa and listen to music through giant headphones, we sit there for hours with our Australian friends and make discoveries. We stumble into a free gig by Amina, four girls who have supported Sigur Ros on tour. Downstairs thumbing through the records is a French musician who invites us to his gig in an old

BORDERLINES

cinema. The promise of free wine and a string quartet is enough. An old black and white silent film plays on the screen behind, as the French Musician sings the words and the strings create the kind of atmosphere you want to melt into.

Tuesday, Wednesday, Thursday, Whateverday:
The days become one, we lose track of the times we wake up with new people in our room and the light lacking. One morning we fly to a northern town with a cinema and another coffee shop, the next evening we go to an outdoor spa at midnight and accidently share a hot tub with a fat man in Speedos. It was too steamy to see we weren't alone. The day becomes blighted with the horrible moment.

Last Day:
Before we leave for Keflavik airport the commercial lure of the Blue Lagoon reels us in. It was an interesting experience, walking out shiny spaceship doors into a barren rocky landscape, and stepping into a milky blue puddle. It wasn't hot enough for our liking, ten o'clock in the morning and it was freezing outside. We wanted it hotter than bath water. Railings led out of the pool and down over the rocks the other side. We'd heard about the hot pools, and guessed they were in that vague direction. We climbed out and shivered in our bikinis, grabbing the railing and walking bare footed up the icy path. We supposed the lack of comfortable paving was to match the spas natural look. It took us a few minutes to realise the path led nowhere. We stood mortified, scantily clad and shivering as a family of hikers strolled past. We almost had to chip our feet off the rocks before we could return to the extremely appealing sky coloured bath.

As we fly home, we chase daylight. Iceland remains dark behind us and the line of light ahead of us suggests Scotland. With one last sweep of turquoise cloud, we're gone. We never ate rotten shark, and didn't get to sit next to Björk on the bus. But our names swirled around a little message in the hostels guest book: Sharon and Aby left their hearts in Iceland, we'll be back to get them one day...

BORDERLINES *Travel*

Rachel Kay
A VISIT TO KAREN VILLAGE

Rachel Chan visits a Karen hilltribe village to witness and reports on the Rice Merit Ceremony.

DAY 1: The Village Buffoon Cometh
There is a famous cartoon of natives hiding their television sets immediately upon sighting some anthropologists. Seeking to break this pattern, the first thing I did upon setting foot onto the doorstep of the hilltribe village was to watch the dogs, chicken, and livestock of this Karen settlement. The hosts were gracious and led us into their home, a cottage lined with teak. Teak formed the riches of the land, and the Karen who lived there were careful to guard the sacred timber from the cash-tainted hands of the capitalists. Timber was not a cash commodity here. I wandered off into the cooking area, where women and men were busy with preparation of the day's meal.

The sprightly dog I followed into the territory of the hens. A rooster crowed, wary. A newcomer on the horizon, large and ungainly. Gulliver had come; and he was about to put his clumsy feet down.

Hearing bustling behind me, I turned to see the group preparing for an evening walk. Around the village we would go. I fiddled with the thought of taking a leak first. Nature won, and in an instant I lost the crowd.

No matter, said I. It was best to wander off alone. That way I could better absorb the surroundings. A comfort zone was the last thing you needed when on adventure.

The village was much more developed than I had imagined. Before arriving, from what meager information I could scrape from the Internet, I was excited at the thought of living amongst hilltribes who ate lizards caught with bark. But here there were systematically constructed school buildings, a football field with children in it, buffalo pens, as well as carefully planned roads.

In front of me was the group. They had stalled to marvel at the building of a house further down the road. And that was nearly as far as we went before we turned to the other side of the village. The vast lands housed paddy-fields and buffaloes. I had my photo taken with buffaloes

BORDERLINES

for the novelty, forgetting that I could as easily take pictures of myself alone with the same effect.

Buddhist Shrine
As the sky ripened the evening skyline, we marched in the other direction to the smell of fresh tobacco. Tobacco was rolled in teak leaves and sold dirt cheap. There was a fresh green smell to it and I was glad it repelled me when I took a puff. The hills were rolling and we walked till we reached some huts. A man who looked like Gandhi to my night-blind eyes stepped out to greet us. It turned out Gandhi was the priest of the village temple. Closer, I could make out his garments and admired its tribal design. Was this how a warrior priest would have looked? Night loved its tricks on my nearly sightless eyes. The priest wanted to bless us and if we would, make donations. He and another monk were building a temple for the villagers and they had recently arrived. We entered the sacred space and saw that it was spartan save for the elaborate altar. We worshipped, and our priest blessed us with holy water. He wished us well on our journey.

Fish sauce and dinner
The Thai do not enjoy their meals without fish sauce. Once when Zakee, our Thai friend and translator studied abroad, he couldn't live without the vital ingredient. For a while, everything tasted bland. Our meals were served on mengkuang mats on the floor. The womenfolk scurried to lay our dining things on the floor. Bidisha remarked that she had never been treated like a king as such. The food was largely fish-based, made of stew, stir-fried vegetables, and soup.

The meal was marvelous save for the fact that I suffered a throbbing pulse in my head due to the four-hour journey to the village. It was made worse by the knowledge that I was to take down notes for the group for our project. The throbbing increased as I, unaccustomed to sitting on the floor, stretched my back into the late hours of the night. Glancing around, I attracted the attention of Tabassum, our chief medic (for what would we do without her indeed, she who had all kinds of medicine in her bag) who gestured to me that she had a headache as well. Later on it was confirmed that at least a few of us had similar discomforts due to the rumbling journey.

BORDERLINES

Sleeping Tight
The solid teak house glittered with the echo of insects. Therefore we had to fasten our windows shut, three of us in a little room, one of the two shared by girls while the men and the family slept in the open. As it had been a tiring journey everyone decided to call it a night early.

There were murmurs of excitement coming from the next room, probably from those who still had the energy to socialize with our hosts. As my headache was an avid companion, I had no option but to save my own excitement for tomorrow.

DAY 2: Mischief:
Binge-eating or Sweater Wearing?
As friends alike clambered out of the communal shower (or none at all for some) into their multilayered sweaters, I shoved down gulps of steaming chicken porridge in the verandah, where breakfast was laid. Here was my one chance to eat without feeling guilty, as I expected we would be travelling somewhere colder than the already cool hut we were staying in. After about five bowls I gave it up, and headed off into the kitchen. There I had another two slices of bread.

While everyone was getting ready I pondered over how many sweaters to bring. Then I remembered that although it was cold now, the climate of the place was one where it would soon get hot. In the afternoon, I did not want to be encumbered with excess textiles. So popping another snack into my mouth at the expense of my waistband, I headed straight off into the truck, which would take us off uphill, to where the Rice Merit Ceremony would take place.

Guerilla Travelling, or Wished it Were
Middle class kids, straight from the sophistication of the city. Thrown together into a single truck struggling its way up a dodgy hill, sinking into broken seats and chilly air. A hands-down winner for a reality show script? No, not really. As we tumbled our way into the back of the pickup truck, then tumbled our way along the mountain, we felt as though we were brought into a whole new world. If there was any rivalry at all among the ten of us cramped together like stowaways into the gas guzzler, it was to see who could stand unaided by the safety railings unaided.

The Rice Merit Ceremony, backstage

BORDERLINES

Backstage, we sat around, milling over the newfound Karen language which we could not really comprehend. The hope of the group lay on the shoulders of Cece, our group facilitator, and Thai member Zakee. They would translate for us into Thai. I caught sight of a remarkable looking young man who showed us how to trap chickens using a complicated looking bamboo contraption, straight out of a Leonardo Da Vinci-like sketchbook. Anyway, what interested me was his intelligent countenance and spirited manner. Later on we were to find out that he was the priest who would lead the harvest ceremony and that a friend of mine had a crush on him. (This of course I only realised after we had returned to our respective countries and had kept in touch online. I think the conversation is still recorded somewhere).

The sun began to rise as the ceremony began. There were ceremonial dances performed by the villagers, who escorted a shaft carrying a symbolic sack of rice around the village, in a long procession. There was a knife-dance; drums were beating and elders sat around smoking on their pipes carelessly (with not a small amount of style). Then we were led to the village hall, where the priest (the one who unwittingly caught my friend's eye for some reason) led the prayers. Dressed in his white frock he appeared completely different from before, seemingly more authoritative. He began an explanation of the whole belief system behind the harvest of rice for the village; it was believe that rice had a spirit, and that rice, earth, and human are related. We create rice from earth, as food rice creates us, in turn we return to earth when we pass on, and create rice in turn.

Therefore it is a principle for them not to sell of rice for prodigious profit. Rice was to be shared as though it cost nothing monetarily, if a neighbour who fell on hard times asked for some from you, you it would do well to give, and received in the future in return. Unless there was really an excess of rice there would be no obligation to sell for profits. This nearly autarchic economic system was to be threatened by the presence of neoliberal forces in the country who attempted to subjugate their practice to the capitalist system by condemning their rotational farming practice as harmful to the environment.

Taking opportunity of this conflict some years ago there was a counter influence from the Marxists who tried to cultivate the Karen to their cause. But this was to fall flat as well as the Karen are a peaceful tribe who believe in restoring balance with nature, irrespective of political ideology. The conflict is largely resolved by now; nevertheless

BORDERLINES

there are minor glitches cropping up occasionally along the path of development.

It turns out, rotational farming is not at all detrimental to the environment, but merely a ruse generated to lure the public into thinking that the land would be better put to use for farming pine trees for commercial purposes. This actually did more harm than good. Anyhow, it was soon time for lunch, and just before, we managed to perform some rather strange business behind the hall.

Sneaking off in the middle of the ceremony to hide from the sun, we encountered an elder from the tribe who was backstage as well, smoking. This adorable looking old man was clad in full tribal regalia, and we say 'adorable' because of his good-natured charm. Being the sugar high trio that we were, we immediately rushed to take some photos together with him. And all this in the middle of a minor yoga session which we somehow got to performing while backstage before our elder appeared.

Lunch, and Stealing Bamboo Cups
By now it seems we were there merely to make mischief. I would not be too miffed were you, my reader, to call me a pirate by now, judging from the antics I had got up to. But beware, for this is nary the end. Shortly after a scrumptious lunch with all varieties of fish (and rice of course, being a sacred commodity), we took to, of all things, stealing bamboo cutouts.

It all started with Aleem, who began to develop a strange craving for these very 'obscure' mugs, which were used to serve tea. It wasn't as though he'd never seen a bamboo tree in the Philippines. But never mind. What got me pulled in into this partnership of sorts was not that I hadn't seen a bamboo tree in Malaysia either, but that Aleem was too 'shy' to collect these mugs (or at least he claimed to be.)

So there I was, shamelessly asking for seconds. Boy, was I glad I wasn't Oliver Twist.

A Time for Farewells
While we spent the first night rather tired out and dreamless, we made up for it by the second night. We still do not recall what got into us, but apparently the dancing bugs must have bitten us as we lay sleeping the previous night.

Being the group's DJ, Bidisha turned on her laptop to the sound of Hindi pop music in an effort to entertain our hosts. Before long it turned out that everyone in the room was an aspiring dancer and so a dancing competition began. Everyone moved their bodies to the sound of Bollywood's latest hit, Rock and Roll Soniye. And that was when we were shown up by the Karen family's young heir, who whipped out his collection of Linkin Park CDs and blasted them on his Hi-Fi.

The neighbours even today must still be talking about our first mountaintop disco session.

BORDERLINES_Travel_

Tiffany Lee
A BITE OF THE APPLE

We had congregated outside the gates of Central Park, all fifty three of us eager and wide-eyed tourists shivering with either anticipation or sheer coldness as the dirty snow seeped through our incapable shoes. Perfectly in line like Victorian school children, we epitomised Englishness. In our polite conversation we all avoided the fact that we were late to enter the park and instead commented awkwardly on the excessive weather compared to the blandness of home. The bitter air didn't seem to have effect on the morbidly dressed, impenetrable 'New Yorkers' that passed us, whereas it seemed to invade our bodies with ruthless urgency.

Clinging to each other for warmth and stability from the icy foreign ground, we were ushered through the gates. As I entered, the dreary, business orientated state evaporated and America led me into its proud wonderland of idealistic beauty and colour. Toto, I don't think we're in Cornwall anymore. Inside the park seemed peaceful and the sound of tourist appreciation drowned out the hostile growls from the hundreds of thirsty taxis that were circling us. It was as if we were encaged by an invisible dome where the reality of New York life was far and we were safe.

The ground inside had been polished with alluring, undisturbed snow that sparkled under the sky's wide, welcoming grin that began to push aside the clouds. A wide pathway had been rescued to accommodate us through the proudest aspects of the park and it rolled into the distance like the royal carpet. We were led at a pace that forced us to absorb our surroundings, but I began to feel as if I was in a museum having to occupy my expression with false fulfilment. The further we were threaded through the park, the more dissatisfied I became. Instead of admiring the view, like the less scrutinising members of the group, I felt an immature desire to kick the disguising quilt of snow and expose the real American soil. I wanted to shake the base of the trees to investigate whether the perfectly gleaming icicles had been fashioned by an intervening adhesive.

I hadn't travelled to the city for meaningless tourist attractions; I was more interested in the culture, the truth. But it seemed no-one would let me in. I didn't ride the 'elevator' a hundred floors, my ears popping six times on the way, to be greeted by a gift shop on the Empire State

BORDERLINES

Building. There was no doubt that Central Park was beautiful, but it wasn't nature. In fact it seemed to epitomise the deluded manner that my British cynicism had detected in many of the New York people. The park was plastic, an edited version of America that gleamed like the artificial looking donuts at breakfast. The insincerity of the sparkling white toothed culture that had already begun to suffocate me evoked an overwhelming need to put on a cockney accent and promote my country.

Instead, I composed myself and pushed the volume switch on my iPod. Perhaps this was disrespected to the trivial and uninteresting words of the guide, but it filled me with compensating lyrics of British kitchen sink culture. My iPod, a product so wholly American it advertises itself with the fruit of its capital, was a disappointment to its makers. It was a homage to the unashamed truths of Britain produced by the poets of my generation.

Not only did I begin to miss the gritty quality of British life but I sensed an unpleasant familiarity. The all-American extras that gave life and energy to this theatrical façade were sledding in the snow. The children laughed through twanging accents under their mop of silky hair. I felt as though I was standing in the pathetic setting of a Tom Hanks romance, but then again, I probably was. The ghosts of Hollywood legends haunted the park, their former presence forbidding me from taking this well devised set seriously. I began to wonder what the parks would smell like in China.

Surrendering, I followed the group as they tiptoed onwards, capturing every image with high definition cameras that would represent their journey flawlessly to friends and family. I looked at my footprints that lay helpless behind me. Falling snow had already begun to repair my sabotage of the immaculate American ground, ready to accommodate the next batch of tourists. I glanced at the guide, who grinned unconvincingly, fuelled by New York's gluttony. I could feel him stuffing stars and stripes down my throat with every word he spoke.

BORDERLINES *Travel*

Brian Appleton
FORTY DAYS IN THE WILDERNESS OF HEARTLAND

With my heart full of love beyond the breaking point
I lay my youthful head in Leila's waiting lap,
The familiar scent of her like Tuber Roses
I breathe in long and deep.
Safe wrapped in her arms and legs I surrender
To sweet dreams of bright tomorrow,
With her fair turquoise gemstone
And I, old silver in betrothal ring
Of life promised together.

Under cover of full darkness the moon loses her shyness coming out
to play…
Kneeling over me, she kisses my eyelids into sleep, perhaps trance.
Resisting, I long to bury my face in her full snow white bosom,
Her soft black hair tickles my face, gazing at me with silent burning
desire like still waters running deep, but I too tired to raise my head.

Twenty seven days later I awake alone wandering in the Lut desert
following the tracks of her camel endlessly to the West,
where are my cucumbers and melons, grapes and dates
no figs, no cherries, no egg plants, no pomegranates
here there is only hot sand scalding my feet.

What has become of her, my youth, my love, where is she?
Like saffron's mother crocuses waiting beneath spring snow will she
Come out again to bloom on the 40th day of lent and
Shower me with a 100,001 stolen kisses
While jealous bearded deities above
Are not looking.

And is her name Iran…
Or am I destined
For madness?
Majnun.

BORDERLINES

BORDERLINES *Travel*

Brian Appleton
SOUNDS OF SIENNA AT DAWN

Silently the darkness turns to light
And then the swallows begin to stream
Their whistles, the first sound to greet the day
Followed by the drone of courting male pigeons
And the shrill chirping of baby sparrows in the eves.

The air is clear, still and cool in early morning,
And now the Tuscan hills are rolling to the horizon
In every direction, studded with dark majestic cypress trees
Amid a tapestry of golden wheat and silver gray olive orchards,
Here and there fields of red poppies and the portent of jade vineyards.

Now the clatter of rising metal shutters,
Shopkeepers' repetitive sweeping of stone pavers,
A row of vespas suddenly parked in front of Garibaldi
As well as a few blue city buses and the sound of footsteps,
Buon giornos, the rattle of coffee cups and hissing espresso machines.

Another day begins in the heart of this medieval town
Like every dawn has risen looking for me these past long years,
Thirty-five in all, the only difference now is that I am here this time,
In the place that I have never left in my nostalgic heart and longing soul,
In the Contrada of the giraffe, a woman dear to me awakes and readies for work.

In a few hours all of this I know so well,
A family name for every house and palazzo,
A memory of someone's laughter at every corner and alley,
Recollections flooding my mind like the wheeling swallows above,
It will all return into the treasure chest I carry in my mind and I am gone.

BORDERLINES *Travel*

John Edwards
THE FINNISH CONNECTION

"That guy is pokerfaced. Don't you think he's pokerfaced?" Apparently the American woman was talking catty, in an exceedingly loud voice, to her husband about me. The boat sliced through the cold blue waters of the Saimaii Canal, built in 1856, in what seemed like a preposterous spot. Nowhere. I inhaled and exhaled the novel frontier: "Scandinavian wilderness," plus a snoutful of flies. I felt bad. I couldn't really manage a conversation with the Swedish tourist sitting next to me, other than, in answer to her friendly questioning, slurring a lugubrious yawp. Amidst the droning hum of the ship's engines was the low languid gurgle of the Finno-Ugric language, which is related to Estonian, Hungarian, possibly Turkish—and not much else. Everyone sounded a little like Foghorn Leghorn with laryngitis.

Lake Saimaii is Finland's largest lake, and the American couple were quick to slowly outloud this nugget phonetically from their guidebook, as if speaking to a kindergartener. I could tell they thought I couldn't speak English, thinking I was probably Finnish or Russian. The reason for my extreme facial rigidity is what the French call "guelle de bois" (face of wood), meaning the previous night in a Lapeenranta campground I'd polished off a couple of six packs of Finland's finest beer, Lapin Kulta, and was feeling it.

We were on our way to Vyborg in Russia, a dreamscape that was once Finland's second-largest city before part of the province of Karelia was lost to the Russians after World War Two. In a country with over 187,888 glacial lakes, the Saimaii no longer seemed great shakes. I was laked out. You can only swim naked in the pristine wild with flickering water sprites so many times before you crave something new, such as dog sledding or reindeer-hunting. Or in my case, why I was here in the first place, unraveling an ancient secret perhaps older than civilization itself, and more dire than the Da Vinci Code.

It was during the Springtime in Paris, France, that I first heard about "the Statues." I was staying with my French friend, Annick, who was a member of Servas, a hospitality-exchange organization affiliated with the UN, whose aim was to foster mutual understanding between nations and

BORDERLINES

world peace. I called Servas "Serve Us," because it was a convenient way to get a free place to stay the night. (Servas guests were also supposed to leave a gift, which in my cost-effective case involved proudly procuring a stolen pen and leaving it dangling meaningfully from the bedside table.)

Anyway, one night a Finnish Servas couple came to stay. They turned out to be Pagans. Which to the naked mind's eye conjures anything from false idols to real gods (with a little nature worship and Medieval tapestry-like orgies thrown in). When they arrived at the Rive Gauche apartment with their backpacks they seemed, well, "frosty" and blinked with bewilderment under the artificial lights. One of them shyly adjusted his aviator sunglasses as if to say 'nice to meet you.' The Finns seemed glad to be in 'Mediterranean Paris" and were interested in everything under the midnight sun, ranging from Renaissance art to Asian cuisine to African dance.

After everyone else was asleep, the Pagan guy turned to me, casting a spell with his somewhat commanding voice. "You know, they've found these statues that are older than anything else ever discovered in [_secret location in Europe]."

"Really, what are they like?"

The Pagan's eyes were aurora borealii. "One of them is a golden boy," he related. "The others you would not believe . . ." It almost seemed as if the Pagan had been sent on a secret mission to specifically tell me about the statues; he even hinted that one of the statues might resemble yours truly. He then capped it off with, "Some people think that white people originally came from Finland," his wine-stained tongue a wagging blue ribbon. We talked and drank far into the night.

Getting from Paris to Helsinki was a little like receiving bum directions from Santa Claus to take back Christmas gifts from miserable lout miscreants' houses. (Jolly St. Nicholas's family could possibly have Finnish origins.)

With my heavy backpack, I felt like I was hauling a sackful of Nokia cellphones. But I had an invite from a French friend and her Finnish boyfriend, Pasquale and Keri, to stay at their place in Helsinki, if I could find it.

O'er land and sea my travel girlfriend (whom shall remain virtually anonymous) and I found ourselves at a confusing Legoland-like complex of apts in Stockholm, pacing the wood floors in our socks (most Scandinavians ask you to remove your shoes) and getting briefed by my

BORDERLINES

friend Asko, a Finnish-Swedish ex-UN Peacekeeper. Asko's building had a badstad, the Swedish equivalent of a sauna, which was invented in Finland. Luckily, Asko's brother worked for Viking Lines, so we found ourselves with free tickets, then not much later drunk and dizzy in the disco of a spotless high-tech vessel which delivered us to Helsinki. Looking out over the expansive blue-white ocean bile of the Baltic, I felt like a character from The Sagas.

At the harbor in Helsinki, I squinted at the Senaatintori (Senate Square) overlooked by CL Engel's stately domed and pillared Tuomiokirrko (Lutheran Church). The first thing we did was visit the kauppatori (market). I bought a Russian sandwich (with saucy Stroganoffy filling) and some smoked trout.

Tastebuds tantalized, we wandered into the Centrum and entered an atmospheric luxury restaurant whose postmodern décor was dolefully reminiscent of IKEA on lysergic acid. Here for the first time in my life I dined on fresh reindeer with Arctic cloudberries, picked by hand by Finnish Laplanders. I toasted the gods with a digestif of Lakka Liquor, also made of Arctic cloudberries. I decided I'd try to get as close to the Arctic Circle as possible. I had my reasons.

Sandwiched between Sweden, Russia, and Norway (and throughout history often incorporated within them), Finland has been a jigsaw-puzzle piece of geopolitical real estate swaps.

Inhabited for at least 10,000 years (note: at least) by a number of barbarian tribes, including the native Sami (Laplanders), Swedish Rus (forerunners of Russians), and the Russian Finns (does that make sense?), the country seemed perfect for investigating prehistory. (I was going to keep my mouth shut about the Statues, though.)

During the Cold War, Finland was kind of an East-West link, and the atmosphere could still be a little like slipping into the pages of a suspense novel. Occasionally I'd be sitting next to elaborately mustached men in green suits (whom I identified as "Yuri") with briefcases stamped "I want you!"

Eventually we arrived at the abode of my friends, Pasquale and Keri, who cautiously welcomed us with a smorgasbord and Sibelius on the CD player. Keri, a photographer for the Finnish tabloids who specialized in shooting women with massive groodies, resembled a skinny blond-haired Santa. (Finland majored in producing Santa doubles.)

After an hour of catch-up, the reunion talkfest sputtered out. Someone had broached a topic which my girlfriend and I were quick to evade: how long were we staying. We sat in stony silence, all the good conversation used up, then the embarrassing silence was broken when Pasquale and Keri left to pick up another surprise guest from France. True to the Servas "Serve Us" code, I refused to take the hint and check into a hotel.

In the two weeks that followed, as we toured lakes, exhausted topics of inquiry, mildly eyed our naked bodies on our sauna excursions, and had heart palpitations over high beer prices, Pasquale, shaking her raven Hester Prynne tresses, would get a bit surly. So what if we mooched flatbread and smoked salmon from the refrigerator every day to save money: that was part of the cultural exchange, right? I, fathead that I am, was waiting for the proverbial Bruce Naumann boot: "Get out of my house!" But the dismissal never came.

One Wednesday (derived from "Woden's day in Norse myth), after spending a surreal day surrounded by topless supermodels with high cheekbones at Hietaniei Beach, the five of us went to a flash restaurant. The scenery had made some of us frisky. The French friend with a blasé "Boeuf!" began a rigamarole about how married women should be allowed to have affairs. "Zey must have zis secret garden," he insinuated with Maurice Chevalier indifference.

Surprisingly Pasquale agreed.

Not Keri. Looking hip because of his retroactive flowered shirt, he countered, "I don't. I think when people go out they should be loyal!" (And this from someone who photographed bare breasts for a living.) I now sensed the real reason for their cool manner. I felt less like a friend than a freeloader. Perhaps we had arrived at the wrong time?

Unsure about how to approach the subject of actually wrenching ourselves away from Pasquale and Keri's unique hospitality, we returned to the apartment one Thursday (derived from "Thor's day") after what we thought was some last-minute bye-bye sightseeing. Upon return we found the house completely empty. (Finland is so safe that many people don't lock their doors.) On the table was a note: "Here are the keys to my car. Go wherever you want. Have fun. –Keri."

After a whirlwind Henry James tour of the countryside, grinding gears and Amexing petrol at deserted automated gas stations, we traced our path backwards on the fold-out map. What had we missed? Somehow we had sped through the 13th-century town of Turku (believe it or not, the former capital of Sweden!) and Brothers Grimm forest-fringed small towns with brightly painted clapboard houses and solid Lutheran churches. All a

BORDERLINES

blur. We returned nevertheless invigorated to Helsinki, dropped off the car, and prepared to go north towards the Arctic Circle.

I went to the CPO to make an international phone call, to warn my friends and family I was running out of money, and ran into the female half of the Pagan couple! This seemed a little too weird to be a coincidence. The male half arrived soon after, his smile a portrait of reptilian mirth, and we soon found ourselves in their favorite café. The Pagan pointed out a shaman friend of his who had inducted him into the mysteries. Of course, it was also a coincidence that he happened to be in the café as well, and wouldn't I like to meet him?

I glanced over at the shaggy shaman, brushing off crumbs from his beard, the spitting image combination of a Hell's Angel and Rasputin. Inexplicably, I felt a little creeped out and said that no, I didn't want to meet him. I gave being too tired as an excuse. Once again, I was reminded of the Statues. Were people watching? I waved goodbye to the Pagans. Their friendly smiles suggested that perhaps we might meet yet again.

Next we took a train to Joensu, planning to eventually reach Rovaniemi, gateway to Arctic Lapland, and cross the Arctic Circle before the long winter set in. We checked into a campground in a pleasant forest. The campground had a sauna, where you could steam and slap yourself with birch twigs. My girlfriend thought I was crazy when she saw me maniacally digging a hole in the permafrost with a hard rock. I had a hunch, you see. (I thought of the many layers of civilization stacked up, the mysterious statue of the "golden boy," and wondered if it might be Tintin?) Once again, I felt like a friendly freshwater stream, mankind's natural state. And then I caught sight of these strange lights seemingly moving overhead. But when we woke up the next morning in our tent, teeth chattering and toes numbing, we knew it was time to leave this land of northern lights and winter dark. Finland was beginning to freeze.

BORDERLINES *Travel*

Bryan David Blake
TRASH, TRAINING AND TRAUMA

Adventures in Marathon traning in Naples, Italy

I'm on a street near my apartment in Pozzuoli, Italy, a small seaside town adjacent to Naples whose bay is actually a very old and thankfully very extinct volcano. For all intents and purposes it is considered to be one and the same as Naples - much as Brooklyn residents would call themselves New Yorkers, I guess - and its people are Neapolitan to the core. It shares the same fate and characteristics with its larger neighbor (the most densely populated city in Europe, by the way, as well as the only major city in Western Europe situated next to an active volcano), for good or bad, and it's where my wife and I call home for the time being.

Since rounding the bend and coming onto my street, I've had five cars honk at me (I've been on the sidewalk, mind you), narrowly dodged seven scooters (both on the sidewalk and on the street), been chased by one stray dog and playfully nipped at by two more, Olympic high-hurdled two massive piles of uncollected garbage that are still steaming from last night's rain, received innumerable hateful stares from older Italian women and in general have been glared at by every group of Neapolitans I pass, simply by virtue of the thinning blond hair on my head.

And this is just since I got off the train on the way home from work; I haven't even started running yet.

Anyone who has ever had the privilege of driving on the autobahn in Germany will tell you it's a driving experience that really can't be beat anywhere outside of the Bonneville Salt Flats with a jet engine strapped to your trunk. Anyone who has ever driven in a Middle Eastern country knows what it's like to drive among people with an enviable disdain for other human lives, be they pedestrians, cattle, other drivers or themselves.

Those who have driven in Italy, though, know what it's like to drive among one of the most finely organized forms of chaos in the world.

Speed limits are suggestions, one way street signs are really more of a 'heads up,' and the horn becomes your most valuable weapon in your daily battle to get to work on time.

Anyone who has ever driven their battered Fiat Punto or woefully

BORDERLINES

undersized Smart Car FourTwo in Naples, however, can reliably describe to you firsthand what it's like to fly a high speed fighter jet in the middle of a heated dog fight, where you have no wingman (and even if you did he'd be on his cell phone), all the other planes are trying to shoot you down (even the ones from your own country) and the aircraft carrier you just took off from expects you to find your own landing and parking space on deck because the flight deck crew decided they're going to go on strike that afternoon, then charge you one Euro to park there anyway.

All of which only adds to the rich flavor of living in this, the black sheep of Italian cities. Travel outside of Naples, even someplace as close as Rome (just two short hours up the peninsula), and you'll be greeted with the same response every single time someone asks you where you're from:

"We live in Naples."

"Ach. Napoli!" your new friend will say, while two hands beseech the sky for advice as to why someone like you would deign to live there. "Napoli non e Italia!"

So there you are, forcing yourself to begrudgingly defend the city you call home against those snobby northern Italians you have nothing against except for the fact that their trash is collected on a regular basis and they have all the good football clubs.

Which comes easily enough to anyone willing to look beyond the graffiti, the garbage *everywhere*, the [apparent] general sense of disdain for any sense of order, the unwillingness of your average Napolitano to stand in a coherent line to wait for anything, and so on and so forth in an endless list of gripes. The inadequacies and irritating traits of Neapolitans are too numerous to spell out here, and we've all heard the usual Italian stereotypes, so it's not worth mentioning the differences between Italians and the Rest of the World.

Like I said, if you live here long enough you learn to love it, as long as you can see beyond the obvious shortfalls. The food is phenomenal, the people will give you the shirt off their back as long as you're willing to chat a moment or two now and then, and there is a sense of unity here that permeates everything: we're not Northern Italy (spit!), we were doing just fine before the unification of the country (and later Mussolini) stole all our revenues and built up the North, thank you very much, and to hell with you if you don't like the way we do things. This is Naples, and we've been marching to our own beat for a lot longer than wherever you're from has been a country, in case you forgot, so kindly leave us the hell alone.

BORDERLINES

Which is all well and good, until the first time you decide to start training for any type of athletic event that you must prepare for outside the comfort of your own home or local gym. Once you take the plunge and commit to a marathon or triathlon, for example, you've now entered a realm few here dare to tread, and one no guide book will tell you about.

To stride down a Naples street in running clothes is both a brave and foolhardy deed, mainly because the Neapolitans don't really view anyone wearing running clothes and actually running as being interesting enough to pay attention to beyond a piercing stare for a few seconds. That's why it's so dangerous: cars assume that you'll get out of their way, because roads are for cars and cars alone. And you will, every time, if you want to make it to the next run. You'll learn that running on the side of the road that faces oncoming traffic is only good if you want to look into the passing cars for good looking women. You'll grow eyes out of the back of your head, because that watchdog you just passed may very well be trotting right behind you waiting for the right moment to bite clean through your Achilles tendon. You will learn to suppress a very strong urge to vomit on the side of the road after you pass your first hillside sulfur vent, dead dog or cat, two month-old pile of uncollected garbage, or the wondrous sight of said garbage on fire.

I first experienced the fun of running in Naples while training for the Venice Marathon. I began training during the summer, with the race in October. Southern Italy gets fairly hot in the summertime and especially humid around a big city like Naples, but the heat and the humidity are not really the climate problems, so to speak, that you really have to worry about.

Running in general in Naples is seen as an anomaly, something nobody but soccer players do, and even then they only do it with a ball and while on a field. Soccer is the official religion here after all, and Catholicism the national pastime and anyone else is either from out of town or from a family that doesn't care about their welfare, because no sensible Italian family would let one of its own out of the house looking like that.

I realized this the first time I managed to actually bring a church processional to a screeching halt, single handedly – one of those dropped-in-the-middle, "what the hell are you doing?!" sort of hateful stares from everyone in attendance that day – by running right through the middle of it half naked, albeit still on an unoccupied sidewalk and in broad daylight. Normally it's an uplifting, somewhat motivating feeling to have everyone

BORDERLINES

looking at you and no one else, but that only counts when they're actually cheering, not invoking the curse of San Gennaro and trying to bore pure death through your upper torso with their eyes, which was clearly the case here.

After that it would be smooth sailing, or so I thought, since I'd be out in the free and clear on the country roads away from town. I realised, though, that this was wrong the first time I had to choose between having my left arm threshed into pulp by the large green tractor/bailer combination barreling its way towards me, or running ankle deep through last month's garbage. Hoping against hope that there was nothing slightly hypodermic, overly rusty or mildly rabid beneath the surface, I trudged right on through that trash pile, cursing viciously that old Italian hillbilly on his beat up Landini that couldn't give me one foot more of road room as he sent a text message to his cousin while lighting a cigarette and ignoring me completely.

I realized that this was to be the theme of the rest of my training time: choices. I would be forced, day in and day out, while out on the road running, to choose between the lesser of two death defying cultural barriers.

Case in point: I'd be running along next to the sidewalk (anyone who's been here long enough knows that pedestrians don't belong on sidewalks, only scooters, parked Smart Cars and uncollected piles of dog merda are welcome) when suddenly I look up and see a four door Clio with no hubcaps bearing down on me from the other direction, aiming for the empty spot I happened to just then run through. Narrowly avoiding a total collision (there's always a little scrape or two in these cases, but you learn to quickly brush these off) a sense of understanding washes over me: for all that guy knows I could have been running to that spot to hold it for my beat up Rover while my uncle drops off his dry cleaning and grabs a coffee.

At this point, spouting curses does you no good unless you know the really good ones in Italian, and even then the guy that nearly launched you into the nearest coffee bar has already forgotten you existed and moved along.

What you have to realize, sooner or later, is that cars are just as confounded by your presence as you are of theirs. Italian pedestrians don't run across the street, offer a courtesy jog or even walk fast; to do so only confuses and scares drivers, who have no idea in which direction those sneaky street walkers are going and can't decide if they should speed

BORDERLINES

up and go ahead of or behind the person in the road. So they always, even in the heaviest, fastest traffic, whether it's pissing buckets or sunny, all get out, walk at as leisurely a pace as can be across the road, in order to ensure that every driver knows beyond a shadow of a doubt exactly where they're headed.

So a runner going along parallel to the flow of traffic just throws everybody off their game, since the drivers now have no idea if this idiot is going to dart out into the road, try and cross it or attempt to hurdle an oncoming hatchback doing fifty at a dead sprint like a whitetail buck during rut.

They'll always expect, and are in fact always prepared for, the walking types to step out into the road at any point: that makes sense. It's the damned runners that give 'em the willies.

It's strangely soothing to not fully understand the local language while running in a country that doesn't approve of you doing so. When you can't understand the taunts and jeers of the scooter-riding teenagers zipping by you, you really lose any sense of self consciousness, and a Zen-like blissfulness surrounds you and you're off to ponder the deeper things in this life.

And then a side view mirror shaves the hair off your forearm as you round a corner. The horn blasting and three miscreants hanging out the back windows hoping you were carrying a backpack they could grab, bringing you back into reality. The cars don't need to speak your language to let you know you're in their way and they're not gonna do a thing to change that old 'law of gross tonnage.' He who hath the most tonnage wins. The way they see it here is that it's not their fault you decided to jog down the side of the road instead of driving like a normal human. Don't you have any parents?

So once you learn to master runner-to-car diplomacy your experience becomes slightly less stressful, although you still run with your head on a swivel at all times. Trying to predict how the pedestrians sharing the sidewalk with you will react is a crapshoot every time, and no two Italians on a sidewalk act the same way.

Sometimes they'll take pity on your foolish self, out there in the heat for no good reason, and step slightly out of your way as they exhale a cloud of smoke right in your face (this is just about the highest form of courtesy you can expect, by the way). Most of the time, though, they'll be walking five abreast and silently challenge you to a game of 'Red Rover,' and the only way to get through is to drop off the sidewalk and onto the

BORDERLINES

road – bad idea if you're near an open or potentially open parking spot – or lower a shoulder, pick up some speed and barrel on through as hard as you can. You'll be met with adolescent grumblings, insecure teenage tough-guy posturing in front of friends and another cloud of smoke, but you're through and on your way down the street when these come at you, and besides, who cares? You don't know any of their curse words anyway.

This isn't really a good idea if it's a gaggle of old ladies, a group of nuns or well-dressed old men (one never knows the connections one's adversary may have), but anyone else is fair game, and I always enjoy those occasions when I get to plow on through a group of teenagers intent on sending me to the street rather than break up their party.

It's not out of rudeness that they ignore you, Italians tend to walk with a sort of tunnel vision, and anything they're not directly talking to isn't really worth bothering with. So when you're jogging along a narrow sidewalk and someone is walking towards you, you might as well just bite that bullet and squeeze to the side or stop and let them pass by. Or if they're younger than twenty just strap on a thousand-yard stare and keep on running – they probably deserve it anyway.

So if you've got a weak stomach or sensitive gag reflex, or care at all about your image while running, stick to hitting the elliptical or treadmill at the gym. The folks in such places will regard with awe and fascination your goals and achievements, but this will get you nowhere come race day. Outdoor Naples presents its own unique aromas that challenge even the hardiest of stomachs. To find yourself inhaling pure sulfur exhaust from a volcano one minute and three week-old uncollected garbage the next will only serve to enhance your cardiovascular system's capacity for punishment.

I like to think of it as a poor man's high altitude training center. All that smoke, exhaust, volcanic emissions and garbage can do wonders for your lungs, making you all the more grateful when you run through a stretch of clean air, or at least what passes for it here. Not to mention the benefits to your sense of situational awareness – dodging cars, dogs, nuns and scooters can do wonders for your reflexes.

And all that while on the way home from work. Just think of the wonders you'll see when you decide to actually go run.

BORDERLINES *Travel*

Josephine Green
THE LONG WAY HOME

In the far distance, Simon saw two figures slowly making their way along a rough path. He looked at them with fascination and wondered whether it was his eyes deceiving him. They looked like children; a slim figure with long, dark hair he supposed was a young girl, while the other he could see was leading the way with strong shoulders and a determined step. He thought this figure a boy.

Then Simon heard a voice. A small but powerful voice was whispering through the wisps of wind around him. It was a woman's voice and it seemed to be calling out to him, wanting him to do something. Simon did not understand it though; she was speaking persistently in another language. It was the same voice as before, that same one that kept whispering. Simon wanted to capture it. He wanted to hold it around him so that he felt safe. It was always there and he didn't want to lose it, not up here. With this voice he could stay here, he could continue to shut out the rest of the world.

He looked at the space where he had seen the figures. They were getting nearer, but they still looked like dots on the horizon. He had time to work out what to do before they would see him. He stood up and walked to the edge of the path knowing that he had to be very careful, be certain that he wanted to be found by them. He decided to creep down to the lower ledge of the hillside where he was perched. He hunched his back as he walked down through the light snow and retreated behind an old, empty tea house as he watched the two figures getting closer and closer. He was drawn to them somehow and then suddenly he noticed their faces; they had seen him.

Manju looked at Pradeep and then back at the figure in front of them. Simon stood quite still. The air around them all seemed to tighten and the frosty, cold breeze held itself around the three small children. They all stood; no one spoke. You could hear the faint cry of a vulture in the distance. Simon looked at the Garhwali children before him and wondered what to do. Still no one spoke. Manju looked up at his brother, twisting a stray hair on her shoulder around her forefinger. She stepped forward, noting the young, but mature looking, foreign boy looking at them expectantly.

BORDERLINES

She said hesitantly,

'Mera nam Manju hai, apka nam kya hai?' Simon looked at her nervously and replied anxiously,

'Mera nam Simon hai. My name is Simon.' His Hindi was not very good. He wondered if they spoke English, 'Kya aap angrezi aatee hai?'

'Haan. Yes,' Manju tried. 'Yes, we have a little English.' She smiled innocently, knowing her English was very limited but wanting to try it out. 'Maybe you teach, yes?' Manju asked keenly. Simon grinned.

'Maybe. Perhaps you can teach me more Hindi too?' He looked at Pradeep as well this time. Manju took the initiative and tugged on her brother's shirt sleeve,

'My brother, his name Pradeep.' Pradeep looked at Simon questioningly.

'His name is Pradeep, ah, I see. Pradeep and Manju.' He smiled at them both and then looked down at the snowy ground. He was not sure what to do; he felt very uncomfortable and slightly afraid. Pradeep looked Simon up and down, taking in all he could see; Simon had curly, ruffled hair that was a dark blonde colour and was wearing a white and red polo-shirt, underneath a thick, blue, woollen jumper with khaki trousers below. His heavy walking boots were obviously made of real leather and he looked about twelve years old. Simon looked around him as he felt Pradeep staring at him. He knew he did not want to be asked any awkward questions but he felt he had to break the silence. He put his hand out to shake Pradeep's.

'It is good to meet you Pradeep.' Pradeep looked at his hand and for a second Simon wondered if he would reject his offer. Instead, Simon was suddenly offered a warm, gentle hand over his.

'Namaste, Simon, milkar xusi hui.' Manju tried to translate the words as Simon's puzzled face suggested he did not understand.

'To meet you, it is good.' She grinned. Simon slumped with relief at their kind words. Manju was so excited at finding someone up in the mountains like them. As they all looked around and began wondering what to do next, feathery snow began to fall.

'Let's go into the tea house?' Simon suggested as he set off into a steady run up the path as the snowflakes started to settle on their clothes. Manju and Pradeep ran after him, their eyes wide open at where he might be going.

When they got there, the kharak was completely deserted, with just a couple of hearth stones lying in the corner of the room and a doorway leading into another.

BORDERLINES

'This is like the one I was in up the mountain.' Simon said as they made their way inside to shelter from the snow. He looked at the two staring at him and predicted that they would start asking questions. He was right.

'Why are you here, please?' Manju looked straight at him. She could not quite understand why such a young boy was up here alone. She could understand it more if he was Indian, that would not be so out of the ordinary, but it was strange to see someone so young. She wondered how he would know his way through these mountains.

'I am living up here.' Simon hoped this might lead them away from the question of his reason for being there.

'Why?' Pradeep asked this time, as Simon shifted uncomfortably on the floor. He looked at them with their gentle faces and trusting eyes. He decided there and then that he would tell them why he was there. Perhaps not the whole story, not yet, but he would try and tell them what had happened.

'I have run away.' Simon looked up at them, the brother and sister looked at each other.

'Runaway, this means?' They looked puzzled. Simon fiddled with the lace on his shoe and wound it around his finger.

'It means I have run from my home,' he sighed deeply, remembering his home.

'You run from your home, why?' Still they looked confused. Simon realised that perhaps they might not understand why he had runaway.

'I was unhappy at home.' He looked out of the door and watched as the snow continued to fall. 'Home is not like these mountains.' He glanced at the peaks that stuttered across the window ledge.

'Where is your home?' Pradeep asked, growing increasingly concerned. Why would a boy run away from his home? And why to here, these harsh mountains, when he obviously did not live here, he did not speak Hindi and was foreign.

'I live in Udrapaag with my father. He is a businessman. We moved here when…' Simon stuttered, not wanting to finish his sentence, 'when my…when I was just nine years old,' he corrected himself, knowing that he did not want that much of his past told to strangers yet.

'We live near Suraithota,' Manju gleefully stated, recognizing that they lived very near each other. Simon looked at her harmless smile and felt a wonderful sense of warmth run through his body. He suddenly felt very safe, safer than he had done in a long time. Perhaps the voice that spoke to

BORDERLINES

him had been trying to tell him something about these children. Perhaps someone out there knew that he would find these children and they would help him.

'How long you are in the mountains?' Manju questioned him.

'I have been here for four days now. Up there,' he pointed towards the ridge, 'Up there behind that small pass.' They both looked and saw a snow covered mountain top and assumed that behind it lay a small hut snuggled into the mountainside that probably looked much like the one they were in now.

'You have food?' Pradeep wondered.

'I have a little food, yes. Are you hungry?' They didn't understand, Simon tried to recollect some Hindi, 'rotee?' he remembered. Their eyes lit up.

'You have rotee?' they said as Simon pulled out a bulging plastic bag with layers of chapattis rolled inside.

'Here, have some bread. It is good.' He could see they were hungry as they each munched their way happily through a chapatti. 'We must stay here tonight I think. Do you agree?' He raised his eyebrows at Pradeep.

'Haan. Stay here. Good.' Simon pulled out his two blankets from his rucksack and laid them on the ground. They would have to share the blankets; he could see the other two had no sleeping material, only some spare jumpers.

'We can share these,' he suggested to them both, 'one underneath and one over the top?' He indicated his thoughts by preparing the blankets on top of one another.

'Naa,' Manju stated firmly. 'You have one blanket. Pradeep and me have one blanket.' Manju would not dream of sharing a blanket with this foreign stranger and, although Simon seemed slightly put-out, she assured him that this was definitely how they would be sleeping.

The children all lay in their beds with their minds drifting into different thoughts. Simon was wondering whether he had been wise in trusting the two children so soon after meeting them. Manju was thinking how lucky they had been to run into such a gentle boy, who seemed so eager to look after them and join them in their trek home. Pradeep was thinking rather negatively. He thought that it was all a little suspicious finding this boy in these mountains and he didn't quite trust what Simon had told them. He could see that Simon wasn't being completely honest with them and he thought that Simon already felt too comfortable with them, particularly with his sister. Nevertheless, one thing they all

BORDERLINES

subconsciously agreed on was that they were all exhausted, and eager for a good nights sleep.

The morning soon appeared with a fresh winter breeze and, thankfully, a warm burst of sunlight too. All three quickly packed their things away, Manju and Pradeep eager to get back outside and onto the pathway home. Simon was not quite as enthusiastic but he had offered to help them get home, even if he wasn't going to return home himself. Pradeep spoke to Manju of the village where their uncle lived, Gartoli. He was sure it was just a little further through this valley, and then descending into the Milam Valley. He recognised the east side of Nanda Devi now in the light of the day, and reassured the other two that they would soon find some life somewhere in this basin of mountains.

An hour past, and then another. On the verge of Simon thinking he should make a suggestion of a plan 'B' the youngsters unexpectedly saw the sight of smoke pouring out of the ridge in front of them. They all hurried forward and looked down from the pass. There, lying in the midst of snowfall, they saw a small town full of wandering people. They ran down the hill towards it and then suddenly Simon stopped them in their tracks.

'No, wait. Stop.' The siblings came to a standstill and looked intriguingly at Simon.

'A problem, Simon?' Pradeep asked. Simon looked down at the village.

'It is just that…' he faltered, 'well, there may be people looking for me and I do not want to be found.'

'You are afraid someone sees you?' Manju suggested.

'Yes, exactly. Haan. What if they have been looking for me? For us, even.' They all stood in the snow wondering what to do.

'Maybe, we go down.' Pradeep pointed at himself and Manju. 'We check. We get some food. We must ask someone how we get home. You understand.' Pradeep was sure this was reasonable.

'Of course. Ok, well I'll wait for you down there, by that bridge crossing over the stream.' Simon pointed to a shaky looking set of tree trunks that had been placed precariously across the river below the town. 'Take this money,' he said, pulling out fifty rupees from his pocket. 'Chai, yes.' They all smiled at the thought of warm tea trickling down their throats.

'Ok. Come, Manju.' Pradeep grabbed Manju's hand as they continued on down the hill, while Simon headed for the other side of the town.

BORDERLINES

As Manju and Pradeep wandered into the town a sudden waft of burnt charcoal and sweet chai drifted past their noses. The stone cobbled path meandered through rows of wobbly stalls that sold every kind of daahl and chai. Their mouths began to water and their stomachs began to groan.

'We buy a cup to fill with chai,' Pradeep told Manju as they neared one of the stalls.

'Haan.' They exchanged thirty rupees for a big canister of delicious, steaming chai and then asked for two samosas to share between them all with another ten rupees. Manju held the hot cup with the tips of her fingers as she blew gently on the whirling, light brown substance, while Pradeep stepped forward to ask the old, kind-looking man standing behind the stall, where exactly they were,

'This is Chaponni. You are not from here?' the man asked curiously.

'No, we visit from another village. We try to find our way home.'

'Where is your home?'

'Janumla. Kya ye bahut door hai?' Pradeep asked the man.

'Haan. Yes, it is still far. But you come from where? Are you not porter, like the other boys?' The man seemed confused.

'Naa. We just visit, we are stuck when a bridge fall down. Samujtha hai?' Pradeep was certain this didn't sound at all suspect.

'Theek hai. Well, I help you go back home. It take maybe another day. But, you wait here tonight, I come with you in morning.' Manju looked at Pradeep who seemed to be juggling with the idea.

'You take us home?'

'Yes, I take you home,' the man replied. Manju's face lit up, but then she remembered Simon. She pulled at her brother's hand to urge him to follow her. Pradeep thanked the man and said that they would think about it. They walked off and wondered what on earth they were going to do. The best thing right now, they knew, was to take the tea to Simon and ask him what he thought. They wanted to get home, but they knew Simon did not want to be discovered yet. They must find him first before anything else.

They ran to the bridge, Manju holding her hand firmly over the top of the cooled down tea. Their eyes scoured the landscape but Simon was nowhere to be seen.

'Where is Simon?' Manju asked her brother. Pradeep looked around, checking behind the large rock that sat next to the edge of the river.

'I do not know. Ah, sshhh, listen Manju.' Pradeep thought he heard a

BORDERLINES

faint whisper coming from under the bridge. He walked over to the ledge and, low and behold, there, beneath the tree trunk, leaning against the muddy river's edge, was Simon.

'What are you doing?' Pradeep knelt down and held out his hand for Simon to hold onto and pull himself up.

'Quickly,' Simon said, 'we must leave quickly. I'll explain behind the rock. We must not be seen.' Pradeep and Manju detected the urgency in Simon's voice and followed him swiftly towards the rock, crouching next to the large, snow covered object. Simon glanced back at the town to ensure no one had seen them and then continued, 'The man I told you about,' he took a breath, 'the man I was running from, he is here, in this town. I think he may have seen me.' Manju and Pradeep uttered a slight exclamation.

'Which man?' Pradeep dutifully asked. Simon lowered his head.

'The man who thinks I stole something.' Simon's voice had become quieter.

'You steal?' Manju exclaimed.

'No. Naa. Naa.' Simon looked deep into her eyes, hoping that she would believe him. 'Naa, Manju. No, I did not steal. The villagers think I did, but I didn't. You must trust me.' Manju did. She knew he wouldn't steal and she could see that he was upset. She gave him the cup of chai and watched him drink some of the warm tea.

'It is ok, Simon. I trust you.' Manju looked at her brother who was saying nothing. She imagined he was thinking about the offer of help home. There was no time to find out what he was thinking though, as Simon suddenly cried,

'Quick! They have seen us, they are heading this way. We must run.'

BORDERLINES *Travel*

Loree Westron
THE ROAD TO REPARATION

I pulled the telephone away from my ear, anticipating my mother's sigh. "Abby," she called faintly from my left hand. "Abby, are you listening? It's time the two of you sorted this out."

The stroke had been a mild one, by all accounts, and my father was expected to make a full recovery. At the end of his sixth decade, he was still strong as a mule according to the doctor, and had a temperament to match according to Mom. But this first evidence of his mortality had scared my mother into action, forcing her to look at the broken pieces of their lives and attempt to glue them back together.

"There's nothing to worry about," she said. "But I wish you'd come home all the same. Just for a visit."

For my twenty-first birthday, my father had given me his prize possession, a 1970 cherry red Chevy Cheyenne that he fondly referred to as The Old Chief, the pickup he'd bought the year I was born. He believed in handing things down the generations as a way of keeping continuity in life. "If you remember where you came from, you'll never get lost," was his favored piece of wisdom, parcelled out by way of praise and admonition so often that the meaning of the words became lost.

And somewhere along the way, I got lost as well.

It had been five years since I walked away from the farm and the argument I knew I could never win, five years wandering from one city job to another, unable to stick or settle to any occupation or man. In all that time, my father and the farm had never been far from my thoughts, blighting my expectations and turning my efforts at living away from them rotten before they had time to mature.

My mother was right. It was time to get things sorted out, time to deal with my father, my brother Patrick and the family farm; time to stop running away. I looked at The Chief, parked outside at the curb, and knew we were ready for another long drive. Daddy would be glad to see his truck, even if he wasn't so glad to see me.

Leaving was easy. It always was. I'd drifted east to Pennsylvania for no particular reason, so I'd no particular reason to stay. Early next morning, I slung a pack carrying the meagre contents of my life into the

BORDERLINES

truck and made my way through the back streets of town, left on Elm, right on Constitution, through the intersection and onto the freeway heading West.

At a gas station near the Pennsylvania Dutch Folk Culture Center on I-78, I opened a road atlas on The Chief's hood and examined the continent spread wide before me. In states where populations are high and dense, and paper space is limited, towns with fewer than four digits worth of inhabitants usually get missed off the maps, but Idaho is not such a state and Nezperce stood defiantly on the page, daring me to call it home. I poked it with a stiff finger then stretched my hand to measure the distance. From where I stood, it was one hand-span to the Missouri and the best part of another to the Idaho border. Twenty-five hundred miles. I gave myself a week to get there.

Gunning it past R*oadside America – Indoor Miniature Village – Established 1935* and the turnoff to *The Greatest Christmas Display in the Whole USA*, I was halfway through Ohio by nightfall. On the outskirts of Columbus, a cheap motel gave me shelter from the city and I spent the dark hours dreaming about mountains and asphalt and Mama's potato salad.

"Your father only wants to do what's best for the family." My mother's position as mediator and her constant deference to the head of the household, felt like a betrayal.

"What's best for Patrick, you mean."

Like a bad tooth, I'd learned to live with the memory of that day, pushing the dull ache of it back into the corners of an earlier life. I wanted to forget about it, move on, but the root refused to shrivel up and die, and from time to time, the infection still flared.

North along the 33, through Dublin and Marysville, past Mad River Mountain and Bellefontaine. The further west I traveled, the more certain the lines on the pages of my atlas became until west of the Neil Armstrong Air and Space Museum at Wapakoneta, the roads stretched out straight and flat and inviting. One small step. One giant leap. In a news-clip lodged forever in the collective mind, the astronaut bounds slowly across the surface of the moon in a time when the world's hopes still outweighed its fears.

Its three hundred and thirty three miles from Columbus to Chicago, but after detours through Hicksville and Albion and Warsaw and Mishawaka, just to say I'd been there and held their names in my mouth, I'd added on a hundred more. By the time I reached Joliet, ten miles south

BORDERLINES

of Romeoville, I was ready for a roadside diner and a Motel 6.

Patrick was still in diapers when Daddy gave me a job picking rock in the South Forty. He paid me a penny for every chunk of granite bigger than my fist and joked to neighbors that my wages would break him. When I overheard him brag to Mama that the ground I'd worked was the cleanest piece of property on the ridge, I knew he was pleased. And when he said I'd make "a damn fine farmer one day," I convinced myself that he was as proud of me as he could be of any son.

Joliet to Davenport. One hundred and fifty miles on I-80, taking a brief detour through Peru, and East officially became Midwest across the Mississippi at lunchtime. Over the border I opened the atlas and propped Iowa against the dashboard. My heart leapt at the logic of all those lines, precision cut along homestead boundaries of sections and quarter sections, divvying out the prairies to make a checkerboard of wheat and alfalfa.

Moscow and Muscatine. Bonaparte, Milton and Mark. Mount Zion. Lone Tree. Morning Sun. Norway. Oskaloosa, Independence, Pleasantville and Prairie City. Nevada, Indianola, Correctionville, Early. Lucas and Le Roy. The Birthplace of John Wayne and the Grotto of the Redemption. Murray, Mount Etna, Tripoli, Story City. Shenandoah. Mystic and Macedonia. Albert City and Arthur. Elliot, Melvin, George, Lester, Maurice, Craig. What Cheer. I checked my watch, four states, five days and eighteen hundred miles to go, and lit out for the Missouri.

In May of 1804, Captains Meriwether Lewis and William Clark accepted the challenge of exploring the western wilderness of the newly acquired Louisiana Purchase. Seventeen months later, The Corps of Discovery paddled canoes down the Clearwater River, passed parched and dormant land that one day would blossom beneath my father's sweat. And mine.

My father didn't approve of Ryan, the boy I took back to the farm after my junior year of college. I had grown weary of Idaho farm boys and the way they seduced with conversations about acreage and animal husbandry. Ryan's folks weren't farmers, but I supposed he could be guided in that direction. New ideas, I thought, might not be a bad thing for the farm, but Daddy made it clear that ideas, especially new ones, were not what he wanted. Following my mother's example, I complied with his wishes, cut Ryan loose and let him drift away.

BORDERLINES

Eastern Nebraska, as far as Highway 281 which runs from Lebanon, Kansas in the south all the way up to South Dakota in the north, is wrinkled by rolling hills of soybeans and sorghum, and scored through by the gullies of a thousand creeks and rivers which feed the ravenous Missouri.

To the west lay the Great Plains.

Four hundred miles wide and three thousand miles long, the plains gouge through the continent like a new footprint in old snow. If you slice across the middle of North America, on any line of latitude you choose, and look at it side on, you'll see the basin-shaped contour in the earth. Eighty-five million years ago, this trough – for it is more akin to a pig trough than a bowl – was filled by a vast inland sea. That's why people find sharks' teeth in the cornfields of Nebraska.

From the air the plains unfold like a rumpled sheet of parchment upon which ribbons of asphalt and water flow, unfurled on the breeze and bent to the shape of the land. Following the curved cicatrix of the Platte River, I paralleled the interstate on Highway 30, through Grand Island and Odessa and the dusty streets of Gothenburg.

"You're listening to KKIC, Country With a Kick, coming to you out of Beaver Junction. Up next Chad Wilmott and Your Cryin' Eyes."

I gave up looking for an Oldies station in this land of manicured cowboys, and irritated by the whine of other people's failures, I switched off the radio and tried to ignore my own.

"How can I be with someone who doesn't trust me?" There was no answer of course, and after a few weeks or a few months, men eventually discovered how to read the silent spaces between my words. I learned to let go quickly and not look back.

Across the freeway and south of the river, half a million emigrants rolled west over the plains in the middle years of the 19th century. In the name of progress they sought new lives in a new land: fortune, fame, adventure. Together they built one nation's future and brought about another's demise.

Before me stretched a great big nothingness 'to be raced across, not savored' unappreciative travelers had warned me, endured not enjoyed, but emptiness fits me well and by the time I reached Ogallala the plains wrapped round me like a new skin. When the first white settlers crossed this great expanse they wrote in their journals and letters back home of surging black seas of buffalo hide that took a week or more to pass. What they witnessed was the essence of the continent, the sustenance and soul

BORDERLINES

of its first people; what they saw was an obstacle to their progress, something to be controlled, utilized or destroyed. Within a generation, the buffalo – untamed and unprofitable – were gone.

    The sun was down and the stars were up by the time I pulled in to Bridgeport, stiff-kneed and sore in the shoulders. At a campsite west of town I unrolled my sleeping bag in the bed of the truck and lay down beneath the heavens. I was dreaming about fishing with my grandfather when beads of sudden summer rain tore a slick-bodied trout from my fingers and drove me to shelter inside the cab.
    My mother had been the perfect farmer's wife: ready to sacrifice her complexion to the demands of the land; willing to take on the dirty work of mucking out barns and birthing cows; able to stack hay bales as high and neat and secure as a man. She was the ideal laborer, strong and cheap and pliable. What's more, she knew her place. While she provided the kisses and band-aids for blisters, it was my father who made decisions about the land, when to plant, what to plant, on whom to bestow his trust.
    Highway 385 cuts across the high plains, rolling red and arid into South Dakota. By 10 o'clock, I crossed the state line and passed through Buffalo Gap. To the east lay the Pine Ridge and Rosebud Indian Reservations, where the grandsons of Crazy Horse still wait for justice to turn full circle (time harbors all wounds), and to the north, the Badlands and the sacred Black Hills.
    The rain which fell in the night did nothing to cool the air and in the morning, the wind that blew through the windows of the truck burned as if from the blast furnace of hell. "Pockets of rain expected in the afternoon," a voice on the radio announced.
    Through Rapid City and Sturgis and Belle Fourche, then across the corner of the Wyoming rectangle and into Montana. One state to go. And this, the biggest of the lot.

    "I've made up my mind," Daddy announced over breakfast on Patrick's twenty-first birthday. "Won't be long before your mother and me are gonna want to retire. Take it easy for a change. Maybe move into town." I looked at my mother, then back at Daddy. Patrick, bent low over his plate, continued to mop egg yolk and bacon grease with sliced white bread as if the conversation had not turned from leaf rust and root rot and the cost of new combines.

BORDERLINES

"Time Patrick took charge of things round here, started making decisions hisself." Patrick's gaze never once lifted from his plate. For him Daddy's words were no surprise.

Wind rustling through prairie grass makes the sound of white noise, the kind that televisions used to make when they went off-air at night, like a rattlesnake warning to keep off its ground. From the top of an unextraordinary hill I looked across the eastern end of Montana. In all directions I saw at once nothing and everything there was to see.

"You weren't meant to be a farmer's wife," my mother finally said. There was a soothing quality to her voice, even when the words she spoke were thorny. It was that softness I resented most, the way she found no fault with others as she tried to nudge me to their point of view. "And Patrick's gonna be a family man, soon. He needs the security of knowing the place is his. Outright."

Through the passenger window, I watched steely clouds suck together on the horizon then roll and churn and boil up, brimful with electric rain. Farmers take out crop insurance against such clouds. Within minutes, the sky to the west and south and overhead which had been pale but pristine in the morning, turned ashen and black. The sky to the north turned the color of a week-old bruise. Purple thunderheads belched and resounded and stabbed the earth with daggers of light. On the road The Chief rocked in the wind as an obsidian finger unbent itself from the sky. It danced across the horizon pointing with discriminate accusation, first here, then there, then further along before withdrawing into the clouds again.

Near Tongue Creek, I pulled into a campsite and slept curled up inside the truck again, the distant rumble of thunder lulling me to sleep.

"Quite a storm last night," a woman said the next morning as I washed away sleep at a standpipe. "Heard about them poor folks up at Pine Lake?"

I shook the excess water from my hands and rubbed them across my face.

"Tornado cut through town," she said. "Nine people killed in their sleep; two children still missing. Guess none of us knows when oblivion is going to strike."

Highway 212 runs straight through the Little Bighorn battlefield. For half an hour, I was the only traveler upon it, rolling through prairie grass, looking for ghosts and finding plenty. With a cassette tour guide

BORDERLINES

incorporating authentic sounds of bugle charges and Sioux war drums (available at the Visitors Center for $12.95), tourists can travel the route of the Seventh Cavalry's destruction in the air-conditioned comfort of their own vehicles, experiencing the desolation of that other day when the world changed forever.

When a way of life, the very means and the meaning of life, is taken away, what comes next? Sorrow. Rage. Resentment. Don't speak yet of forgiveness. If there is some fragment of good in all that has happened, where is it? Remember where you came from and you can find your way back. The words sounded nice but I wondered if they were true.

On I-90, running north and then west towards Billings, I watched the earth take shape on the horizon, a dark ripple at first, hardly noticeable, but growing all the while. As the road climbed out of the basin, all the round softness of the prairies exploded into the Rockies, ragged and reaching for something in the sky.

The heat of the lowlands fell behind me as I climbed through timber, up to Bozeman Pass and by the time I reached the Continental Divide, the air was chilled and clean and the edge of the world was in sight. In a snag, above the road, I spotted an eagle surveying the mountainside. Heavy bodied but weightless, he lurched into the air and made slow circles in the sky. Another day's drive and my journey would finish where it began, my own circle complete.

Eighty years before my father plowed his first furrow, his grandfather broke through virgin sod and carved his descendents a new homeland, each generation passing it father to son, father to son. Nobody recorded what happened to the daughters.

The road dropped all the way to Missoula, then rose again as I turned onto Highway 12, towards Lolo Pass and the Idaho border.

For centuries, the native people of the Northwest traveled through the Bitterroots along the Lolo trail. In September of 1805, The Corps of Discovery passed this way too. It took them three weeks to negotiate the mountains and by the time they were found, fed and befriended by the Nez Perce, the men were half-starved and crazed by thoughts of death.

If the Nez Perce had known what was to follow, might they have allowed these pale strangers to die?

As the miles unwound alongside the Lochsa – fast-flowing and foamy white over rapids – the river stripped away the burden of time. To the north and south and east of me stretched deep green wilderness, Thoreau's

BORDERLINES

forest primeaval, simultaneously ancient and new, untouched by logger's ax or farmer's plow. The thought of its existence, that something survives untamed in this man's world, gave me then and still gives me hope.

The waters of the Lochsa feed into the Clearwater and those of the Clearwater feed into the Snake and the Snake's waters feed into the Columbia and all of these, with all of their memories diluted, wash into the sea and are reclaimed.

Around me rose familiar hills of cheat grass and sage and wheat stubble, swelling like the amber hips of a reclining goddess. I eased the truck off the road and sat for a time, watching the wild river empty the mountains of distant rains.

After losing themselves a while, The Corps of Discovery emerged from the wilderness and found a way to go forward along these turbulent rivers. I swore, when I left, I would never return, but as I looked around at the tinder-dry hills I knew there was nowhere else I would ever belong. Over the next hill and around the next bend, the grain silos of my family's farm would come into sight. I shifted the truck into first and turned off the highway, crunching gravel as the tires bit into the county road. In the mirror, I watched a plume of dust rise up behind me and disperse into a cloudless sky.

BORDERLINES *Travel*

Quentin Bates
ASTRAY IN ICELAND

Bordeyri and the Banded Men

Iceland is a peculiar country, a primeval land where steam and history come out of the ground at your feet. As you come down the long road over the heath that leads from Reykjavik, Hrútafjördur nestles like a long cobalt tongue between brown hills to east and west. At the bottom there's the truck stop of Brú and taking the road out towards the Strands, there's Bordeyri, the last stop before Hólmavík.

Bordeyri's hardly even a town. These days it's a collection of houses, a shop, a couple of workshops and a hostel with a bare patch of ground between it and the beach. Even the satellite dish on the upper floor of the shop looks as if it's been there since the 1960s.

The telephone exchange was shifted down the road to Brú when British soldiers arrived to occupy Iceland in 1940 Bordeyri had been gradually shrinking ever since. Even the petrol pumps are gone now that Brú at the crossroads and Stadarskáli east on the Blönduós road are where the traffic stops.

On a summer afternoon when we draw up outside Hrútakaffi, the village shop that doubles as a café, the sign in the window reads 'closed today,' with no explanation. It's not easy to see if this refers to the shop or to Bordeyri as a whole. It's a fly-blown, dust-blown little place that sits on the western side of Hrútafjördur around a spit of shingle jutting out into the fjord while houses and workshops cling to the hillside above.

It hasn't always been like this. Some of the first settlers made their homes in Hrútafjördur and the place must have buzzed with activity. Vatnsdæla Saga tells us that the name itself, Bord-eyri, literally 'log-spit', was given to the place by Ingimundur the Old when he was searching out new territory and named the spit of land after the driftwood piled up on it. Grettir the Strong's forbears made their homes at Melar, on land at the bottom of the long strip of fjord amid sheltered waters that yield good fishing, plenty of fertile grazing land and long strands that pile up with driftwood. There's still a farm and a homestead there, the first one on the Strands side of Hrútafjördur past the crossroads at Brú. On the July afternoon we passed through, newly mown hay lay in thick blankets

BORDERLINES

across the pastures at Melar, drying for the winter under summer sun. This is the way it has always been – hay meant that the livestock lived through the winter, and if the livestock survived, so did the people.

A thousand years ago, Bordeyri was a place where heroes returned to their homeland, dragging their fat-bellied wooden cargo ships up onto the beach for the winter and caulking them for the following spring's sailing season.

According to the *Laxdaela Saga*, when Ólafur Feilan the Peacock returned to Iceland from his triumphant voyage to Ireland to claim his kinship with King Myrkjartan and Norway, where King Harald gave him a good welcome and Queen Gunnhildur an even better one, he made landfall in Hrútafjördur in the ship that the king had given him.

News of Ólafur Höskuldsson's arrival at Bordeyri travelled fast and his father rode north for a joyful meeting with the young man and to invite him home to Höskuldsstadir away south in the Dales, wearing the fine scarlet clothes given to him by the King of Norway which gave him the Peacock name that stuck with him for ever.

Most of the action in *Laxdæla*, regarded as one of the greatest of the Sagas, takes place south in the Dales. But here in Hrútafjördur and a little way west in Midfjördur, as well as being Grettir the Strong's territory, is where one of the lesser known tales is centred. Bandamanna Saga, translated either as *The Confederates* or the Saga of the Banded Men, takes place right here.

One of the central characters, Oddur, was a man with money, an eleventh century self-made millionaire who left home as a young man with little blessing from his father, to make a fortune first in fishing and then in shipping before buying himself a chieftainship. These days Oddur would be Armani-suited with a blackberry in his pocket, a platinum AmEx, a top-of-the-range car and some cripplingly expensive hobbies.

Although it's short, *The Confederates* has many of the ingredients of the ancient Sagas – hubris, much legal wrangling and some violent death. Oddur lived at the farm at Melstadur. Today there's a farm and a church still there, the quiet of the churchyard and its lines of new and old gravestones broken only by the unobtrusive songs of the unseen birds.

Oddur feels he has been wronged, takes his case to law and through a 'technical error,' finds himself set to lose everything to the Confederates of the title, the eight judges who are appointed to adjudicate the case. By luck at the law courts, Oddur runs into his crusty old father, Ófeigur, who tells him in no uncertain terms what a fool he's been and takes on the task of

BORDERLINES

winning the case himself. It's hard to believe that the two men had been estranged for all those years, considering that Melstadur and Ófeigur's farm at Reykir are within a half an hour on horseback of each other – virtually next door, even by today's standards, let alone those of a thousand years ago.

Ófeigur wins the case for his son by paying handsome bribes to two of the judges to act in his son's favour, and Oddur lives to a ripe old age at Melstadur on good terms with his now increasingly prosperous old father. It's an oddity among Icelandic sagas. *The Confederates* pokes sly fun at the rich and powerful, their greed and their willingness to bend the law and abuse their positions to line their own pockets. Oddur's technical error is even eerily reminiscent of some recent political manoeuvring.

The loser of the story is Ospakur, Oddur's friend who looked after his lands and chieftainship while he was away abroad. When Oddur returned from Norway, the two fell out and Ospakur found his way east to Vididalur where he found a shapely lady called Svala who farmed at a place known appropriately enough as Svölustadir – Svala's Homestead. Ospakur's undoing was to either steal a few of Oddur's sheep or else be fingered for someone else's bad deeds. Whichever it was, and in spite of protesting his innocence, Ospakur found himself outlawed after the killing of his friend Vali. The fatal blows had been meant for Oddur and Ospakur had little choice but to run for the hills. When nothing had been heard from him for a good while, a new man took Ospakur's place in Svala's bed.

Eaten up with jealousy, Ospakur arrived at Svölustadir, murdered Svala's new man and was himself wounded by another man on the farm before taking to his heels. A body found in a highland cave the following spring was judged to be Ospakur and the story ends there, although the reader is left not knowing what became of the shapely Svala, with one husband outlawed and dead and the second murdered by the first. At any rate, there is no longer a Svölustadir in Vididalur, so at some time over the last ten centuries, the place has changed its name to suit a new occupant or else been abandoned in hard times like so many homesteads, the old turf walls reclaimed by the landscape into a row of barely-discernible hummocks.

Back at Bordeyri, Tony the photographer is trying to get everything into a single frame, and a middle-aged lady in a thick fleece wraps her arms around her and comes across to chat.

"There's always a wind blowing down Hrútafjördur, I find. It's always windy here," she complains as her husband stretches stiff legs walking

BORDERLINES

around their big Toyota jeep and the caravan behind it, as big as some of the trucks that roar along the country roads since the state shipping company that served country towns was closed down twenty years ago.

The woman shrugs deeper into her fleece. She's right, and there is a sharp wind coming off the strands that's at odds with the bright blue sky. Maybe that's what made a landfall in Hrútafjördur so attractive in the days of sailing ships, always a breeze one way or the other to get in and out of the sheltered fjord.

"God help me, I could have been brought up here," the woman sighs. "My Dad used to be an engineer and blacksmith for the State Herring Company in Siglufjördur and we used to go back and forth past here. Once he told me he'd worked here for a while," she adds.

There's hardly any more activity that there would have been when the eccentric Baring-Gould rode into town with his no less odd guide and their tired train of ponies. It's a hot Saturday afternoon if you can keep out of the wind, and 4x4s with and without caravans and trailers bump down the hairpin bends to Bordeyri to find Hrútakaffi closed, each one sporting a film of brown road dust as perfect as if it had been sprayed on professionally at a body shop.

Apart from me and Tony down at the beach with his cameras, there's apparently nobody about apart from a pair of women in the distance, chatting over the cold barbecue that stands outside every house, ready to be sprung into action.

"Hæ. What's your name?" demands the more daring of two small girls on bicycles, cycle helmets crammed on top of woolly hats. "Where are you from? Are you a foreigner? My name's Helga and I'm eight and that's Thorgerdur." she announces, not waiting from an answer. "I'm from Iceland and Hungary as well," she adds seriously before commanding her friend to make tracks as they decide where else to go. Speed is clearly of the essence and they have better things to do than hang around chatting with passers-by.

It's safe enough to let children play out here at all hours. Bordeyri has a population of only a few dozen nowadays. In its prominence in ancient times and into the 19th century, the place was one of the busiest in Iceland. Sheep on the hoof were exported from here to England and Bordeyri was where a great many country people made their way on board sailing ships at the start of their journeys to the New World in Canada. Times were hard in Iceland and prospects in Manitoba were tempting.

Now there's a convoy – three jeeps and two monster caravans between

BORDERLINES

them, rolling to a halt. From the first a thickset man jumps out and lights a clearly long-awaited cigarette while the drivers and passengers confer.

"Closed? God."

"Hell."

"Brú, then?"

The driver hardly has time to drop his smoke, stamp on it and jump back behind the wheel before the others are off to find hamburgers, coke, cocktail sauce and cartoons on an endless loop at Brú. That's where there's petrol for thirsty 4x4s and a washing station to get rid of the fine brown dust of the Strands roads.

Bordeyri is closed today and as soon as they have rumbled back up the twisting track to the main road, the silence falls again, broken by little more than the cries of terns sending warning signals to Tony on the beach, and the faintest rumble of traffic across the fjord in Húnavatnssysla.

Vatnsnes

Oddur Ófeigsson left his home at Reykir with not much regret on his father's part. In his rise to a chieftaincy, Oddur made his way out to Vatnsnes to work as a fishermen pulling cod from the waters of the wide Húnaflói Bay. He went from fisherman to boat owner and from there to running a trading boat across to the Strands, before running trading ships abroad that made him a wealthy and respected man by the time he was able to settle at Melstadur as a chieftain.

The peninsula of Vatnsnes is an out of the way place. There wasn't even road out round the point until after the war when Marshall Aid brought tractors and bulldozers to do the work. Close to the tip of Vatnsnes, Gudmundur Árnason walks stiffly down the rocky beach at what was once the family farm – now closed up and used as a holiday retreat by a Reykjavík family.

Down by the sea are the boat, shelter and the boat winch that the brothers, Gunnlaugur the eldest, Gudmundur, and the youngest, Skúli, used to work before the road was there. The boat never had a name – it was just their boat and for close to forty years it stayed on the beach since their last fishing trip together in the sixties, after which Gunnlaugur and Gudmundur found themselves drawn away to sea on ocean-going ships and Skúli to trucks.

"We used to push the boat off and row out to fish with hooks and lines. At the end of the day we'd row back and bring the boat back up the beach. There's an art to it, landing in the surf."

BORDERLINES

The boat winch, made of stout timber dry and crumbling with the years, was what all three of them turned between them, bent over at the long bars slotted into the pillar of the capstan, and on every circuit stepping over the rope that brought the boat up the shingle and into its shelter.

Gudmundur Árnason recalls the old days of hard and healthy manual labour as if it were yesterday. Once the boat was up the beach, there was still the fish to be dealt with before they could go home to the farmhouse. The cod had to be painstakingly split and salted, or else headed and hung to dry in much the same way that Oddur Ófeigsson a thousand years before them would have done before success took him elsewhere.

The brothers also built the shelter themselves. It's two straight and level dry stone walls, tightly packed to perfection, tapering gradually from broad bases each side to narrower tops, man-high and just the right distance apart for the boat to nestle in between through the worst winter weather.

Seen close up, the skill that went into the building, and the size of the stones, is remarkable. From rocks the size of a man's head to some as big as, and much heavier than, small pieces of furniture.

"This one was a bit of a weight," he says with a wry smile, slapping a rock perfectly shaped by nature to form a corner of one of the stout walls, a single stone with a straight square end, the size of a large suitcase, lifted by hand and cajoled perfectly into position all those years ago.

BORDERLINES *Travel*

Jane Anderson
THE BEGA VALLEY, NEW SOUTH WALES

The wheels scrabble for a purchase on the dusty road, and I am gazing dizzily back down a ravine choking in a blue-green miasma, exhaled by a tangle of eucalyptus. Ahead the red earth switchback leaps jaggedly uphill, and behind the ample sweep of the Bega Valley luxuriates in its own fecundity. The van swings drunkenly from side to side, clashing gears grating against the whine of brakes. We are travelling to Canberra, if we ever get over Brown Mountain, and I am rediscovering a tendency to travel-sickness. My nephew and nieces obligingly make vomiting noises, just to help in my moment of crisis.

I am here because my sister Ann and her husband moved to Bega in 1995, three of her four children were born here, and it is my greatest pleasure to visit them, when I can, and gut-wrenchingly awful to leave them waving at the airstrip. Still, today my return is two weeks away, and there is plenty to look forward to before leaving the Australian spring for a dismal grey English November.

The Bega Valley was first settled in the 1830s by squatters, pushing south over mountains and through bush, sometimes on horseback, or in wagon trains dragged by oxen. For at least two years there was only one white woman living south of the Moruya River, the northern boundary. She was accompanied by her 'husband and some sheep'. The squatters staked their claims, and their descendants live and work in the Valley today. The day after my arrival I was privileged to meet a Bega name – Mr Wayne Hegarty, head of one of the original families.

The Hegartys still occupy land in Angledale, on the opposite bank of the river bordering Ann's land. At dusk, I could just see their house lights glimmering through the bush, but in daylight I was unable to discern any tracks leading to their farms. So how do they get there? After dinner, with the children in bed, seemed the best time to have a meaningful discussion.

"If there are no other farms off your track, you probably don't see any headlights at night then Ann?" I ask.

Ann thinks for a moment, then replies. "Well if the Angledale lot hit the golf club, they usually come back up our track, then ford the river

BORDERLINES

further up, just to avoid the random breath tests on the town bridge." We step outside, dragging chairs onto the veranda, before continuing our conversation.

"I'd have thought the river was a bit on the deep side to ford, you could drown yourself," I observe.

"Well yes, but if you want to keep your licence … and the worst of the lot is that bloody old pisspot Wayne Hegarty." So says my sister, as she pours me another gin. We fall silent, dominated by the swiftly changing landscape.

There is no dusk in the Bush, a red glow burns for an instant along the horizon before sudden darkness obscures the land, followed almost immediately by handfuls of diamonds glowing icily from above. Sitting on the veranda, we enjoy the still calm; for a moment no insects are shrilling, and the starlings' harsh croak has been silenced.

A distant set of headlights peers through the gloom, dipping and rising, swinging towards the house; a thudding, growling diesel engine obscures the rumble of the cattle grid. A sand-streaked white ute veers crazily up the drive before shuddering to a halt close to Ann's car. The driver nonchalantly climbs out, cigarette drooping between his lips, lager tinny in his hand, and waves languidly in our direction.

"I don't believe it! Wayne Hegarty! Don't say anything," Ann hisses at us through a clenched smile as he approaches with a crab-like walk. We suddenly become incredibly British, standing to greet Mr Hegarty, who introduces himself to me as 'a typical pissed Australian farmer'. A major social dilemma, to agree might be rude, and silence could be interpreted as antisocial behaviour.

"Good to meet you, Mr Hegarty," I reply. The correct choice as his face cracks open to reveal a graveyard of blackened stumps. He has just dropped by on his way to ford the river, it seems, and within ten minutes heads unsteadily back to his vehicle, which is soon eclipsed by the warm velvet night. We are left contemplating his probable fate, yet our fears are not to be realised; two days later I meet him in the town Post Office, not surprisingly I remember him, although he can't quite place me.

We all have our version of the real Australia, ranging from lifeguards at Bondi Beach to the sacred sites of the Aborigines in the Red Centre. Bithrey inlet, near the town of Bega, provides the unedited version as viewed from the first convict transports.

The metallic tinging of bell birds bounces off the trees, interspersed with raucous shrieks from magpies, violently louder than their northern

BORDERLINES

cousins. We pass through claustrophobic bush, overhung by massive swathes of blue-green eucalyptus, lending much-needed shade. No-one lingers; lizards flit under our feet, snakes may not be far behind. A scalding blow as we emerge from the trees, soft white sand heated to touch point by fierce light, a rush to the creek, the tide flowing inwards. The primeval inlet basks in its own isolation, guarded by massive serrated rocks, ready to rip apart any seaborne invaders. Was this what they saw at Port Jackson? The bush broods, surrounding and enclosing us; there is only one path out. In the nineteenth century shipwreck survivors often set up home on the coast where they landed, as the bush was impenetrable. The town of Port Albert, down the coast in Victoria, is still inhabited by the descendants of one such disaster.

Modern visitors appreciate the seclusion of Bithrey; we are here by choice, and yet it is sometimes too solitary even for us, with the car ten minutes' walk away. Nevertheless I will always return, it is a part of the Bega Valley that has an uncanny appeal.

Two days later I head south to Eden, on the Queen's Highway. Ann had warned me that it is the Australian equivalent of the M1, and to watch out for other vehicles; I count five cars and two tractors in twenty kilometres. Enhancing this unreal situation, the occupants of two cars wave and flash headlights at me; are they warning of a major traffic hold-up perhaps? No, there are no delays, they merely recognise Ann's car and assume that they must know the driver.

The broad, clean road glides smoothly between emerald verges of well-watered grass, impeccable lawns surrounding pristine bungalows. In Europe people would be sunbathing, here we know our limitations; the sun assaults the landscape, smashing onto pavement and grass alike. Slowing down, I am confronted by an expanse of white-tipped sapphire ocean. A painted toy fishing boat smacks through the waves, heading for the harbour entrance below. This is Twofold Bay, the sea inlet of Eden, first discovered in 1797 by the survivors of a shipwreck, later to be developed as a major whaling port by the Imlays, one of the most influential families in the Bega Valley. The Imlay brothers were given their squattage by Governor Burke in 1833, after working as surgeons in the Sydney Infirmary, and their house, still standing, is the oldest in Bega. I occasionally find the concept of history in Australia difficult; I grew up in York, where it is possible to buy knitting wool in a shop built in the twelfth century. Nevertheless, Eden has its own heritage and I intend to search it out.

BORDERLINES

I drive towards the sea, and a bright white tower guides me to the Whaling Museum, a square stark building backdropped by azure waves. This area is known as the Sapphire Coast for good reason, colours of sea and sky sing through the sparkling air; the landscape is thrown into sharp relief. Perhaps this is caused by less pollution in the atmosphere, or maybe my northern eyes are unaccustomed to the unforgiving sunlight.

Whaling made Eden, and its history attracts visitors; while in the museum I meet many Australians, mostly from Sydney and Melbourne, searching out their own colonial pasts. Yet whales were hunted long before the Europeans arrived and generations of Yuin people used every ounce of the giant mammals, even lying for hours in their rotting carcasses in an effort to cure rheumatism. The killer whale, or Orca, was so named because he guided the other whales into the bay to face death by harpoon; the skeleton of the last Orca at Eden, Old Tom, hangs on the museum wall. When he died in 1930, the whaling industry of Twofold Bay died with him.

The museum also has an exhibition dedicated to shipwrecks, which provides grisly reading, and a spectacular look-out over the vastness of the Tasman Sea. Yet what I remember most are the truly friendly Aussies I meet there; admittedly most are in holiday mood, but their interest and sheer goodwill is humbling. Cynicism is not in their vocabulary, and they are determined that pommie visitors will not only enjoy an action-packed holiday, but will return to Australia in the future. So, armed with a fresh list of places to see, I leave the coast behind and drive towards the Snowy Mountains.

It is sometimes possible in this part of Australia to surfboard in the morning and ski in the afternoon. I have no such ambition; by November, spring is well into its stride, and August snows have melted into the bilious green marshes surrounding the foothills. But the opportunity to climb Australia's highest peak has to be grasped, so I purchase my ski-lift ticket, hop on, and set out on the first lap to the summit of Mount Kosciusko. Towering above the ski resort of Thredbo, and named after the Polish surveyor who discovered it, Kosciusko initially appears to be a very domesticated mountain, even to the extent of having a built-in boardwalk for environmental reasons. I am also very surprised and quite relieved to find a portaloo perched precariously behind a large boulder – further evidence of civilisation.

On reaching the snowline there is a palpable change in the landscape. The boardwalk evolves into a stony track bordered by yellowing slush. At the summit, intrepid climbers, including myself, clad in shorts and fleeces,

BORDERLINES

begin to regret leaving our trousers behind. Sudden whoops startle our little party.

'Snow you guys!' A party of teenagers thunders past and launches themselves into a greying patch of snow, all of three metres square. Again I am impressed by the Aussies' enthusiasm; this school party from Queensland may be seeing snow for the first time. They opt for chill novelty rather than gaze at the lunar panorama of peaks diminishing into a purple haze. This may be a wise choice; shading my eyes while looking around, I fail to notice bright green moss on the path. I perform a humiliating totter, followed by clutching at air, as the track rises to meet me. Knees remarkably unscathed, scrambling up trying not to give anybody eye contact, I am horrified when a teenage girl runs towards me, brandishing a handful of tissues.

"Your mouth! Your mouth! You poor duck!" she cries, attracting an embarrassing amount of attention from concerned bystanders. My chin feels warm and wet, and I swiftly realise that a large part of my front tooth has gained an independent life of its own. My ascent of Mount Kosciusko could well become more expensive than I had planned. I gingerly make my way back down the mountain, climb carefully into the car, and drive back to the relative safety of Bega.

The following morning, sitting on the veranda, tenderly sipping tea, I eavesdrop on a family conference.

'Ann, I'm not happy with that town dentist. If he screws it up she'll be in agony on the flight back.' My brother in law William, an anaesthetist, has provided me with pain relief and definitely has my best interests at heart.

"Well I thought he was OK, the children liked him," Ann replies distractedly over a measured clunking noise indicating a foreign body in the washing machine.

"Now look, you saw him at last New Year's party, he sat behind the barn all night singing the More Beer song. Trust me Ann, he has definitely got a problem. You should go to the bloke in Canberra, you can always stay the night and do Parliament House afterwards," William suggests.

Eerie mists drift toward the river, allowing spectral grey bushes to take shape in the paddocks. A black bootlace slithers silently from under the house. Yet this ancient land does not menace; it imparts peace, soon to be shattered.

The children erupt onto the veranda, pile into the van and we roar off into the dawn. In the dental debate, Canberra has won.

Rachel, my eight-year-old niece, looks round at me. 'Aunty Jane, Mummy says we can go to the Nimmitabel pie shop on the way. But you must try not to be sick going over Brown Mountain.'

Bibliography
W A Bayley, *History of Bega*, [Bega: Bega Family Museum, 1987].
Robert Hughes, *The Fatal Shore*, [London: Collins Harvill, 1987].
J A S McKenzie, *The Twofold Bay Story*, [Sydney: Eden Whale Museum & Historical Society, 1991].

BORDERLINES

Freya Scott
COLOUR

AMBER

1.

The day she left was yellow. The sky gave way to an early sunset. I watched from the warm wooden steps of the front porch. I have always found them fascinating. The sun, dragged daily into a burning horizon and melted, the remains spread across the sky, the colours seeping into the blue. There is nothing calm or peaceful about this to me. To me it is painful. The colours stretched across the sky stretch within me also. I am pulled backwards into darkness. The dying of the day reaches in with claws, into some depth of me I cannot reach myself, and pulls, pulls and stretches, as if to pull me out of myself, as if to turn myself inside out and colour the ground.

Still, how easily the sky is washed clean. How quickly the colour fades into nothing. How smoothly the night sweeps through to cover the remains and how willingly the sky settles for transparency.

The day she left it was yellow. The sky gave way to an early sunset, and Amber was gone by the time the darkness had thickened around me.

My father drove her to the station that day. It must have felt heroic. I stayed on the porch long after he had returned. He walked past me up the steps, ruffled my long hair and walked silently into the house where my mother was crying into the dinner. I sat there long into the evening, and many evenings afterwards, accentuating my loss with sunsets.

Amber wasn't the start. For me she was, but it had begun long before her. The world had taken her, and I could not argue with it. A force outside of nature and choice had taken her, and how many of us were powerless to stop it. She was mine but the power to protect and keep her was not. This realisation buried itself in my mind and there it grew in the absence of Amber, who had left me because the world had labelled her imperfect.

BORDERLINES

SOAP

2.

My mother was the smell of soap and the colour of straw. She was the sound of the breeze, soft and gentle but wavering. Her mouth was unnaturally red in colour and often in speech. Her eyes were brown, but dull. She was affection and disappointment, though never at the same time. I hoped I would never be like her.

She was mine in the absence of Amber, although some days I wasn't sure whether I wanted her. With Amber gone, I was automatically thrown into the empty space left by her. It was a dark space, dreary without her light. It was a space into which my mother desperately wanted me to fit. If I had been the kind to adjust my base ingredients, to sweeten my person to please, I'm sure I would have done it, and she would have adored me. As it was, I was stubborn, and clung to the things that frustrated her. I daily felt her disappointment, and daily saw my own in her. Sometimes it was blue. Sometimes it was the red of her mouth, or the yellow of her stupid words.

"Some good will come of this," she said the day Amber left. She spooned some runner beans onto my plate. "We are still living, and breathing. We are still safe. Some good will come."

"There is no 'good'," my father muttered some moments later. For him, all good in the world was lost with the first fallen angel. He stood up and took his plate to the kitchen, shaking my shoulder gently on his way in what he imagined was a comforting way. Instead it made me feel ashamed, like I was responsible for this sudden lack of goodness in my mother's life, and the eternal lack in my father's.

ROHAN

3.

I wake up and there's a storm beginning outside. A summer storm, wild with electricity and the dry sound of wind rushed fields. It breathes heavily over the roof. The darkness in the room starts to sway, to swirl, suddenly warm. The darkness takes on a purple hue, the colour of the clouds, clouds I can't see, but I know the colour, the way they move. I know the thunder waits, and I know the lightning will split the sky, and I know the morning will bring coolness and the smell of burning pine trees.

BORDERLINES

Rohan stirs beside me, as if disturbed by the change in the world outside. He sleeps with his mouth always slightly open. It is something I have come to love. He always looks as if he is seeing something. Sometimes he looks amused, and sometimes, more recently, he looks concerned. I do not know what he sees, and I don't ask him. Some things I let him keep.

The storm erupts inevitably, and I fall into uneasy thought. I realise then that I am afraid. Is he too?

We never saw it coming. I don't think many people did. Like with the storm, we saw the warning signs, heard the growing impatience behind the clouds, felt the quickening pace of the wind and hoped it would pass us by. But here it is. And there they are, only a few miles away, stretching their grey fingers towards us, clutching at our clothes like smoke, potent but unable to hold us. But soon the fire will spread, and we will be caught in the flames, as so many others like us have been.

It was never meant to be this way, I think.

"It was never meant to be this way," he said the night before, holding me close, underneath the sheets, his lips in my hair. "It was meant to be the daydream. Remember?"

"Yes," I'd replied, smiling to myself, feeling him smile too. I was silent for a time, and the smile faded. "I wish we weren't here. Wish we could be back home. Wasting all our time. Making all our plans for the future."

"You liked that?"

"Didn't you?"

"Yeah," he said animatedly. "It was... real."

"And this isn't real?" I said, squeezing his hand, kissing the corner of his mouth.

"Oh, it is. Just some things make it unreal. Something takes the edge off reality. Keep thinking one day I'll wake up and this will all be over, or it will never have even happened, and we'll actually be able to do what we said we would. That will be real. When it's just you and me again. It wasn't meant to be like this." He slept then.

When I wake again, it is still dark, but it is morning. The clouds choke the sun with puffy grey hands. I get up, and open the curtains to allow a small amount of light into the room. The world outside looks fresh and ruffled from the storm.

"You like the dark," Rohan mutters and buries his face into the pillow for a second. He glances up at me. He screws up his eyes to see me

BORDERLINES

properly. I smile, but I know my eyes remain dull.

"Not today," I say, and sit beside him on the bed. I know where he is going today, and the time has come too quickly. He reaches up and with a touch of his hand meets my fear with sympathy.

"Do you not want me to go? Do you not want to do this?" he asks after a while. For a minute I look at him, and I see a safe way out. I wonder if he has asked me in order to test me, or maybe because inside he too wants to get away.

I want to get you out, I think to myself, staring hard at him. I will the words into my eyes. I want to keep you here.

"I guess sometimes we don't get what we want," I say, and he understands, because he gets out of bed, and goes to shower.

I am still in my bedclothes when he is ready to go. I am still desperate and cold inside, and afraid, and longing for him. He is distant as if he had not shared a bed with me last night.

"I'll be back late Friday," he says, picking up his hat and jacket from the kitchen table. He hugs me hard and walks towards the door. I wish I could lock it. "Only three days. Not long."

He knows that it will be an eternity. I am afraid that he does not care for me, or worse, for himself, for his life.

He walks out of the door, and it is then I know I am wrong. He looks back at me for a time. Memorising me with such intensity I feel his stare lightly graze my cheek.

And suddenly the doorway is empty. I feel suddenly wide awake. I walk about the house, barefoot, hugging my elbows, staring at doorframes, at the corners of windows. I get back into the coldness of our empty bed, and lie on my side, and imagine he is next to me sleeping. With his mouth slightly open. Seeing something. Concerned. I never ask what he has seen. I tell myself it is because I want to let him keep some things. The truth is I don't want to know. The truth is he does not ever dream of me at all. He sees the future. He sees ideals and struggles for justice. I am not in front of him to see. Behind, next to him, maybe, but never in front. It is not me he fights for.

I get up and walk back through the grey light of the house, to be alone and thoughtless. I want to starve this insecurity but I can't, I can't escape him.

*

I cannot get used to passivity. I cannot help but want to scream at my helplessness. I sit and I watch the people I love being ripped from

BORDERLINES

underneath my fingertips, too weak to hold them. How has this become?

I think it started many years before me. Even my mother found it hard to recollect the beginning. If there was one. The way I saw it, it was like a single ant at the edge of the blanket that slowly became a swarm wanting to take over the entire picnic.

They took over the south first, on the east coast, where they took control of the ports. Of course, years ago there were countless strikes – the fishing industry took a dive and never recovered – but soon enough these were reduced by means that I still suspected were underhand. People reacted in different ways. There were book burnings in the bigger cities, which at the start were against the propaganda, but soon enough the purists were burning books themselves, and after that it was difficult to tell who the bonfires were for. There was uproar in the larger towns and cities when the curfew was put in place, though apart from Rohan, I never knew anyone affected by this law. Other than that, there was little resistance.

"Like a slap in the face," my mother always said. "We were so surprised we couldn't react." I didn't believe it. There were too many supporters by that time to warrant it being any kind of surprise.

"They were voted in," my father said one afternoon as he fiddled fruitlessly with dial on the old radio. "People asked for this."

"How did they get in? Surely someone would have realised what they were doing?"

"Of course. The leaders of the other parties. Johnson, for instance. Was preaching against the purists for years. Fat lot of good it did him, he was dealt with pretty quickly along with the rest of them." My father shook his head. "Perfection. Something we all strive for, darling. Something that will always be out of our reach. But this – this is no search for perfection. This is a culling, a stripping down of humanity into something else, something - " He stopped short when he realised I did not understand what he was saying. He stared into space for a time. Then, "People want this," he said incredulously.

Part of his incredulity was always disappointment. My grandparents lived far south, where support for the purists was strongest, and I had never met them. I never would, and he would never forgive them.

"Don't worry," he said finally. "There's time enough for worry."

"Are we safe?" I asked, against my better judgement.

He smiled. "It'll be all right," he said, although his eyes told me that he didn't quite believe himself. I did not stay to question him further. Instead, I ran out into the garden where Amber was waiting for me. She wanted me to go down to the paddock with her where Jesse and Rohan were mending fences.

It was the last unbroken summer, Rohan's second and Amber's last with us. He was from one of the cities in the south where the purists had already taken over. Orphaned and without much in the way of responsible family, he lived under the protective wing of a minister and his wife from the age of ten. Birth certificate lost, Rohan had escaped the fate of many of his kind at the age of sixteen when the purists took hold; but he suffered traumas of his own as the purist regime tightened its hold on the city. Rohan was brought up knowing the ways of the church and was raised like a son alongside the minister's two daughters. His wife doted upon her adopted son and she taught him to read and write in the spare hours between meals and church services.

It had been a strange, but happy existence, he assured us. He told us about it in the darkness of late evening behind the woodshed, where we gathered most nights to talk away the day's events into clean, blank sleepiness.

"I love this time of night," Rohan said once, at the end of the summer. It was getting cooler by then. The night was clear.

Amber leaned into his shoulder and sighed, contented. Jesse leant back on his elbows, his legs entangled in mine. I lay back against the wall next to Rohan, loving the pressure of his shoulder on mine, knowing at the same time that he did not feel it.

"I love this time of night," he said again, to no one in particular. I shifted my gaze to his face. Lazily Jesse looked up.

"Why?" he said.

"I never got to see it," Rohan replied. "Back home, no one was in the streets after 7 o'clock, except the patrols. I used to watch from the window. Kept a few rocks on the sill in case I got daring enough. All I had was a house of candles and dodgy electricity, especially in my room. I practically lived in that pokey little room. But here," he said, and spread his arms, "Here there is dark I can move in. Nothing like this at home. Not since the invasion."

He liked to talk about 'home'. He liked to talk about hardship, how he endured it. I look back and think that he said it to impress us, but at the time it did. Our hearts went out to the image of a young boy, sat at the window, gazing out onto a moonlit street from darkness. The young boy labelled imperfect by his dark hair and heritage.

"Yes, but this is your home now," Amber said, winding her arm

BORDERLINES

around his. He grinned at her, humouring her, responding to her flirtatious giggles by squeezing her hand.

"I wouldn't have any other," he said to her, bending his head close. Then he leant back against the wall again and stared into nothing. "Here I have friends, a decent home and the freedom to kick back in the dark and enjoy it."

I loved the dark as much as daylight, but what I loved more was that Rohan saw the dark as I did, somewhere to be free, somewhere to enjoy the things that we lived for, things that sometimes life denied us.

Amber never really understood. I don't think she really listened. Her eyes were in love, her heart followed, blind and deaf. Consequently, Amber grew up – and backwards, at the same time. Two years older than me and twice as pretty, she was everyone's favourite – Rohan's, Jesse's, my mother's. I think she thought that this gave her the right to do anything and do it her way.

She decided to fall in love with him, and she did it her way – wholeheartedly, without thinking. He became everything to her. Everyday was for him, for the glimpse of him in the morning when he walked through the house at breakfast time on his way out with my father, for the afternoons we could bother him in the fields, or out in the cowsheds, for the nights where we sat and lit fires, or sat on the porch, or ate in the dining room with all the windows and doors open to the twilight. Those nights we would all dress up nicely, and my mother would use the nice plates and watch her red mouth. Amber used these nights to her advantage. As time went on, she dressed up more nicely, spent longer making herself up, stopped helping me tie up my hair. It was all calculated. She had decided to love him, to make him love her, to have him no matter the cost. She adored my mother's disapproval, and my father's indifference gave her the freedom to manipulate, to scheme, to play.

I had not known this side of Amber before. I suppose I had never before had the chance to see it. From the very first night it became obvious, and I was at once unsettled and accepting, in the kind of way only a child can be when she recognises her age as an obstacle.

"Lend us that skirt," she said, waving her arm impatiently at me. It wasn't a question. "That brown one, with the stuff along the bottom."

I was stood at the wardrobe, deciding what to wear. Luckily I'd already seen it and didn't have to rummage around. I flung it at her.

It was Friday night. Amber and I were dressing in our shared bedroom. Her half was decorated with yellow paint with a neat border of orange

BORDERLINES

leaves. Hung up in plain wooden frames were a photograph of her in a ponytail and another of me, my mother and father, dressed for church. They were cliché photographs, nice enough, but I took little pleasure in them.

My side of the room was also yellow with orange leaves, but in place of the photographs, I had paintings. My father's paintings. They were as far from reality as the earth is from the moon. They were vibrant and beautiful, canvases of shape and colour and meaning. He never drew outlines. He painted with light.

"If you break up white light with a prism," he said to me once, "you get all the other colours. Light and colour go hand in hand." So it was in his paintings. He spent hours getting the base colours right, only to paint over them with new colours, brighter, fresher, building up layer upon layer of paint. Sometimes he mixed sand with the paint, or deliberately made stippled effects so that the paint rose in sharp little points. I guess that meant something too.

My mother didn't know they had meaning.

"Child's play," she'd mutter. "Wish your father would go and mend that chicken coop instead of messing around with his finger painting." Sometimes she wished he would help with the tea more often. Sometimes she wished he'd get a real hobby. But really I think she wished that he would show her what he meant.

Amber wriggled into the skirt and put on a white shirt. I glanced up at her enviously from my place on the floor where I was trying to put my best shoes on. I'd grown during the spring and the shoes were now miles too small. Even my feet were growing ahead of me.

"Does that look ok?" she said, twirling around in front of the old speckled mirror hanging on the back of the door. She flicked her long auburn hair back from her face and wrinkled up her nose. She twisted her hair up behind her head and searched around for something to hold it in place.

"Come on, come on," she whispered impatiently. Finally her perfect fingers rested on several tortoiseshell hair grips. Within seconds she'd secured her hair in place. Hours and hours of practice had made her expert at this kind of manoeuvre. She grinned at me in the mirror. "Good, huh? Eye-catching enough?"

"Depends who's eyes you want to ensnare," I said slowly, pretending to struggle with the miniscule shoe, knowing exactly who's attention she wanted.

"Rohan's, of course," she giggled. "He's perfect!"

"If you say so," I said, feigning disinterest, standing up and trying to walk even though my toes felt like they were being bent double.

BORDERLINES

"Oh, come on," she smiled, poking me in the ribs, "I've seen you staring after him, you like him as much as me."

"No, I don't," I said, desperately trying to keep my face from turning red. I pretended to be deeply interested in my reflection.

"Yes you do," she laughed, twirling away from the mirror.

"Don't."

"Do."

"Don't."

"Do, do, do!"

"Shut up," I said, irritated. Because she was right. She stood behind me, grinning over my shoulder at the mirror. She started fiddling with my hair, which was the same colour as hers, and almost as long.

"Hand us that brush," she said, and then proceeded to style my hair. I was grateful to her for that; my clumsy hands could manage little more than a rough pony-tail.

"I'm going to marry him," she said matter-of-factly after a while. I looked at her in the mirror, not sure if she was joking.

"What, Rohan?" I said, my stomach jolting. She nodded. Smiling. "Don't you think mum will have something to say about that?"

She shrugged. "Probably."

"Dad wouldn't much like it either."

She thought for a bit, and then rearranged her ideas. "Ok, so I won't marry him. We'll just have a wild, passionate affair. Then maybe I'll get married."

"To who?"

She shrugged again. "I don't know. I'll get mum to help me on that one."

I wondered what Rohan would think of being unceremoniously pushed aside and replaced by another man of my mother's choice.

Amber finished my hair and stepped back to admire it. I turned my head this way and that to look at my hairstyle. It was cute, but I wasn't as striking as Amber. I wondered if that had been her intention.

"You look lovely," she said, smiling genuinely at me, and I forgave her at once for being beautiful.

Just as we were ready and about to leave the room to go down to dinner, I said, "What if Rohan doesn't notice you?"

She stopped brushing her skirt down, and looked thoughtful as if that eventuality hadn't occurred to her. "He will," she said firmly, and my heart sank. He would notice her, and she would make sure of it.

BORDERLINES

"He will," she repeated. "Mind you let me sit next to him," she said, and I thought I heard a warning tone in her voice. Her mouth was almost as red as my mother's even then.

We barely knew Rohan and already Amber had claimed him as her own. I didn't mind at first but I still felt bitter that night. It wasn't that I resented Amber for disregarding my feelings; I resented her because she knew that I'd really wanted to wear that skirt.

Anything for love I suppose. Anything for him. She was in love with him from the beginning. There was little before him. She loved him; and I could not.

TOAST

4.

A year later, my mother was sat at the breakfast table, reading a letter, eyes involved with words, mouth involved with bread and butter. The kitchen smelled of jam and burnt toast. A rack of black bread sat in the middle of the table untouched. She had used the new toaster instead of the grill.

I sat down and took a piece of toast, smothered it liberally with jam, something I knew she would disapprove of. She barely glanced up. I crunched loudly, childishly. She frowned a little.

"From Amber?" I asked, mouth full, crumbs spraying. I knew I could get away with this today. She nodded, and smiled a little. Finally she looked up at me, eyes shining with something I could not name, her red mouth stretched over her teeth.

"She's fine," she said, holding out the letter so I could inspect it. "Living with a couple in St. Antoine. Older couple apparently, in a little town house. She sounds quite happy." She nodded approval. "Lots of parties," she added, with a touch of envy.

"Anything for me?" I asked, hoping for an extra note addressed to me. My mother moved the newspaper and other various items spilling out of envelopes and shrugged.

"Don't think so, honey," she said, but she didn't sound too disappointed for me.

The back door opened, and my father and Rohan walked in. My father ruffled my hair, and walked on through the kitchen and down the steps to the cellar. Rohan remained near the door and nodded at my mother before turning his gaze to me. I felt suddenly the soft weight of my hair on my shoulders and the gentle tendrils about my cheeks. I breathed in, aware

BORDERLINES

suddenly of the exposed skin of my neck and of my tongue behind my lips, felt the muscles in my body tighten and relax into graceful curves. I uncurled the fingers of my left hand, felt the fluidity of the movement, laid my hand flat on the table. Everything in the room seemed positioned for me, waited for me. I held his gaze, steadily. Every shred of my skin held fast. Every bit of me felt perfect and living, as if every move and every breath had been written, had been made for these moments, had been carefully planned and woven into each passing second. Amber disappeared from my mind.

We neither of us smiled. Why should we, when smiling conveys so little, when even words and touch are meaningless and hollow.

Then he was gone. I sat through the rest of breakfast pretending not to feel my mother's knowing gaze, crunching black toast crusts. I felt reckless. Let them think what they will. I have done nothing wrong.

*

I sit in our kitchen for a long time after Rohan has gone. The wind, calm after the storm, plays around the corners of the house. I think about making toast and eating it with jam. I know I will not burn it though, so maybe it is not worth it. I can't eat my way through memory. For a moment, I almost miss my mother. I miss Amber more. My heart gives way to an aching for her, for what I have done to her. *I have done nothing wrong.* It was easy then, under the disappointed gaze of my mother, to be stubborn and childish, to pretend I was right, to pretend I had done nothing. There is nothing to hide me now. I am plunged into responsibility, into recognition, to realise that I have taken something that was never mine. How she must hate me. How I have wronged her.

I feel torn in two – how is it possible to ache so much? And how is it possible to love so hard, and so blindly, that I would hurt my own, destroy the happiness of the only person in the world to have loved me? I am cursed now, to be loved by a man who does not know me, to be hated by a sister that I have hurt and can never heal.

I wish for a clear day, and a sunset, and pain to settle me into the night. Relief from my guilt comes from this. A sunset, a loss; my punishment.

BORDERLINES

Emma Callan
LOSS

I was thirty-four years old when I died. I'd never thought about dying before. My friend Cassie used to be pre-occupied with the notion of death. I always put it down to her Catholic background. It was an entirely blank subject for me.

So what's it like? I still don't know if I can explain it. I must be in my fifties now (if we're still adhering to an earthly concept of age). Twenty years on and I'm none the wiser.

Maybe I could try smells, tastes. There's so little here. How can I describe the glorious stimulants of the senses if there's nothing to stimulate them? My eyes are open and see things - blocks, lines, forms, profiles, contours of things. I'm holding a photograph but I can't really feel it. Sorry I can't be more use. But if I close my eyes, that's different. Bear with me, let me go and I can hear everything - bird song, the cracked laugh of our fire, a single raindrop hovering on the leaf tip of my geranium plant. Just let me go back, I can give you the touch, the taste, the smell of their sandy curls blanketing my cheek that early June evening. Let me go, just for a moment.

When I first found out I was going to have them, I had just had a job interview at NatWest. It was for a position I thought I was under qualified for, so I assumed a laissez-faire attitude that gave way to a confidence and eloquence I never knew I had. Evening drinks with Cassie and Jade became a 'pre-emptory celebration of my new job'. I remember that they were the exact words I used as my friends stood and clinked their glasses with mine. Despite my tongue in cheek self-indulgence, I was genuinely bursting with a glowing belief in my job prospects and myself. I was the type of person who never pushed themselves for fear of failure and yet inadvertently I thought I had pushed myself into a damn good position. There's nothing like death to incur regret. I regret the cowardice I let myself live with till that point. At least I want to regret it. I'm not sure I do. I can show you the true meaning of regret. Then you can decide for yourself whether you think I give a shit about anything else at all.

I don't know why I'm writing this. I don't want anyone here to read it. I've tried to make them listen when they've asked. It's very simple – I want to be alive, alive with my girls. They don't have to do anything, just let me go.

BORDERLINES

Shortly after my smug toast, I was lying in the back of an ambulance. I'd fainted and taken my dinner and a bottle of bubbly down with me. In my half conscious state I remember thinking that maybe my body had conspired with providence to kill me so I wouldn't get my job. In a way I was right. Pregnant, twelve weeks gone, twins. My first life ended there. I saw my profile - single, mediocre wage, stunned. I didn't speak for a good twenty-four hours until I uttered a word that, as I scratch on to this page, makes me wince – abortion. It was a question more than a statement, one I thought I had answered until I saw them; grey and blotchy, electronic and beautiful, together as always. That was the first and only time I fell in love.

When I rub my thumb and forefinger together I feel the soft, plump pink of two year old skin. April would only sleep if I used my two fingers, no more, no less, to stroke the palm of her hand for at least five minutes. As I sat there, my other hand would stroke Sara's forehead, smoothing the unruly locks away from her chubby cheeks. I would tell April that this would have to stop soon, that she can't rely on mummy to get to sleep forever. She would just squeeze the hand that was stroking hers and make warm, comforting noises on her dummy. I knew it was the right thing to stop, so three months later, I fought my maternal instincts. After several calls from April and one from Sara, there was silence. Both relieved and perturbed that my girls had adjusted so quickly to the absence of their mother at bedtime, I peered round the door. Both sets of eyes were shut. April's fingers were nestled in her sister's hair, dragging it over her face rather than holding it back. In turn, Sara had her hand round April's, her thumb and forefinger gently stroking her palm. If I could have foreseen what was to happen the following year, I would have ignored my sensible parental instincts. If I could change what was to happen, I would still ignore them. I would spend every night with my flesh on their flesh. I would spend an eternity listening to the quiet breath of my children's sleeping innocence.

Do you ever think about decisions and consequences? Parenting is full of them: which nappies avoid nappy rash, when is best to stop breast-feeding. Simple decisions can steal sleep. Even simpler decisions can steal lives.

I decided to drive my twins to Norwich to my friends Linda and Simon. Since the birth, my friends had been substitutes for a father and grandparents. It was a cold but clear February day and the drive was familiar to me. When I go back over my choice to go I search for reasons, signs I should have spotted to deter me, alert me to the fact that a

BORDERLINES

depressed drunk would smack his Volvo into my old fiesta. But there are none. You may think this could alleviate my conscience. You're wrong. I cannot bear to think that it just is.

They need to let me go. But they won't and each time I'm nearly there, where I belong, they pull me away. I've been so close, several times. They try to convince me that I must stay, make the most of the rest of my life. Yes, they call it 'life'. What a fucking joke. They thought the photograph would help to convince me.

Well, I'll wait with my eyes closed and try to be patient. I'll drift back to plump pink and wispy sand. Occasionally I'll look carefully at the photograph of my daughter's graves. One day I'll live with them again, for now I'll wait for my death to end.

BORDERLINES
Linda Albert
A FABLE

Once upon a time there was a woman who spent her life trying to keep a beach ball under water - a task given to her by a wicked witch when she was born. The witch warned her something terrible would happen to her mother if she were to allow the beach ball to rise above the water. The beach ball was very buoyant, filled with an explosive family grief. The woman didn't know this, but she used all her energy to comply with the task. She was a rule-follower. Her hair, which was pitch black, and stood straight up from her head, fell out the next day, and eventually grew back in the softest shade of yellow ever seen. She had a pale, clear forehead and a look of sweetest innocence. Her eyebrows were so fair they couldn't be seen. She was convinced these were a sure sign she had been chosen for something.

It was a hard life, forever having to keep the beach ball under water, through every minute and every hour of the day and night - through adolescence, high school, college, marriage, the birthing and raising of her children. On the surface, she looked just fine. No one would ever have guessed how hard she was working, how very unusual were the circumstances of her life (or maybe they were typical. It was not for her to know.) The yellow hair didn't help much either; didn't bring her any sympathy. Innocence is not always a useful trait.

Finally, an old woman came to her, beautiful in her ugliness, and informed her it was time to let go of the ball. And she would help. The woman with the ball was afraid. She had held it for so long it was almost second nature to her. Then there was the question of her mother and the witch. The old woman laughed and turned into a beautiful white wolf. The ball shot into the air, drenching everyone for miles around. It was a regular tsunami, but amazingly and despite complaints, not one person actually drowned. In fact, some people found it refreshing, and those who didn't were ultimately cleansed in spite of themselves. Except for some unusually well developed biceps, and a tendency to bursitis, the yellow haired woman lived happily ever after.

BORDERLINES *Poetry*

Tessa Foley
AN APOLOGY TO A FORMER SELF

When Mummy met Daddy, she used to live there –
No, not that one there,
That one there, yes, the one with the green door,
Old number sixty-four.
Yes, it is only small, not at all like our nice house now.
No, not even a phone, did Mummy live alone?
Oh no, there were four
Of us living behind that green door,
How did we fit? Well I know it's not big,
Half the size of our house and there's only three of us,
And you are little, yes.

When Mummy met Daddy, she used to work there,
On that corner there,
Uh-huh in a bar, oh yes, it was hard, but a laugh,
I suppose, do I miss it?
Oh no, not at all,
Daddy wanted more for me than pulling a pint,
He said I was too bright,
Uh-huh, Daddy's like the prince in your bedtime book,
He took one look at my terrible life
And swept me away to make me his wife,
A wife who needn't work,
Oh yes, Sweetie, he's a prince, a prince in a tie.

When Mummy met Daddy, she went drinking with them,
Uh-huh that collection of strange looking men.
The one with the long hair is Generous John,
Did I like him? Well yes, but I was wrong,
Daddy taught me that burping isn't fun,
And the one with the hat?
That's Mummy's friend Matt,
He sent Mummy flowers but Daddy told her to send them back,
See, when daddies love mummies,

BORDERLINES

Only they buy them flowers,
Oh no, Sweetie, no, mummies don't always get flowers and if they do,
That means someone else is getting them too.

When Mummy met Daddy, she was happy in that house,
In her tiny room, in her lousy job that left her poor,
With her silly, stupid friends who loved her more,
Than Daddy ever would.
Uh-huh, she has her three-piece-suite,
Synthetic heat, enough to eat,
Her garden chairs, her spiral stairs,
Her locked away, day after day,
Right way to live –
So, Sweetie, please give this letter to Daddy.
He'll be home soon, well, maybe,
And so long, Baby, you're eighteen now,
That's old enough to work in a bar.
Make Mummy proud.

BORDERLINES *Poetry*

Tracey Leach
FIVE TIMES TO MARKET

To market, to market, to catch your soul
And steal it back from her.
To plant it in the deepest pot -
And the widest for its roots.
No money exchanged in this transaction,
I am taking what is mine.

To market, to market, to buy some ice,
And freeze you until it burns.
The only thing that will drip now
Is your blood - when I decide.
No money exchanged in this transaction,
I am taking what is mine.

To market, to market, to buy an orange
That will never be opened or touched,
It may have been, if brought by another
But instead it was grasped by a selfish hand.
No money exchanged in this transaction
It is my thoughts that buy this piece.

To market, to market, to buy a star
And name it after us.
I'll look out our window every eve
And point to it and never forget.
No money exchanged in this transaction
For who can own the stars?

To market, to market to buy a sharp knife
And hold it to sacred skin,
Tempting and teasing watching scared eyes
Unsure of how far I will go.
The money matters little anymore,
My blood surges out, now you can have her.

Anita Sheard
DEATH AND FORGIVENESS

(Decrescendo – Gravë ♪)

As I did hold you dying
My hand upon your brow
Your breath became as nothing
I wondered then as now.

Why oh why had you to go
Allegra, vivace, I loved you so.

The glutton in your brain
Had been a little lump
With vengeance back it came
Your life thereby to stunt.

Why oh why this cruel loss
Rubata, staccata, your life away did toss.

I never had so touched you
But suddenly the fear
Of losing you so very soon
Made everything quite clear.

Why oh why must pain be borne
Ritardando… now I mourn
Perhaps the reason for your fate:
To show to forgive is never too late
And though it took so many years
It made my love felt through my tears.

Why oh why no second chance
Glissando, morendo, ends life's dance.

As I did sit and hold your hand

BORDERLINES

Its fingers frail, your skin so sore
I hoped and craved you'd understand
How much I wanted your love before.

How oh how can you now know
Dormendo, sognando, I must let it go.

 gravë

Nikesh Murali
GIRL FROM IPANEMA

The girl from Ipanema – the green eyed dove.
She walks like there is no worry in the world, like the earth that moves for its celestial lovers in a slow graceful rotation, so that they may relish every inch of her with their sparkling eyes of heat and light.
She kisses the breeze on its way, turning it into the sweetest scent that you would ever smell and make you dream of warm love that will linger forever in the cold regions of your heart.
Her hips sway as she walks past smitten suitors and debates rage in the Veloso bar about why God is so cruel to them, while the strings of a love struck guitar try to imagine the chords for a song that just might reveal the reasons for her divine presence on earth.

The girl from Ipanema – the offspring of Aphrodite.
She walks to the beach in her low cut skirt and a carnival of love follows her to the ocean. The waves perform a samba in her honour, the contagious rhythms of which travel to the mountains which pine for the embrace of pure clouds.
She sits ever so delicately on the sand as if to not hurt their fleeting souls, as the moon begins its eager climb to the stage of the heavens so that he may impress her with the complex harmony of the bossa nova.

The girl from Ipanema, when she goes walking, the whole world is in rapture and the sighs from her lovers grow louder, but she only has eyes for the sea and the transitions of day and night.

She just doesn't see.

BORDERLINES *Poetry*

Freya Scott
WATERMELON FOR BREAKFAST

I remember
though you do not,
that before we were strangers
there was a warm, peach-coloured morning,
when we had watermelon for breakfast,
big, thick slices
fat juicy smiles
that we ate with our fingers.

There was tenderness
and promise in your eyes
as juice from a shared breakfast
clung clumsily
and sticky
to my lips
ran over my mouth
and blushed my cheeks.

You leant across the table
and kissed
the corner
of my mouth.

How I wish
that the second you pulled away
I could have reached up
to peel it off
and stick it,
like a sticker, or stamp,
into my diary

As proof
that once
for a second

BORDERLINES

for one moment in time
you leant across the table
your sleeve in a melon puddle
to kiss my mouth
the corner of my sticky mouth

to put your lips
over a melon kiss

as if this were something
as if I were loved.

BORDERLINES

Victor Manley
WHEN WE WERE YOUNGER

When we were younger, in that first flush of a nervous, youthful love, before we knew exactly what the other would say and do and think and feel at every moment; when we were young and we bought that house in the city. It was that time of faith and beauty in judgement, when we started to see the bearing, the frame of each other behind the words and conversation, to understand something more than the speech and basic purpose of expression.

I remember that house, just a stones throw from the river, which is really why we bought it. Because apart from its proximity to the water it was dark and cramped, the doors and windows creaked in the night and neighbours argued from between tiny cracks in the wall. But it was ours. That was what kept us there, what made it brighter.

When we were younger we used to go for walks along by the current on the banks of the river. And the weather would split the days in two. If it was fine, and simple clouds interrupted the blue only gently, like pike flicking their tales idly from below the water, then we would consider walking the longer way. The 'coastal path' you called it, because of the one or two worn green signs that pointed along to some distant coast, one which we never reached. It was always one of my great desires to follow the 'coastal path' till we reached the sea, to watch the promised waves and rocks which had been so long anticipated by those green signs. And to see the river here, as it ran along the banks and circled its way around its currents and undercurrents, or between the legs of a striding bridge or two, was to see what would soon become part of the sea. And, if on a day when the sun seemed to moor its brighter self on the water and a fresh wind drove towards us, I could almost fancy there was a taste of salt in the air, or the sound of a dragging wave upon the rocks.

I dreamt that one day, as we rounded a further corner, where the path started to be broken with dusty stones and dry, seeding grass rose tall beside us, that as we rose above a gentle incline, a quiet and forgotten inlet would open before us. Here the aggressive rocks of the coastline were broken, and calmed to allow this spiralling river to lose its momentum, its purpose, and slide along sandy ridges and pebbled banks. Filtering, sometimes in sight and catching a ray of sunlight, or slipping below view

BORDERLINES

to run some way in shadow under stone and the collapsed coastline rock, before returning to sight to splash gently around the foot of a stone that still rose defiantly to meet it along the middle of its path, breaking the flow at the point where the tides salt water stood and swirled to meet it. And upon that rock, as if he had as right a part as nature to be there, stood a fisherman, letting his line hold in the current; who would wave a greeting to us, though we did not know him, as much to say, 'Don't we all see the beauty of this? And shouldn't we be glad for it?' And then, having dropped his hand, would continue on his leisure in case his sudden inattention should lose him a catch.

But we never did make it that far. By the point where we may have been tempted to explore further was another path that branched off, pulling us slowly back, first by the mere suggestion of life, a few houses that seemed to break up out of the arable land, or perhaps by some barking dog who would appear as we approached before leaping away towards its home again, back into the city. And we would follow its direction, heading for home, if we had not turned back already. Often the sky would have changed, the gentle ripples of cloud gathering into a wave that now strode across the sky and out of sight, being ploughed by the same wind that had begun by sifting through the branches of those beech trees that hung so low we had to bow to them at times, and had finished by ruffling your auburn hair. Or perhaps we had already strayed from the path at some point, sat by the river and watched the course of it as you rested your head on my shoulder, and it grew late and the orange sky started to threaten darkness.

It was on one of these days, as we sat and trusted an hour to the river, that I take my memory of you. Now whenever I want to watch you smile, I go there, into that hour, as an explorer who stumbles upon heavens plains, and entrust my mind to tell me exactly how you looked, the scent of your wind-brushed hair, the taste of your breath. I am frustrated initially by a romantic glow, a rosy haze that blinds that picture of you, and only finally does your smile appear as if from a mist, softly drawing back its subtle veil to admit that look, that look I see now. Like a collector I selfishly store it away, valued not as an artist would do with an eye to its details, its faults, perfections or frailties, but rather admired and given pride of place in that shifting gallery of memory.

If, when we looked out from the pale wood doorway, the clouds already stood bold upon the horizon or threatened with dark majesty above us, we would, unlike upon the days when the sky stretched clear

BORDERLINES

and brilliant, take the town way. Following the thin beaten path which broke a line between the river and, at first, the road which wound quietly beside us, or the very backs of houses from which the gentle humours or hostilities of life would issue to flood towards the far banks.

We would let the array of sounds and sights bear us along, sometimes hand in hand, though often, when the path narrowed itself, one by one. You leading, me following. And I would watch your skirts as they were flicked by your heels, or your thin waist pressured by those simple ribbons you would tie there, or your auburn hair that fanned out from where it was gathered at your neck. It was easy to follow while I watched you walk. And sometimes I would suggest going back before it was really time just because I had been watching too long, I had been watching as you flicked your skirts above your ankle with your stride, or the fabric tied in at your waist would twist as you walked in such a way that I would catch you up, and kiss your neck so you stopped walking. It was like a reassurance of my futility, your walk, I knew that while you led I would follow anywhere.

It was sometimes that these town walks would be caught by a blustering rain, or a faint wind may bring white snow to bear. It was twice that we were caught by a storm, and once that the lightning forked across the river as we sheltered in a crumbling boat house, where the rain dripped in through the rotting wood and rising ochre paint. And you were beautiful with tracks of water rushing down your face and excitement in your eyes, and I kissed you there in that fragmenting place.

This chance of ill weather was why we took the town way, or rather the better chance of finding shelter on this route rather than the 'coastal way', where the river, rain and land met without interference.

And so it was for me that the days came to be called. Firstly those bright days, and then those with such a chance of rain or wind. Firstly coastal days and then town days. And it was with the same peculiarity that anyone may attach such words to mean things other than their original purpose that we used these terms which would be nonsense to a stranger. It was our language and code. It kept the world at bay a little.

I was thinking of that day, that day which I can reach into and produce your smile, when we sat by the river on the 'coastal path' and a strange excitement rose amongst the notes of your voice as you spoke. This time, as always, I had to fight through the haze, like pulling back sheets of condensation coloured with rose water, before I could see you properly, and not just some romantic glow but really you. I do not remember exactly

BORDERLINES

what you said, like any other day and any other words I merely remember the general substance of it all and the rest falls from how I knew you, how well I saw your soul. You see, I did know it so well.

'Soon I, well I don't think I'll be able to walk this way for a while,' I pulled my eyes from the water rushing away to meet its end at the sea. She was looking down but I could see the half-smile and the anticipation making her bite her lip as she glanced up at my face as I turned to her, shifting my weight now to my left hand. I made a noise in the back of my throat of some interest, some concern. I guessed it was what she wanted. 'I've got something to tell you.' Now she looked steadily into my eyes and I creased my brow at the sudden intensity there. I knew already what she would say, her secret. I could not have done otherwise, I think I saw it before she did - that new spirit in her, that strength, but I had said nothing.

'I know,' I said before she could speak again. I turned back to watching the river and laughed as the silence built up beside me.

'I don't understand.'

'I can see,' I turned back towards her and could have laughed again at the surprise, almost the consternation there. 'I love you. I can see the change. And so will he.' She shook her head and then, as if forcing herself towards understanding, she smiled.

'Or she.' And now she laughed as tears rolled from her eyes.

'Or she' I agreed. This is my moment to keep of you. The memory I treasure above all. That smile as I kissed the tears from your cheeks.

It is better by far than many of the others. Better by far. I doubt much of what is in my mind now, like it is all scratched together from dreams and fairy tales, snatches of old songs, adventures in a book. I see myself in my memories and take the place of others there, looking back at myself. And want nothing more than to break my own skull with whatever is at hand.

My own face has become like a scar to me. I hide it away inside this dark, damp cupboard of a house and fidget as the shadows reach for me. And when it does seem that the gloom rises up at me, when the fingers are reaching for my throat and the weight holds me like knees upon my chest, you come. There with your hazy glow, that rose hued mist, rising with the sunlight the stretches through the window, to harry the dark away, to chase it from the room and lend me your strength while the day lasts. But, my God, how long the nights.

I stand there, on the river bank where we once sat clinging to each other. I watch the waves and currents spend themselves on the banks and then hurry on and away. I watch the far bank. I watch the path, both

BORDERLINES

behind and before me. I watch the sun and, when it appears as an emissary of the night, I watch the moon. I watch, and I wait.

You left that morning to walk along here. We had argued as the wind gusted and clouds, like the forebears of an ailing sky, began to gather. I would take the town way then and you, against the judgement of doctors who said you should not stretch yourself, would walk your 'coastal path'. I had strode frowning along beside the river and before long, just as it had promised to do, the wind rose and rain broke the rivers surface a thousand times in a moment. I ran for cover under a willow that hung from beyond a fence some hundred yards away. The wind almost tore the coat from my back as I huddled dripping beneath the half-cover of the tree. Away in the house behind me I heard sudden exclamations, laughter and the sound of windows being closed. A shutter crashed against its frame as a dog's barking was silenced with an impatient shout. Suddenly the sound of the rain was all. Even my breathing rose hollow in my chest, it was a strange kind of natural silence. The birds had hidden themselves and their songs beneath cover, the city behind me stopped to admire the superior strength of nature's rush, there were no clocks to tick or bells to chime. The tide of the wind and the dash of the rain became the world, and I could only look out from my net of vanishing cover and worry that you were home.

I searched the city over the next days. I searched the path and the fields that tried to hem in the growing streets. I searched until exhaustion took me to bed and then, when I could stand again, I searched some more. They found something after weeks, a face, a body. And it looked like you. Yes, it looked like you in as much that a box of paints can resemble a portrait. No soul, no spirit. There were your eyes and your lips and the curve of your waist, but it was your shadow. A shadow you had cast off to remind me you were still there, to make sure I was still searching. And I did. And I do.

The sun sets, it gets late and soon the night will reach for me again. One day, when I am sure you walk before me, when I see the hem of your dress flick up above the ankle, the ribbon tied so sure at your waist and the flow of your hair, I will follow. I will walk in a storm and slip upon the riverbank, just as they said you did. And then the currents and undercurrents will pull me. Maybe a fisherman standing alone on a rock will pull me in as I catch his line, or maybe I will finally reach the sandy ridges and pebbled banks and walk calmly to the sea at last. To finally know that view as I have dreamt many times before.

I remember my youth. Maybe you would say I am still young, though I feel as old as the tides.

BORDERLINES

Dean Borok
GHOSTAL REGIONS

Havelock switched off the TV and went into the bedroom. He peeled off his clothes and jumped into bed, though it was not yet seven P.M. What he needed was a good twelve hours' sleep. Then he would be able to get to the factory early and re-check all the work that he knew he had fouled up that day. In less than a minute, he was out cold.

The world of dreams is an eternal infinite universe inside each person. Though it may to some extent be driven by the unformed expression of neurotic impulses and sexual repressions of the dreamer, it is also informed by conversations with the dead: voices of the Unanswered, the Unresolved, the Unredeemed, who struggle to make their desires known to the material world by using living voices of those fortunate enough to still possess them. By what method of selection is one chosen to be a vessel for the revelation of these programmes? That is a question that has long intrigued such illustrious deities and savants as the world has produced.

The eternity of dreams can act as a soothing "Doctor Without Frontiers", or it can be a manifestation of a satanic dimension of hell; a fount of philosophical profundity, or a bottomless oubliette of gibberish; a rocket to the celestial paradise of desire, or a subway ride to the terminus of consummate suffering if one should endure the misfortune of boarding a train conducted by the infernal motorman of Orphean malediction. This was the train Havelock found himself on, the solitary passenger of a fluorescent-lit express barreling through diabolical stations with names like "Hiroshima," "Auschwitz," "Ypres," and "World Trade Center." As his train flew by on the express track, Havelock was able to catch a glimpse of the crowds of dead souls jammed together on the platforms; rotting, monstrously deformed victims missing limbs and faces; fountains of blood spouting from open arteries, people retching and vomiting from gas intoxication, wailing from the suffering of unendurable agony as herds of rats gorged themselves on maggot-ridden body parts that had been kicked onto the tracks by the ever more crowded mobs of victims compressed onto the narrow quais, waiting for a local which would never arrive.

This train ride went on for hours, passing through an infinite number of horror-ridden stations. Tiled walls announced the names of stops: Nanking, Krakatoa, Srbranica. Havelock, who had at first been revolted

BORDERLINES

and horrified by the monstrous scenes of suffering he was passing through, eventually became habituated and even impatient. At length, he was only stirred to interest by the most grotesque manifestations of atrocity, chemically mutated birth defects or people who had become fused together from the heat of nuclear explosions. Finally, he lost interest completely as his train progressed mile after mile, station after station, hour after hour, the monotonous clacketing of its steel wheels against the rails pounding out a metronome rhythm of tedium. To amuse himself, Havelock composed a little song:

> *The death train through hell, it sure is swell,*
> *Mutilated corpses smell,*
> *It's got its own beat,*
> *Of rotten meat,*
> *Landmine victims got no feet...*

The train slowed and switched tracks. It pulled into an empty, garbage-strewn station. The mosaic-tiled sign on the wall said "Avenue X. Gravesend." Havelock thought to himself, it figures that the train to hell would end in Brooklyn.

The doors opened. A voice announced. "Last stop. Everybody off the train." Havelock picked up his duffle bag and walked out. He looked for an issue and saw the exit sign at the end of the platform. Hoisting his duffel bag over his shoulder, he made his way to the sign and ascended a flight of stairs.

He found himself on the deck of a troop ship mobbed with soldiers that was being nudged into a docking berth under the scorching Mediterranean sun. Havelock found that he was wearing a soldier's uniform as well, in camouflage green with a peaked garrison cap.

A sign on the side of a corrugated storage shed announced to him that he was in a port named Philippe. A French flag hung limply from a pole in front of a colonial-style administration building at lands' end.

Havelock and his fellow soldiers smoked cigarettes and watched over the side as Arab longshoremen dressed in long robes secured the ship's ropes to the dock. Gangplanks were set up and the soldiers, each bearing his duffle bag and carbine, filed down to the wharf where they mustered in platoon groups to await their transport assignments. They stood at parade rest, their kit bags in front of them.

The sergeant of Havelock's section came up and addressed the group. "While we're waiting for the trucks, I'll just say a few words.

BORDERLINES

"Welcome to Algeria. Remember that you are still in France. Our job is to maintain order and security until the government in Paris arrives at a disposition concerning the future governance of this territory. Remember that all the inhabitants, European or Arab, are French citizens and entitled to all the guarantees of the constitution.

"Having said that, I will remind you of a fact that you already know – that we are in a war zone, although with the exception of certain sectors adjacent to the Moroccan and Tunisian frontiers where the adversary maintains standing divisions, it is an unconventional war, a shadow war. Certain of you who have served in Indochina know what I am talking about. For the rest of you, that means that the enemy will not fit any normal combatant profile. It could come in the form of a woman with a knife or explosives concealed beneath her clothes, or a child with a hand grenade. Do not be deceived by a smile or a friendly greeting. Always be on your guard.

"Right now you are attached to the Eighth Parachute Regiment. You were trained to jump out of planes and kill people. But that does not mean that that is what you will do here. It's possible that some of you will be transferred to infantry or intelligence battalions, depending on the needs of the service orders, maintain discipline and work as a team with your comrades, and hopefully you'll avoid any undue misfortune."

An officer wearing a round kepi approached with a clipboard and summoned the platoon leaders. In a minute, the sergeant, whose name was L., returned. "All right, the trucks are here. Platoon, attention!" He marched the soldiers to a staging area filled with idling trucks and they clambered into the backs of them. The canvas tops had been rolled down, and as the convoy rumbled out of the port and onto the streets of Philippe, the troops were able to get their first glimpse of Algeria.

The port and center of town were heavily fortified with tanks and half-tracks. Soldiers manned sandbagged control posts at intersections, and at regular intervals along the tree-lined boulevards. The centre-ville resembled any French town, apartment blocks with ornate facades, outdoor cafés, department stores and boutiques, banks and manicured gardens. Well-dressed Europeans on the streets went about their affairs in seeming normality. Schoolchildren in shorts carrying leather satchels and piles of books entered walled lycées. Blue-uniformed gendarmes armed with submachine guns stood sentry in front of a commissariat displaying a tri-color flag on a flagpole over its entrance.

The town was not large, and in a few minutes the convoy passed

BORDERLINES

through the Arab quarter at its periphery. The contrast was dramatic. Children in rags played in the dust next to fly-ridden piles of trash under a baking sun. Veiled women peered out at the passing trucks from the dark interiors of jerrybuilt huts. Mangy dogs and barnyard animals scrounged for food in the barren yards or looked for bits of shade in the meager shadows of dead trees. Waves of heat rose from piles of manure. As the soldiers surveyed this dismal landscape, which seemed to eerily resemble the stage set of a surrealist left bank theater production, the kid sitting adjacent to Havelock said in a discreet voice: "This doesn't look like any part of France that I ever saw."

Somebody else said, "It looks like a fucking shit house de merde. No wonder they went berserk."

Another voice piped up, "You sound like a bunch of commies. You think this tells the whole story? We're not off the ship fifteen minutes and you're sounding like a bunch of damned defeatists. Why don't you just shut up!"

They rode for a long time in silence, sweating in the dust and heat. The convoy passed through monstrously dreary Arab villages identified by signs in Arabic and French signifying names like Sartir and Bouktir, flea-bitten bidonvilles with food stalls displaying stringy bits of meat crawling with flies, hanging from posts exposed to the African sun. It was a desolate wasteland of a place. Veiled women carrying bundles cringed in the shadows of walls. Children waving sticks harassed pathetic dogs that fled trailing drooping tails and shanks sticking through their threadbare coats. Such men as were visible from the passing trucks were seen working in the fields pushing crude plows through rocky soil, or lethargically breaking stones with pick axes in open-pit quarries. The trucks were forced to slow down to a snail's pace over stretches of highway, which were so rutted and potholed as to be practically impassable. At one point they passed a road crew of Arab workers guarded by a lackadaisical detail of native harkis soldiers. One soldier on the truck remarked, "Did you see how they work? No wonder the road's in such bad shape."

Another said, "That's not the worst of it. During the day they're workers, but at night they come back as fellaghas and tear up all the work they did."

Just when the desolation would reach a stage of such oppression as to consummately shatter any remnant of human sensibility, a scenario of divine loveliness would arise out of the heat waves from the barren, black earth like a mirage. These were the European-owned farms and vineyards;

BORDERLINES

fertile, beautifully irrigated and groomed plantations verdant beyond all comprehension, resplendent with balconied mansions resting on impeccable lawns adorned with manicured gardens and bougainvilleas. The farm structures, barns and equipment sheds were well maintained and freshly painted, peopled by purposeful workers who drove modern farm machinery. Modern automobiles were parked on the grounds, and the occasional chic, well-dressed French woman would wave at the passing convoy from the terrace.

The soldier who had earlier admonished had his carping comrades exalted triumphantly, "You see? That's what we're fighting for!"

Late in the day the convoy reached it destination, the camp at Guellal. They mustered in the courtyard of the barracks building, where they were addressed by the squadron captain, a young career officer named Poisson. "Welcome to Guellal. After you are dismissed you will be shown to your quarters. Install yourselves, shower, and mess is served at 19:00 hours. Lights out at 22:00. Because of the nature of the operations in this sector, you may be awakened during the night for nocturnal sorties. You must be fully dressed and equipped and in formation here no later than ten minutes after you are called. That is all. Section chiefs, dismiss your sections!"

The sergeants called out in unison, "Dis-missed!"

Algeria! The name alone is enough to send one into an hypnotic euphoria of reverie, provoking visions of jangling coins on a dancer's bodice; swaying palms and olive groves; winding alleys of the old town; scimitars and daggers; camel caravans traversing an infinite desert dotted with idyllic oases, Barbary pirates. It has inflamed imaginations through the ages, inspiring the sun-drenched tableaux of Dégas and the existential musings of Camus.

Since the birth of human civilization it has played a pivotal role of the cultures of Africa and Europe. A province of imperial Carthage, it provided cavalry troops for Hannibal's conquest of Iberia and Gaul and his twelve year rampage across the Italian peninsula, later allying itself with Rome during her brutal reduction of Carthage. It was overrun in the fifth century by the Vandals and recaptured for Byzantium by the Emperor Justinian. The Berber tribesmen of ancient Kabylie flooded across the Straits of Gibralter to spread a golden age of Islamic culture throughout Spain, receding like a tide to leave debris of Moorish temperament that still informs the societies of Europe and Latin America. What is Cartagena but the Spanish name for Carthage?

BORDERLINES

The French Foreign Legion, newly formed, subdued and captured it for France in 1830. Rich in agricultural resources, it was also discovered to contain vast petroleum deposits. The French also found a use for its vast, sparsely inhabited Sahara region, using it as a testing ground for their nuclear weapons production

Havelock knew nothing of this except that it came to him as a dream, not so different from the inspiration that affects a writer from an unknown source, compelling him by way of obscure forces to move his hand across a page, guided by impulses of mystic provenance.

Maybe he had been infected by a psychic contagion during his pilgrimage to Jim Morrison's grave in Paris, the spirits flowing to and fro across the consecrated terrain of Père LaChaise Cemetary judging his artist's soul to be a suitable vessel to inhabit with their memories and passions. Maybe something had occurred when he had participated in the procession up Sixth Avenue on All Hallows Eve, New York's psychic ground being turned over to suddenly expose a buried underworld of worms, bugs and parasites better left entombed under the soil.

Havelock was an artist and the furthest thing from an intellectual, but he knew viscerally that the artist's inspiration is mostly stimulated by abnormal shocks and setbacks that crush ordinary souls. The key to survival is to ride the crest of the wave rather than try to resist, hoping that the meaning of the thing will ultimately reveal itself in a fashion that he can shape into a communicable form. This abstraction he would never be able to verbalize in a million years, but it was nevertheless the key to his survival, and the fluidity of his nature enabled him to endure, after a fashion, the sledgehammer blows that his spirit was having to absorb.

The barracks erupted in light as Sergeant L strode down the aisle in full battle gear. "Wake up, soldiers! Let's go! Everybody downstairs and ready to move out in ten minutes! Move your asses!" The soldiers, barely awake, threw on their uniforms, laced up their boots, grabbed their helmets and carbines, and crowded down the stairs to the courtyard. When they were in formation, the sergeant briefed them. "There's been an attack on a farm fifteen kilometers from here on the road to Sidi el Khier. Apparently it's pretty bad. We'll secure the area for the DOP to investigate, and then we'll fan out and search for the perpetrators. They can't have gotten far. Any questions?" Nobody had any questions.

"All right, Let's get to the trucks. Double time, hurry and move it!" The soldiers ran to the idling trucks. From the side of the road, Sergeant L

BORDERLINES

yelled to his men, "Be alert for ambushes. They could be trying to lure us into a trap!" Then he jumped into the cab of the lead truck.

The convoy barreled down the road in the pitch darkness, the trucks' headlights showing the only illumination in sight. The soldiers peered out anxiously from their seats in the rear, rifles at the ready. Like Havelock, most of them were green conscripts. Havelock's neighbor whispered, "We're sitting ducks out here."

Havelock heard himself say, "Quit carping. We haven't even got to the battle yet. Just keep your eyes open." Nevertheless, he was shaking too.

The convoy reached its destination without incident. A sign painted in fancy script announced the name of the establishment: Vignobles LeClerc SA. Etabli 1909. Vins Fins. Appelations Contrôlées. It was a vineyard. The convoy pulled onto a tree-lined private road and halted in front of an ornate mansion. A couple of luxury sedans were parked at the front stairs of the house. Private roads led in either direction from the house to equipment and wine processing sheds, all of which were in flames. Captain Poisson and a detail of DOP intelligence officers were already on the scene, having arrived at high speed in jeeps. They were examining the bodies of well-dressed European settlers that were scattered about the lawn. Some had had their throats cut and others had been shot at point blank range. An elegantly dressed young woman in a peach-colored silk dress lay on her back on the grass, staring vacantly into the darkness, her abdomen sliced open from her breastbone to her pelvis like a gutted fish.

The soldiers piled out of the trucks, Sergeant L yelling "Come on, let's go! Corporal Bouchard, get a detail down that road and secure the area where those buildings are burning. Charpentier, you do the same in the other direction. Detain anybody you find and bring them back here. Schroder, secure the entrance to the farm." He addressed the troops, "The rest of you, I want you to form a line and go into the fields at intervals of ten meters. Don't group together. Watch out for ambushes. Anybody you find, try to detain them without killing them, if possible. We need to interrogate them."

Havelock stalked warily through the vineyard, carbine at the ready. In the starlight he could discern the silhouettes of his fellow soldiers to the left and right. His apprehension at being exposed in unknown terrain, vulnerable to an invisible enemy, was palpable. The minutes ticked past as the column of soldiers marched farther and farther into the field, until the burning farm structures, the only landmarks in their topography of obscurity, had diminished in size to small glowing embers.

BORDERLINES

He was jolted by a flash of light and a small explosion to his left. The flash, lasting only a millisecond, was followed by a man's hideous screams of terror and unendurable pain. The other soldiers quickly ran over and grouped around the wounded victim, who was writhing in agony on the ground.

"It's Millet. He stepped on a landmine."

The man's reddened face was contorted in a grotesque eye-popping mask of horror, his mouth stretched to twice its size in a bizarre smile like a funhouse billboard. His abdomen had been blown open like an over-inflated soccer ball, internal organs bulging out through the shreds of his flesh. One leg was blown clear off and the man's arteries were irrigating the ground under him with torrents of black blood.

Two soldiers kneeled over him, one cradling his head. "There, there. The medics will be here soon. You'll be fine."

The wounded man looked up into the eyes of his friend. "What happened? Oh God, it hurts. Make it stop hurting. Mais pourquoi, pourquoi? Where am I? I have to go home. I have to walk my dog!"

He died.

"Poor devil."

Shots rang out. A man cried and fell as bullets thudded into his body. Flashes of light appeared in the dark like fireflies from shadows rising up that appeared in the dark to be a wooded area about a hundred meters in front of the line. The corporal who was leading the detail ordered the men, "Get down!" They all hit the dirt. "Who got hit?"

"It's Boileau. He's still breathing."

"Blondin, run back and get a medic." The firing from the trees continued, with the bullets whizzing over the soldiers' heads. "The rest of you, this is what I want you to do," the corporal continued. "Five of you, I want you to spread out at intervals of ten meters and return fire. Let them think they have us pinned down. The rest, divide into two groups. One group circle fifty meters to the left, the other group fifty meters to the right. We'll run to the trees and then close in and catch them in a pincer. Don't shoot until you're in position." The bullets continued to zing overhead. "The five men who are returning fire, when you hear us engage them, you'll stop shooting and run in from the front. Any questions?" There were no questions. "All right, now. Speed is essential. It shouldn't take more than two minutes to get in position. We should be able to kill them all. These Arabs are stupid. Now, go!"

The group broke up, keeping low. In a few seconds the line of riflemen

BORDERLINES

was set up and returning fire. Havelock ran with the detachment that broke off to the right. After he felt that he had put enough distance between himself and the skirmish line, he stood up straight and ran with all his strength toward the copse of trees. He could hear the clump clump of his own footsteps and those of the other men, his own breathing, and the firefight to his left and the chirping of the cicadas in the African night.

The men made it safely to the trees without drawing fire and started to close in towards the source of the shooting. In a minute's time they were close enough to see the muzzle flashes from the insurgents' guns. The pressure of the excitement and fear had built up to critical mass in Havelock, and he felt he couldn't wait any longer to start shooting. He raised his rifle to his shoulder and started squeezing off rounds, stopping after each shot to reset the bolt. The Arab attackers stopped firing into the field and turned to confront the soldiers. Bullets flew blindly in both directions as the two sides strained to fix a bead on their enemies. The bullets whizzed by Havelock as he struggled to reload faster and return fire, aiming into the pitch dark.

He felt a hammer blow to the head and was knocked down onto his back as a bullet slammed into his helmet. His ears started ringing, but it wasn't a church bell kind of ringing – it was a sinister, diabolical kind of electric ring, like a condemned man strapped to an electric chair would experience from the metal conducting helmet that had been strapped to his head. The ringing seared through his brain as he felt the life force being drained from his body. Havelock sat up in his bed. It was morning, and the phone was ringing. He picked up. It was Paulette.

"Why didn't you call me last night?" she demanded.

BORDERLINES

Diana Bretherick
THE MUSE OF CAMDEN

Everything about her had been sweet – her smile, her eyes, her perfume, the taste of her. But sweeter still was the sound of the knife slicing through her flesh and bone as he slit her throat from ear to ear. She fell back onto the bed, the blood seeping out of the wound and dripping onto the faded counterpane. It was dawn. The rising sun threw its pale rays onto the curves of her body. He sat back and studied his work with a critical eye. He detected a palpable improvement – his skill was evolving into something with more subtlety than his earlier work. It still lacked something though – a certain finesse that had always eluded him. One day he would capture it and then he would be able to rest.

He thought back to his first efforts – he had been almost overwhelmed by a sense of disgust that mingled uncomfortably with the arousal that can only be produced by the purity of inspiration. His work then had been frenzied, uncontrolled and ultimately disappointing.

Now however, he had learned to use his emotions rather than be governed by them. He felt that he was on the threshold of discovery. A little more practice and he would reach the pinnacle of achievement.

He reached into his bag and took out his sketchpad. He wrote in charcoal at the top of the page – 'Muse of Camden – 1907'. He looked again at his subject and took an inward breath as if gathering his strength. Then, as he exhaled, he began to draw.

As the sun rose over the dusty streets of Camden Town its nocturnal inhabitants began to withdraw. These were shady creatures - over painted ladies, whores, drunks, criminals – the flotsam and jetsam regurgitated by the city. Then there were those who were merely visiting – dipping their toes into the seedy hinterland that provided them with forbidden fruits – so juicy and inviting in the ill lit night but grotesque and unwanted in the garish day. They faded quickly with the moon and the stars – as if they had never been there at all.

As the daylight began to dominate, the market sprang into life and the sound of buying and selling and the usually good-humoured banter that went with it grew louder. People began to come out of their homes on their way to work. As they did so a man left his place of work and merged into the growing crowds, leaving the product of his employment lying

BORDERLINES

lifeless on a bed, her eyes staring unseeing into the distance. She would remain forever a creature of the night, whilst he adopted the day as his own, despite having little or no claim on it in reality. For now, his work was done.

The newspaper headlines leapt out of the page at him.

ARTIST CHARGED WITH CAMDEN SLAYING. IS THE BEAST OF CAMDEN FINALLY CAGED?

He felt assaulted, battered, even bruised by the words. Someone had laid claim to his work. How could that be? How could anyone mistake the work of a genius for that of a mere glass engraver? He strode around his rooms restlessly murmuring the impostor's name to himself as if by doing so the man would cease to exist. He stopped suddenly. What if the impostor lay claim to his other work; all that he had built on to get to where he was now. He sank to his knees, trembling with the horror of that thought. How could he counter such a claim without being arrested? Remaining undetected had suited his purpose. He had left examples of his artistic development all over Europe. His plan had been to reveal his portfolio only after death, on his own terms not by the hangman's rope. Now, unless he acted to prevent it, someone else would take the credit for all he had achieved. He went over to the heavy folders that held the records of his work and undid the ribbons that held them together. Soon his paintings and sketches littered the floor, a symphony of bloody gashes and young white flesh in various poses. Others were more explicit and featured older more broken down bodies, slashed, and in some cases, eviscerated. The only exception was a portrait of a gaunt young man with an earnest expression.

He sat amongst his pictures reliving the memory of their creation. As he did so it became clear to him what he must do. With a heavy heart he went to a drawer and lifted from it his knife – the only other witness to his work.   It was not until some days later, when his landlord came to call in search of the rent, that his bloody remains were found, surrounded by the burnt remnants of a life's work. A few paintings survived – some merely scorched but also some completely untouched by fire.

For a century or more they lay in a vault in a London gallery, gathering dust, waiting for discovery. Their creator also lay in the family vault, waiting to be immortalised by notoriety. But soon the waiting will

BORDERLINES

come to an end. There is to be some stock taking. The gallery's vaults are going to be explored in a search for new paintings for exhibition. When one in particular is pulled out of that mouldering bundle, an infamous mystery will finally be solved. An archivist will select and admire the well executed picture of a gaunt young man peering out of the canvas. Then, in a search for the identity of the artist, they will squint at the barely legible script and gasp at what they read. The irony will be that the artist considered this to be among his least accomplished pictures. As far as he was concerned, his art had grown from its early rudimentary and clumsily executed beginnings in 1888, to something much more sophisticated. But still, it would be this painting that would form his legacy and he was powerless to change it. He hadn't been able to resist identifying himself using the name given by the newspapers to his artistic alter ego. The smudged signature at the base of the painting gave everything and nothing away – Jack the Ripper – a self-portrait.

BORDERLINES

Andrew Williams
SUNDAY AT THE PICTURES

The boy in the wardrobe mirror was an impostor. The shirt and over-brushed hair wasn't me. I'd become an alien. Mum called from downstairs in her giddy-up voice. It was the third time of asking.

In the kitchen Auntie Linda sat smoking, her perfume crowding the air like a contagious disease. She eyed me through black, spidery lashes. 'Very posh,' she said.

Mum fussed over me making adjustments to my hair and collar: 'He is posh.'

'No I'm not,' I said. 'I look stupid.'

Mum tugged my arm: 'Stop it.'

'I just said I'm not posh.'

'I know you,' she said.

'I feel sick,' I said.

Auntie Linda said, 'He's got butterflies.'

She was right but I felt really sick too; the kitchen was full of steam and heat and Mum's roast was repeating on me. I wanted to forget about going to the pictures with Jane. 'I could phone her and say I'm sick,' I said.

'No you bloody well can't,' said Mum. 'You can't let a girl down like that, can he Linda?'

'You'll be alright once you're up in the back row with her,' said Linda. Giggling she ran her tongue over her too red lips. 'No one will notice you there; they'll all be doing the same thing.'

'Oh, don't listen to her,' said Mum. 'You just go and have a good time.'

Linda's perfume settled on my neck like prickly heat. 'Don't do anything I wouldn't do,' she called as I left.

At the front door Mum pressed something into my hand. 'In case of emergencies,' she said.

I looked – it was a pound note. I called through the door to say thanks. She just said, 'go on' through the frosted glass.

My friends were playing football at the end of the street and I wanted to go and show them my pound. I walked the other way instead. It'd keep until tomorrow.

It took a conscious effort to knock at Jane's door. There was nothing to be afraid of; her parents were friendly and I was nice and polite. It was a relief because I was really worried I'd swear. I don't do it at home but when I'm really angry they can slip out, naughty words. Mum went on about it so much that she made me afraid I'd swear in front of them, even for no reason. Mums are experts at that; focusing on something and then blowing it up out of proportion.

We left Jane's house and started talking and soon I realised the awkwardness had followed us, hanging above us like the grey sky.

'Shall we wait for a bus?' I asked.

'No thank you,' Jane replied.

'No, we'd probably be waiting for ages.'

Jane nodded.

'Sunday,' I said.

She smiled but didn't look at me.

'It probably won't rain now, anyway.'

Jane didn't respond. A yellow Cortina drove past. 'That's the kind of car I want,' I said. 'But not yellow.'

We walked the rest of the way in silence.

At the pictures Clive Reynolds was waiting in the queue with Lee Hillier. I would've bet Mum's pound he'd come over and give me a hard time but when he saw me he gave me a weird, quizzical look and a nod of acknowledgement. I felt relieved that they held off the Gestapo routine and then disappointed somehow, and I felt strange and guilty.

At the ticket booth the manager appeared and took Clive and Hillier to one side.

'Alright you two,' he said. 'I've got my eye on you. Any repeat of last week's antics and you'll be out on your ears. Understand?'

'Okay, opeysay outhmay,' said Clive. Hillier laughed.

The manager touched his bow tie and his head jerked forward and back: 'Eh?'

'Okay, opeysay outhmay,' Clive said again. Hillier was in fits and I was laughing inside. The manager's nickname was Soapy-mouth, but he couldn't tell that was what Clive was saying.

'What are you saying?' he asked, screwing his craggy face up.

'Okay opey…'

'Go on, hoppit,' he said, jerking his thumb towards the stalls. 'I'm keeping my eye on you.' He looked after them with a double head-jerk.

I bought our tickets. As we passed the manager he touched his bow tie, jerked his head and said: 'Enjoy the film.' Okay Soapy, I thought.

Jane wanted to sit in the front row so we did. The film was full of

BORDERLINES

references to my situation: The lead had a love interest and they kissed a couple of times. I spent the whole time trying to crank up the courage to put my arm around her shoulder. It seemed I was there for ages, agonising over it, then the film ended. I had the feeling that I'd missed a chance, that a door had opened and I'd just stood there.

As we were going through the lobby Clive went past us riding Hillier like a horse. Hillier's skinny and Clive is stocky so they looked like an ostrich with a fat body. Clive whooped like a red Indian. Then Soapy-mouth leaped out and tried to intercept them. Clive shouted 'wanker!' in his face as they went by him but Hillier tripped sending them both sprawling. Soapy stood over them and you could tell he was trying to say something but his head had gone into pigeon overdrive and he couldn't get any words out. Clive got up and did a pigeon walk, going 'coo-coo,' before running off. I nearly pissed myself laughing until I noticed Jane's expression. I felt sheepish as we left. As we passed Soapy he was trying to wipe his forehead with a hankie but kept missing because it wouldn't keep still.

Outside the overcast gloom had merged with the evening and the street lights glowed feebly in the drizzle.

'Do you want to take the bus?' I asked.

Jane said: 'No thank you.'

We walked to her house in wretched silence. I wanted to talk, to tell her I really liked her and wanted to go out with her again, but I didn't have the spirit.

We got to her house. Without looking at me she said: 'Thank you very much,' then turned and ran up the path. The front door opened as she reached it then she slipped inside and the door closed. I felt like she'd got in a lifeboat and left me bobbing in the sea.

Along the High Street the rain picked up so I hid in a shop doorway until it eased off. A lonely puddle nestled in the middle of the pavement like a miserable sky, where the reflected orange-brown street lights hung like morose stars.

I leaned over to see if I was there but couldn't make myself out.

BORDERLINES

Elke Morice-Atkinson
ELECTRICITY

I'm lusting after someone I'm not supposed to. I remember once I was in town with Jaz at Magma, which was dark club on the strip. I was hanging out by the bar and this person comes up to me and asks for a dance. I say no thanks. But then I saw Fai and my world changed. It collapsed and emerged as something else – something electric and confusing.

No one except Jaz knows what's going on. He saw me look at her that day. He saw the electric green thoughts fly out of my mind and wrap themselves around Fai's shoulders, brushing her cheek with a touch she could not feel.

Now a demon is pinning me to my seat, she's fucking with my head. It's a wonder anyone gets past the twisted thing they call 'youth', where everything, no matter how fucked up it seems, is supposed to be normal.

Those life education classes they made me take at high school didn't prepare me for shit.

"What are you writing?"

I drop my pen and tear the page from my lecture pad. She'll never read the words I wrote for her and if she ever did she'd probably laugh. I want to wish it away, but all the electricity in all the shooting stars I've seen couldn't take it away…

"Just notes," I reply and shift my gaze back to the front of the auditorium.

The class finishes and as I am shoving my books in my bag the lecturer yells that the coursework is due next week. "See ya later!" I call to my friend and spill out of the glass doors with the crowd.

Her skin is like caramel flavoured milk, the kind you buy in the little cartons from the cafeteria. And her hair is a golden wave on a beach. Lips like cupid bows.

* * *

I shiver as a cool breeze through my window tickles my back.

"Sam, food's up!" Mum calls from the kitchen.

I pull on a shirt and run my fingers through my hair. "There in a

BORDERLINES

second!" I yell. I turn off my amp and prop my guitar against the wall, happy to leave the tangle of chords scribbled across my folder. I run down stairs.

She's perfect. I'm not. She'd never look at me twice. She probably has a boyfriend.

"Why the long face, kid?" Mum asks me.

"Nothing," I reply.

Mum slaps a mound of mash potato onto my plate, "If something was up you'd tell me, right?"

I roll my eyes and don't reply.

I can't believe that she lives next door. Less than two metres away and we've never spoken.

"Stop looking into the neighbour's house, its rude."

* * *

"Fuck off Jaz, I don't want to!"

"Come on man, it'll take like two minutes. Promise."

"It's not like I'm getting a Prince Alfred or anything. Just come and help me pick out a bar."

I give in and we walk along the stretch of road where I know Fai will be. She catches the bus here everyday at 4:15. I swear I'm not a creepy stalker. Honestly.

As we near the bus stop I see her. She turns towards us and gives a shy smile as Jaz tells me he wants to get his eyebrow pierced.

* * *

Electric screeching sounds ooze out of my guitar. The breeze sucks the notes and scratches out of my bedroom window where they are whipped away into the dusky sky.

"Turn that friggin' thing down, or at least use your bloody headphones!" comes the usual squawk from downstairs. I place my headphones over my ears and let myself move to the sounds from my guitar.

Floating, whispering, turning. Loud music, smoke and girls dancing to the techno demon. Twisting, gyrating. Fai's there, she's dancing near me. I want to touch her, just brush her hand and hope that she'll see who it was.

I keep playing until something catches my eye. It's her – Fai. I take off

BORDERLINES

my headphones, brush the hair out of my eyes and lean against the windowsill. She looks right at me, but then something distracts her and she dissolves into a mass of white netting. Shit.

* * *

Kiss me quick. Kiss away the demon and make me feel human. Kiss away this electricity.

Fai.

I scribble it again and again on my notepad while waiting for my next class. I'm just doing it so that no one will think I'm a loner, waiting for someone who will never show up.

"Hey," a soft voice says near me. I turn around and she's there.

"Hi," I reply.

"You play the guitar right?"

"Yeah."

"I see you sometimes, through my window, playing it," she says.

"I know."

She looks embarrassed for a moment, but then her hands find their way over to my notebook. "What are you writing?"

"Nothing."

Her lips form a perfect 'O'.

"I see," she breathes.

As she speaks she leans closer to me. I can feel her gentle breath on my face.

Electricity.

Kiss me quick. Kiss away the demon and make me feel human. Kiss away this electricity.

Fai.

"I didn't know you took this class," she says. Her voice is as sweet as cherries.

"I don't," I say. "I'm just waiting for…"

She interrupts me, "Tell me you think it too."

I breathe.

"Yes." Breathe.

Fai.

Spark.

I'm a girl, Fai is beautiful and we're electric.

BORDERLINES

BORDERLINES

Louise Mathewson
MONSTERS OF THE SKY

My four-year-old nephew Max had golden brown hair, tinged with a hint of strawberry, and enormous brown eyes that touched something deep inside me. But behind those beautiful eyes was a boy who was terrified of thunderstorms.

When lightning streaked the sky and thunder rumbled, Max's eyes would grow wide and deep, as if holding a well of fear. One day while I was visiting Max and his family, a flash of lightning tore the sky in two with a jagged line that seemed to connect heaven and earth. The thunder that followed seemed to raise Max a few inches off the ground. He looked like a little tin soldier - his arms folded tightly over his chest, his body stiff. He paced the room, repeating, "I'm scared, I'm scared!"

As I watched him walk nervously back and forth, I searched my mind for something that might calm him. Remembering that when I was young, my mother had told me that thunder was the noise angels made when they were bowling in heaven, I told the angel story to Max. It failed to ease his discomfort. Then I remembered how, when my children had been his age, I used to have them draw the things that frightened them.

I said, "Max, let's go sit down and draw the lightning!"

"I'm scared of lightning!" he quickly reminded me.

"Yes, I can see how afraid you are," I said. "Come with me and we'll draw that scary sky together."

Max looked up at me tentatively, curious about this aunt who wanted to draw lightning. While his family waited out the storm in front of the TV, Max and I went into the kitchen and found a place to draw the frightening behavior of the sky.

Max slowly climbed up on the black and white metal stool at the kitchen counter while I found some drawing tools in my sister's kitchen. I placed a dull pencil and some scraps of white paper in front of him.

In a near whisper, Max confided, "I don't know how to draw lightning."

"Would you like me to draw some first?"

"Yeah," he answered, briefly distracted from his fear. His eyes grew round with curiosity as I quickly sketched a few jagged lines.

"There," I said, smiling. "Do you want to take a turn now?"

BORDERLINES

Max cautiously took the pencil and drew one small sawtooth line. He looked up at me for approval.

"Cool, Max, wanna make another?" I said, handing him more paper.

He made more lightning bolts, each one a little larger and bolder than the last. Max, experimenting with zigs and zags, said "There, that's a giant monster of the sky! This one's gonna be bigger."

As he poured his terror onto the paper, his voice returned to normal, but his eyes continued to enlarge with fear whenever a thunderclap boomed.

"Where do you feel scared in your body, Max?" I asked.

"Here," he said, pointing to his chest.

"Put your hand where you feel it."

He put his hand over his heart. Then I put one hand gently over his, while resting my other hand on his back. "Right here, huh?"

"Yeah."

I paused for a few moments. "How does it feel now?"

"A little better." Max boldly drew a big, dark, jagged lightning streak.

"Are you afraid of lightning, Aunt Lou?"

"Yes, sometimes," I said softly, sensing that perhaps he needed some company in his fear.

Looking up at me, his head tilted slightly to one side, eyes brimming with compassion, Max reached over and put his hand just above my heart. "Does it hurts here?" he asked.

Caught by surprise, I nodded, "Yes, sometimes a little."

The tenderness of my four-year-old nephew touched my soul and filled me with awe at how drawing monsters of the sky together could open both our hearts. That precious memory, created many years ago, sparked a connection between us that continues to this day.

Andrea Bowie
LOSE YOUR WORDS IN A HIGH WIND

Farewells flung at parting trains,
And thrown from cliffs
To sailing ships.
Retorts muttered as asides,
The thees, the prithy's, the thou arts.
Radio's left on;
No one hears, forgotten song.

I asked my granddad where they'd gone,
Where they went
All these squandered, wasted words?
He smiled and winked a knowing eye,
And then he gave this subsequent reply:

"My boy," said he, "these 'wasted words,' as you say,
Are wasted not at all,
For each and everyone of them
Is completely recyclable.
They board passing breezes,
And are whipped up in high winds.

And so they journey to the sky,
To the lexical lost and found they go,
A place of which few humans know.
Here they're stored amongst the stars.
But seldom are they claimed,
Despite being perfectly alphabeticalised,
In cloudy cabinets in the skies."

Here he paused, strangely lost in the cosmos up above,
"But these words do not stay,
To fester and to vegetate.
The plumbing's poor, there's often leaks,
So they return, mixing in the air,

BORDERLINES

Whenever it precipitates.
They amalgamate, they merge, form foreign links,
Only to once again be gathered,
Accidentally, serendipitously,
Into our vocabulary."

I asked my granddad how he knew,
And why he looked so strained.

"My boy," said he. "It's I who edit the dictionary,
And it's just begun to rain."

Catherine Coles
HEADACHE

See this damsel in distress,
Under loved and unimpressed,
Waiting here to be saved
By a man, striking and brave,
But thinking of the hurt before
She clutches onto those unsure
Wanting them to be the one
The man who will show her the sun
But all of these are hesitating
Holding back, deliberating,
And while they sit and think and ponder,
She is left to stew and wonder,
Says that she don't need a man
That she will cope alone, she can,
And this is why she's in distress,
Under loved and unimpressed,
Because her head's been split in two
With all the thinking she can do.
"Giving girls a brain", she states
"Does nothing more than make skulls ache!"

BORDERLINES *Poetry*

Ria Floyd-Berry
ODE TO A PIECE OF CAKE

Forsooth the minotaur did come
And followed in his wake
As rounded as a chicken's bum
A smallish piece of cake.

(Remember, it's always a mistake
To pair a minotaur with a piece of cake.)

And lo, the minotaur did roar
Enough to make you shake,
Almost to make you sorry for
This frightened piece of cake.

While on his way the beast did wash,
He wallowed in the lake,
As careless as to almost squash
This soggy piece of cake.

Maintaining speed the pair did run
Advantage did they take
Of warming in the setting sun
Our beast and piece of cake.

They travelled on throughout the night
But foe! They met a snake.
The enemy then took a bite
Of sweet and tasty cake.

By and by they met a donkey
Whose smile looked very fake
Crept up on them with a sly monkey
And stole our piece of cake.

BORDERLINES

In peril the dessert trembled
A second they did bake
A large table they assembled –
Endangered piece of cake.

Oh woe! A tragic end came fast!
Poor beast could never make
A pudding to replace the last
Beloved piece of cake.

Russell Thomas
EXPRESSIONISM AND A DIONYSIAN WEEKEND

I'm in my room just thinkin bout the weekend
should get a broom, gonna sweep up all these fag ends
thinkin bout the food that I'm gonna be eatin
thinkin bout the moodswings, late nights, beatin
chests like apes, gonna buy a bunch of grapes
cause I can't cook anything like Gordon Ramsey
feelin like a crook every time I miss the damsel,
stayin up late, gonna buy a chain to bearbait
dancing like a crackwhore, don't stop, gimme more
drinkin loads, feelin fine, people drone all the time
crossin roads quick before the green man shows
I'm gonna explode, kickin off, storm blows

walkin down the street with a friendly cigarette
moaning at my feet, gonna find a horse, make a bet
'play it straight, play it safe' – never will listen
buy a crate, break a plate, gold never glistens –
unless you polish it well with authority
gold will demolish all of your morality

kickin up leaves and smiling to the blue sky
all that I leave is a conflict in my mind
wanna get paid, but I just won't get a job
wanna get laid, but I have to wait, dear god
found a horse, won the race, in the money now son
at a loss, clean my face, better runny run run
gonna talk nonsense for a little while now
men have no sense when it comes to why and how
things just pass by easily as traffic
people these days have a lot of things lacking
I'm tryina find a way to keep me from slacking
wanna lot of things so I'm sending me packing
home to house which I thought I grew up in
lonely spouse gonna get a lot of lovin

BORDERLINES

I'm feelin homesick, thinkin bout the weekend
feelin like a trainwreck, feelin at a loose end
thinkin to the future, most likely I'll be laughin
don't wanna pair a bootcut, wanna hem myself in
I'm in a slump an I'm thinkin bout the weekend.

BORDERLINES

Olivia James
INTELLIGENCE CAN BE SO LACKING

"I've always thought it best to be honest, and speak one's mind", she said, exasperated at the lack of comprehension in the man's face. "I'm sorry, but it's time you left. You've been here for almost a month, on my floor without once, well, OK, once you contributed to the Sainsbury's shopping. But I'm not a charity you know. Tu comprends? Je l'espère. Maintenant, il faut que tu parts. Vois-y. Ça suffit."

He looked at her with his huge brown eyes. "God, you're so pathetic," she wanted to say. "You've been here for almost 4 weeks and you still think you can be excused simply because you're French and you've never lived away from home for so long?"

She had helped him find a job, set up a bank account and make some friends. She'd picked him up from the airport and provided him with accommodation since he arrived. He was totally incompetent, and yet strangely very intelligent somehow. She really couldn't understand; not a single bone in her body understood how anyone who was obviously so intelligent sometimes could be so totally basic and one-dimensional on other levels; that is, on a normal day-to-day level.

He was an IT technician who just happened to be a sort of doctorate at economics. That's what he'd told her. She'd never heard of anyone doing a doctorate in economics, but apparently that's what he was doing. Or had done. She wasn't too sure. His English left a lot be desired. She'd met him in Paris. He had been a student of hers just once; just one one-hour lesson. He was waiting in an upmarket Parisian restaurant. Most of the clientele were American, and he needed English. He was pretty bad at it, and left the restaurant. So he never came back for any more classes. But she remembered him because he had told her he had done a degree in IT. Friends in the IT world were always very useful. She hated computers. They always broke down on her, so if she ever met anyone who knew anything about them, she generally kept their details in a little book, ready to be used whenever her computer failed her. So when it did fail her a few months later, she called him. He was quite useful, and came around to have a look. And then they met just one more time. She went to Republic and they went for a walk. They walked all around Montmartre. It was a beautiful day. When he expressed some interest in going to the UK to

BORDERLINES

learn English, she felt so totally pleased. She liked him – he was quiet, obviously incredibly confident (I mean, he is French after all!), and exceptionally good-looking. So she told him he could stay with her for a couple of weeks whilst he looked for more permanent accommodation and a job.

Well, a "couple of weeks" had turned into a month, and he had shown very little sign of actually trying to find anywhere. After two weeks, she had told him he couldn't stay much longer. It was the total lack of imagination that really pissed her off. All he said was that he was happy. He didn't mind being on the floor. OK, maybe it wasn't the most comfortable place in the world, but "ça va". How could he be so egocentric? How was it possible he couldn't put himself in her place; imagine what it must be like for her, having him sleeping on the floor, so that in the mornings, when she got up, she had to climb over him, look for her clothes quietly, couldn't just jump out of bed, naked, turn the radio on and start reading at her desk? She had never come across this attitude before, and it more than puzzled her. She was dumbfounded. The real problem was that she continued to like him so whenever she decided that enough was enough, and she phoned him to tell him that he had to leave, he somehow distracted her, and before she knew it, they were discussing what they were going to eat that night, and he was telling her how he was looking forward to seeing her. She felt quite pathetic. She felt like a typical girl. And yet she was a woman of 34 years. She should not be so pathetic at that age. How sad.

BORDERLINES

Steven Stemp
THE LOVE TAKER

My heart is pounding, feet slamming into the concrete, I'm racing forward, passers-by utter protests in my direction and I pay them no heed. A man steps out from a doorway, I mean only to brush past him but instead knock my arm hard against his. I hear him swear at me, barely perceptible above my own laboured breathing. The sun beats down on me and I feel perspiration bead upon my forehead. Up ahead is the town square, the usual sort of affair, little more than a fountain that is seldom turned on, some yellowed grass that no one cares about, a run down building, bricks stained black; trying to be a Greco-roman temple and failing.

I glance to my watch; I am still running five minutes late, despite how badly I wish I wasn't. Last night was another all-nighter, I still feel the pep pills coursing through my veins, my bladder complains. People tell me they damage your liver, but little in the typical student lifestyle doesn't. A piece of toast hangs from my mouth, and I bite on it, forgetting that in so doing it will fall. Melted margarine stains my blue shirt, and the legions of pigeons flocking around the fountain will find themselves a treat. I glance at the clock tower and my feet stop. I stare at it, disbelieving, and the urge to scream a profanity is being fought back. I fail to stop myself. From the other side of the street an old man glares at me, as though he's never heard those words before.

I slump down indignantly onto a nearby bench and sigh. All morning I knew there was something I was forgetting, and I was right. Today the clocks went forward by an hour. My lecture had finished before I'd even thrown on my clothes and rushed out the door. Fuck.

One would have thought that by the end of the second year of my degree, some form of responsible work habits would kick in, that I'd get my work done in the weeks before the deadline rather than the nanosecond before. Of course, one would be wrong. This town after all, is a student town, and as such breeds student attitudes and behaviours. There's a damn good reason there are so many kebab shops within vomiting distance of each other, and a damn good reason Boots always has a three for two offer on Pro Plus. Of course, in the nature vs. nurture debate, I can't wholly blame my surroundings. I am a lazy twat after all. I arch my neck back, and

BORDERLINES

it responds painfully. Clearly it wasn't happy about the way I fell asleep last night. The rest of me tends to agree with my neck, not happy at all about the one or two hours sleep before the alarm clock blared at me. 'You Are My Sunshine' played with a klaxon, within two centimetres of my pounding skull. You are my fucking sunshine, it's no wonder I threw the damn thing at the wall. Note to self, I need a new alarm clock.

As if today wasn't already bad enough, the sound of a guitar being killed assaults my ears. I glance over at the source. As usual, the steps leading up to the front of the town hall are covered in a sea of baggy trousers and nirvana hoodies, each one a branded non-conformist, filled with pride at just how expensive their outfit was at the exclusive store in Camden. I'm fairly sure the poor tortured acoustic guitar is being forced into playing a bastardisation of Smells Like Teen Spirit. Shame its strings are hanging looser than a porn star's nethers, resulting in what can only be described, as noise. Damn I'm feeling cynical today, more so than usual.

"Sound feckin shite don't they?" A dark sounding voice beside me asks. I start, not realising someone had sat beside me. As my head snaps to meet the source, I find myself dumbstruck. "Sorry there, didn't mean to shock yeh..." Still I'm silent, unable to answer him. I'd never heard an Irish accent sound so rich, it seemed almost as though silk reeking of tobacco had spilled into my ears, strangely beautiful, strikingly masculine. He was about my age, mid twenties at most, his skin was pale, but not sickly, mid length dark hair, green eyes piercing mine like daggers. He was undeniably handsome, or at least I should imagine that he could be considered so. He smiled, soft lips curl into soft reassuring crescent. "Sound shite, don't they? Those lads in the hoods..."

I nod to him. It is only now that I realise the way the dark haired Irish guy is dressed, white silk shirt, frilled at the cuffs and black pantaloons, fine black leather boots up to his shins. Bohemian I think they call it, or like a rejected extra for some BBC period piece. Part of me wanted to comment on how odd he looked, but I was unable. My mouth was dry and I found to my embarrassment that I was staring. I turned from him, and I believe I uttered some apology, though I could barely hear it myself.

"Seems I've made a nuisance of m'self, sorry to have troubled yeh mate..." The Irish guy says to me as he stands to leave.

"No!" I blurt out. The Irish guy looks back at me, he seems surprised and amused. I surprise myself with the desperation in my tone... I find it somehow unnerving, but soon regain my composure, "No, you're not a nuisance, I was just surprised."

BORDERLINES

The Irish guy sits down beside me again and grins, "Surprised, sure. Guess it ain't often yeh get a fella dressed like me unless it's all hallows eve?"

I don't know why I laugh at it, but I do. It's not even very funny, but I chuckle. I smile at him and shake my head, feeling suddenly more at ease with this perfect stranger. My headache is starting to fade, perhaps I'm simply allowing myself to forget about it. It's nice though, to feel the stress melting from me.

"I have that effect, sometimes." The Irish Guy chuckles, "Can see it in yer eyes, like the weight of the world is lifted. Should'n be so young and be so worried as yew seems to be..." There is a note of sympathy in his voice, of genuine concern.

Finally my balls return. "So young? Dude, you're about the same age as me." I'm able to speak without the lack of composure, I sound like myself again. I'm talking as though I've known this Irish Guy my whole life. I find myself wishing I had known him my whole life. I frown at that thought, it's a curious thing to be wishing...

His laughter is deep and soothing, his face alight. "Same age as you? Ah, 'dude'..." He seems awkward with the word, dude, but laughs it off, "...yeh flatter me somethin' awful there!" His laughter subsides, "Not meanin' to be rude, but could you spare a fag perchance? I ain't had a proper ciggy in weeks..."

I shake my head, "Sorry, don't smoke."

"No wonder yez feckin stressed out..." He shrugs, "Ah but where's me manners? Here's me yakkin' on and I ain't even had the courtesy to share me name with yeh!" He holds out a strong hand towards me, "Reynardine O'Connor, pleased to meet yeh."

Hesitantly, I take his hand. Despite the strength of his handshake, his skin is surprisingly soft. "Dave..." I reply, softly, softer than I intend to. I clear my throat nervously, not certain what's wrong with me. My hand and his remain locked for longer than I feel comfortable with, and I slowly pull away. "Reynardine, eh?" I say, trying to break the silence that seems to hang between us, "That's an uncommon sort of name..." I sound like such a dork!!

Reynardine raises an eyebrow, "Rather I'd be named something teh be remembered, than be named something teh be forgotten. All the Daves in the world, like the Johns and the Smiths, all them common names, they all pass away. Smoke in the wind. Yeh can pardon me if I'd rather have something a little less easily forgotten."

BORDERLINES

"Yeah, I guess I can see the logic in that..." I trail off and find myself staring at Reynardine. This peculiar archaism, this strange Irish guy, quite unlike any other person I've met before... Perhaps it's fanciful to think it, but something about him seems beyond human, enchanting... It's with a certain amount of shock I find myself unable to look away from him and again my mouth goes dry.

"Yeh keep staring, Dave..." Reynardine smiles, extending a hand to my face, placing the tips of his fingers against my cheek. My face is growing hot, every hair on my body bristles with his touch and I shudder, I pull away instinctively, but his fingers brush my skin again, soothing my apprehension, as waves soothe a cliff, and so inexorably destroy it. For an instant, I feel ready to embrace that destruction, to give myself fully, utterly...

I shake my head, I blurt out my excuses, "I... I have places I need to be..." I stammer, my mind is racing and I feel my heart fit to burst in my chest. His eyes meet mine, "I have to go..." I insist, pleadingly, trying desperately to shake this wild emotion, this nonsensical surge.

"No yeh don't..." Reynardine replies, allowing this truth to hang between us for a while. "Yeh're scared, confused a little maybe? Not felt this way afore I'll bet? Like I says, I have that effect sometimes..." He draws closer to me, hanging to him is the strong musk of forgotten fields, of lazy summers and wild heather, of wilderness and wildness, I close my eyes and draw his scent in deeply, powerless to do otherwise. "For what it's worth..." he says to me, his breath hot against my skin, "I'm not usually one for the fellas either... But I guess we can't be set in our ways now, can we? Variety bein' the spice o' life and all..."

"This doesn't make any sense..." I whisper to him, "I don't even know you..."

"And yeh never will..." he replies, with what I think is sorrow, regret. "Sorry just ain't strong enough a word fer what I'm feelin'. Yeh have to know, I don't do this to be cruel, not so's I can enjoy it, or get some sick thrill from it..." His embrace suddenly feels less comforting, more of a cushioned vice...

I open my eyes and begin to pull away from him, the enchantment fading, my heart now racing with an uncertain fear. But all my fear washes away in the next instant. Despite his strange words, his strange mannerisms, my own fear; despite it all I forget in that instant all the peculiarities of the situation.

What makes me forget it all is something I'd never have imagined as I

BORDERLINES

ran panicking for my lecture, or last night as I slaved over the draft of my essay and the revision notes for tomorrow's exam. In that skipped heartbeat I forget everything, the world and all its petty and pathetic concerns, melting into oblivion. Oblivion and contentment as his lips pressed softly against my own.

I didn't notice at first as the cold crept over my body. Didn't realise the warmth was slowly ebbing from me, like a bath drained of water, my lips the plug. I began to shiver, decreasing circles of heat bleeding from the edges of my body to my lips in rapid pulses, my body growing colder and colder, and icy chill unlike anything I had felt before.

I tried to push Reynardine away, but could not move my aching muscles, I managed to do little more than open my eyes. As I did, Reynardine pulled away from me, coiling vapours of a barely perceptible energy drawn wraith like from my lips into his. I didn't understand. As my body slumped back down into the bench, I did not understand. I was cold, too cold to even shiver, colder than any human being should ever feel. My eyes were locked with Reynardine's.

"I'm sorry..." He said to me, "But I have to survive. It's nothing personal, yeh understand. Yeh have what I need though, least yez did. Strong soul, strong enough to last me a few days afore I have teh find meself another. Heart attack they'll say, and yeh'll be missed I'm sure. Nothing personal... No hard feelings aye?"

Even though he has ended me, I want to reply, to tell him I forgive him. I'm trying to summon all my strength just to tell him that in that instant, I had loved him. He smiles warmly at me, and I know that he understands...

BORDERLINES

A R Marsh
MAYME

No one dared call her grandma, or mom or Mary. She was Mayme to everyone. Her children, her grandchildren, her friends and her co-workers.

My grandmother, Mayme, was my father's mother; however, I think in her mind she was everyone's mother. She had a cure for all ailments and a solution to every problem. I must have been ten or eleven when I fell off my bike and skinned my knees. She took care of the wounds with prodigious amounts of mercurochrome and aspirin, then disassembled the bike so it wouldn't happen again.

She owned a small coffee shop for a while. Her homemade donuts were the greatest, but she felt everyone should enjoy them – so if you were a little short? Not to worry, she'd get you next time. The word got out and every down-and-outer stopped in for coffee and a donut. Mayme ran out of money and had to close down the shop.

She then decided that she would just make donuts at home and sell them at her friend's place of business. Her friend owned a bar and sat at a stool next to the cash register, cigarette dangling from her lips, and collected bar tabs and donut bills. When the town learned that children were coming into the bar to buy donuts, Mayme had to close down again.

Mayme smoked, drank and loved to play poker. My first bartending job was making sure that Mayme's Canadian Club and water glass was kept full on those nights when the poker game was at our house. The kitchen was filled with smoke and laughter. Lots of laughter.

She had a job in the city one time demonstrating Mott's Apple Juice in a super market. She kept our refrigerator loaded with bottles of the stuff and, to this day, I cannot drink apple juice. She stayed in the city then and only came home on weekends.

She always brought friends to visit, the most frequent being Solly and Ralph who were quiet and never left the house. Sometimes they stayed longer than the weekend and there were a lot of hushed phone calls, but they always left more than enough money to pay for the calls. I had no idea who they were or what they did, but they were Mayme's friends and they always gave me a fifty cent piece when they left. Not too long ago (while watching an episode of the Sopranos) I swear I saw Solly and Ralph.

BORDERLINES

My fondest memory is summer time and the back porch. Mayme was now working in the cafeteria at a nearby mental institution. She brought me up a few times to meet her co-workers. They seemed nice enough, but just a bit off center. She started to bring some of them home for the weekend. It wasn't until I was older that I realized these guests were really patients who were allowed a weekend pass under the supervision of Mayme, the custodian.

Most weekends in the summer our screened-in porch had one or two people sleeping there. I don't remember what they did during the day. I wasn't around that much. My summer days were filled from early morning until dark. But when supper was over and the crickets and frogs began their nightly serenades I never minded going to bed. It was my favorite time because my bedroom window looked out on the back porch and I had a front row seat.

They laughed, they drank. They played cards or just sat around telling stories. I didn't understand them, but I loved to hear them and the great howls of laughter from my family and especially Mayme and all her guests. Their laughter was infectious and rolled and grew until everyone was doubled over.

The best memory is of Herbie. Herbie was small, elflike and he hopped. He didn't walk from place to place, he kind of skipped. Mayme brought Herbie home one weekend and announced that he would provide the entertainment that night. Herbie had produced, directed, and starred in his own film and we were going to view the opening night. He also wrote the musical score and would accompany the film with his accordion.

He set up the screen and his projector and, in his disjointed manner, moved from place to place as he made adjustments to the focus and position of the projector. The screen, which was really a bed sheet, had to be taut and wrinkle free as it was tacked to the wall of the porch. Herbie had to position his tiny body just so, in order to monitor the projector as it stuttered away while simultaneously playing the accordion to match the action on the screen. So there was Herbie narrating his film, playing the music, appearing as the lead role and acting as fulltime projectionist all at once. God, it was awful and I loved every minute of it.

It was the perfect parody of the silent film days. Bad guys hold good girl for ransom. Hero (Herbie) races to the rescue. Watching Herbie racing was a gem. He fought off the bad guys with the best gestures and expressions of Buster Keaton, Charlie Chaplin and Harold Lloyd. The hero won, of course, and the girl fell into his arms to a thunderous accordion finish.

BORDERLINES

The howls of laughter reached new heights that night, but not from Mayme. Herbie never came back and, when asked, Mayme solemnly answered that he had moved on.

I remember a lot of things about my grandmother. I remember rhubarb pie, tapioca pudding and infectious laughter. But most of all, I remember a person who was always ready to reach out a friendly hand to whomever she felt needed one.

BORDERLINES

Ina Albert
LETTER ON BEHALF OF MYSELF

Dear Gulliver,
   I have little to commend me to you, except my fondness for your mistress. My touch is clumsy and I lack even the most elementary knowledge of how to care for you. What's more, I am even nervous about my competence to walk you around the block.
   You must have sensed this when we first met. Though you greeted me effusively, I was reserved, though civil. It was hardly an appropriate salutation to one so young and in need of reassurance in a new and strange environment. I apologize for my standoffish behavior.
   You see I've never been a dog owner. My mother and her three sisters were mortally frightened of animals. Therefore, my cousins, my brother and myself all suffered from a psychological condition often referred to as 'pet deprivation.' We grew up having had no experience relating to members of your breed.
   My response to dogs and cats was reinforced by my parents who decided that my numerous allergies would most certainly be exacerbated by any contact with animals. Hence, every time we visited a home in which pets resided, my mother would insist that they be removed from the room, and preferably from the home, prior to our setting our foot over the threshold. And, even though all these preparations were made, one sneeze would mean my immediate exit from their household and a swift return to our pet-free environment.
   This explains my traumatic response to four-legged creatures from a very early age. However, as I got older the situation worsened.
   I recall one specific incident when I was nine. We were preparing to move from our city place in Philadelphia to an elegant suburb. My mother drove her sister Nan, my brother and me to inspect what was to be our new residence. Mother pulled up to the curb in front of the walk leading to the front door of a large stone and shingle home with a porch that wrapped around three sides of the dwelling. She beamed with pride and waited for my aunt's acknowledgment of the wisdom of her purchase even before opening the car door.
   "Wait until you see the inside, Nan. It has two fireplaces and a beamed ceiling in the dining room. And the staircase is magnificent;

BORDERLINES

complete with an arched window on the landing leading up to the second floor," Mother crowed.

As I gazed out of the rear window, the place looked enormous and forbidding to me. And, since it meant leaving friends and familiar surroundings, I was not enthusiastic about the move.

My mother, a woman whose frame never exceeded 4'10", opened the car door, sliding off the pillow on which she sat in order to see over the steering wheel. She stepped onto the pavement. My Aunt Nan, who stood tall at 4'11", slid out of the passenger's seat and joined Mother on the sidewalk.

My five-year old brother and I pushed the front seats of the two-door Chevy forward and climbed out to follow them. But, as we fell in behind the women, our soon-to-be neighbour came rushing onto her porch to welcome us.

"Yoo-hoo," she waved. "I've heard we're going to be neighbors and I want to introduce myself!"

Right behind her, two Scottie dogs bolted out of her front door and bounded down the steps and across the lawn to greet us.

Mother froze with one foot on the bottom step to the porch and the other on the front walk. My aunt, who suffered from the same animal phobia, stood stock still just behind her and began making whimpering sounds.

Even at my young age, I realized that these adults would be of absolutely no use in this situation. It was fight or flight time. Though I felt panic rising and my breath coming in short gulps, I knew that it was up to me to take action to protect my brother and me from these monsters. Would we be permanently contaminated if they touched us? What if they should bite? The horrifying thought of their teeth bared ready to draw blood propelled me to action. I grabbed my brother's arm and dragged him toward the car.

But, Mother was ahead of me. She had reversed herself and raced back toward the car with my aunt in hot pursuit. They both ignored the neighbor lady who started down her porch steps screaming at us, "Don't be afraid. The dogs are friendly. They won't bite!"

But the poor woman had no understanding of the dread that her loveable mutts could inspire in those afflicted with a terror of animals. Mother and Aunt Nan were in the car with the doors slammed tight before they realized that my brother and I were still outside.

"Please, Mom," I screamed, pounding on the car door, "let us in.

BORDERLINES

They're going to get us!"

Much to her credit, Aunt Nan opened the door just wide enough so that we could scramble into the rear seat. My mother already had the motor running. The minute we were inside, the car shot down the street past the neighbor lady who had dashed to the curb waving her arms in a vain attempt to assure us there was no danger.

So you see, Gulliver, my reticence to stroke your shiny black coat and enjoy your tongue licking my hand comes from an ancestral aversion that I will try hard to overcome.

I ask you to be patient with me. Knowing how fond my dear friend, your mistress, is of you, I will make every effort to overcome my genetic deficiency and cultural deprivation. I ask your indulgence during the debriefing process and promise you that I will mend my ways, face my fears, and take a healthy dose of allergy pills before each visit.

Sincerely,

Ina Albert
Newest member of the ASPCA

Anita Sheard
UNIMAGINABLE CHOICE

In the days of Nebel und Nacht
Of secrets in the face of lies
Choice meant life or death
Simple; conform or die.

Yet Sophie Scholl
Chose life through death
That we might be saved –
Germans, English, allies, axis
For we were all guilty.

The whole world borne
On their narrow shoulders.
You talk about choice?
Which bill can I pay?
My triviality disgusts me.

Liz Barlow
DEAR JOHN (LETTERS TO THE DEAD)

The grief hit me like a spade. The news was words down the telephone. Speech in my ear of a foreign concept; a spade in the tooth that no dentist could fix, and a rush to the stomach like the tubes to your veins.

Should I cry when they push your coffin past me? You told me I'd put on weight – I might resent you still, long enough to hold it all in.

Your tombstone will see through me like you always did in life. Cut the smiles and go straight for the bone, and then make me laugh. But there will be no words from your mouth to rock me to silence, no wisdom of yours to pervade. I always wanted to prove you wrong.

I mentioned you in a poem. I read it out with the voice that you helped me find with after school chats and Tori Amos songs. I hated that you let me rebel – knew I was a good girl trying to break out. You hated the girls that I hated. Said you'd break the legs of any boy who hurts me – who will do the boyfriend bashing now, when I really need it? You who could break me with a sentence.

Will they cremate the razorblade scars on your inside arm, like some middle-class heroin addict? Will they bury them?

You taught me about fine wine.
The taste, the suck, the embarrassing rush to my head when I refused to spit.

You don't die in my version of events. I visit you in a few weeks. I tell you about my life here. I moan about my boyfriend because I think that's what you want to hear. You moan about your boss and trail off on some story from your teenage years.

I never considered your funeral, or me, alone on the sofa, drenched in tears, grasping onto memories that suddenly charge through me in bolts.

BORDERLINES

Ali Shaw
EXTRACT FROM A LIFE

Pia McKenzie loved music. Her favourite toy was a xylophone and for her sixth birthday she had chosen a little stringed instrument, like a miniature harp called a zither. Her family did not own a piano or any other musical instruments, although her father had once played the trumpet. Music was not really something encouraged at home but Pia loved to sing and was hoping to be chosen for the First Year Junior Choir.

Mrs Abrahams, the music teacher was a tall, thin lady with rather a stern manner. She was the kind of person always appeared to be cross about something, even when there was not really anything to be cross about. The children, a mixture of boys and girls all aged about seven filed into the large, light filled assembly hall, chattering and whispering amongst themselves.

"Come along children, settle down, settle down," said Mrs Abrahams, sounding a little bit annoyed already. "Now, I want some of you to stand in a line along here, and the rest of you are to stand up behind on the form which Mr Wilson is going to bring out for you... Mr Wilson!" She called his name loudly with an emphasis on the last syllable so as to catch the attention of the old school caretaker just as he was about to shuffle out of the door. Mr Wilson nearly jumped out of his skin and all the children laughed

"Be quiet!" barked Mrs Abrahams with a stern look that signified she was not about to tolerate any nonsense.

Mr Wilson nodded and then limped painfully to the far end of the hall and lifted one of the heavy wooden benches out of the cupboard. Then he dragged it the whole length of the room at a torturously slow pace, huffing and puffing as he went. Finally he reached the spot at the other end where the children were assembled and he set down the bench in front them by the piano.

"Thank you," said Mrs Abrahams. "You may go now."

Pia looked into the old man's eyes and felt very sorry for him. It must be awful being bossed around by Mrs Abrahams, even when you had a bad leg.

"Now," said Mrs Abrahams as Mr Wilson left the room in silence. "As you know we are here today to choose the choir. The rehearsals will be

BORDERLINES

every Wednesday afternoon and the performance will be on the last day of term at the Parents' Assembly. It's going to be a lot of hard work, so I don't want any time-wasters."

She sat down at the piano and began to shuffle some pages of sheet music before finally choosing a song.

"Now, most of you will know this hymn already so I want you to sing along as best you can and I will listen carefully to see what I can do with you. She sat down at the piano, adjusted her sleeves began to play the first few bars.

Pia's heart leapt. She knew the hymn very well. It was "All Things Bright and Beautiful." She had learned it in infant school and she knew all the words by heart. The introduction swelled and the children began to sing.

Their twenty voices made quite a harmonious sound but it wasn't long before everyone noticed a strange croaking noise coming from the front row. The other children had been quite surprised when Peter Ryan had volunteered for the choir. He was a scrawny little boy in crumpled clothes whose two front teeth had somehow become fused together with all the plaque to form a kind of giant yellow uni-tooth. He couldn't sing at all and was immediately weeded out by Mrs Abrahams who told him he would have to play the triangle.

The song began again and Pia concentrated hard so that she wouldn't make any mistakes. She and the remaining children sang the words at the top of their voices

> "All things bright and beautiful,
> All creatures great and small,
> All things wise and wonderful,
> The lord God made them all."

Pia liked the next part of the song, where the verse shifts into a minor key and she closed her eyes, enjoying the sound of the voices as they all sang:

> "Each little bud that opens,
> Each little bird that sings,
> He made their flowing colours,
> He made their tiny wings....
> All things bright and..."

BORDERLINES

"STOP!" shouted Mrs Abrahams. "STOP, stop, stop, stop."

The children ground to a halt and looked at their teacher in bewilderment.

"No, no, no …this won't do at all," said Mrs Abrahams sounding dreadfully irritated, as though she'd had quite enough of them already. She looked accusingly towards the children, her eyes scanning the assembled group, her chin raised, nostrils flaring slightly. She sharply drew in some breath before finally announcing

"SOMEBODY doesn't fit in."

The children felt a clammy sense of unease. They looked nervously at each other before lowering their gaze so as not to attract any attention, each secretly fearing he or she might be the criminal who was ruining the song.

"I'm going to have to hear you one by one," said Mrs Abrahams crossly. "Now, start the song again on the count of four and this time I'll come and listen to you each in turn to see if we can find the problem."

The song began and Mrs Abrahams walked along the line peering towards each of children, so close that they could smell her musty breath. First she made her way along the front row, then she slowly weaved her way back between the lines leaning her left ear towards those at the back who were standing up on the bench. She had almost circled the entire class without finding any culprits when finally she arrived in front of Pia.

Pia carried on singing, looking straight ahead, hoping very much that the teacher wouldn't find any fault with her, but Mrs Abrahams had heard something. Her brow furrowed and her nose wrinkled and with a look of satisfaction in her eye she turned towards Pia and said,

"It's you!"

"Me?" said Pia.

"Yes, you." said Mrs Abrahams.

"What a very peculiar tone you have," she continued. "I'm very sorry my dear, but it doesn't fit in. Doesn't blend in with the others, you see? I'm afraid you're going to have to play the triangle with Peter."

Pia climbed down from the bench feeling as dejected as old Mr Wilson. Her cheeks flushed bright red as she slunk off to the side of the hall to join Peter Ryan who was still trying to untangle the triangle from the box of percussion instruments.

Pia walked home from school by herself that evening. She made her way down the hill past the railway bridge and then took a turn into the

BORDERLINES

familiar grass verged avenue with houses and trees dotted along it every few yards.

Her family's house was in the village of Westchester in the middle of a long road called the Blueway. Halfway between the village station and the crematorium, a funny smell would sometimes drift across the family's back garden if the wind blew in a certain direction. Pia's father said it came from the "Bone Factory" somewhere on the other side of town. Pia and her two brothers and sister knew that the crematorium was the place where people's bodies went to be put in the oven when they were dead; they often saw the black cars full of flowers and people with sad faces driving past the end of their road and so Pia had assumed that the "Bone Factory" was one of her father's funny sayings, when really he meant the crematorium. She would shudder deeply and run into the house if ever she smelt the smell. She made a point of saying to her mother that if ever she was to die she did not want to be cremated in case she was actually still alive and could not get out of the coffin. This had been her worst fear for as long as she could remember. But then again, what if you were buried in the coffin in the graveyard and you suddenly woke up in the dark and couldn't get out? That would be awful! Pia's brother Daniel said that she would be eaten alive by the worms and that after a few weeks there would be maggots coming out of her eye holes.

Pia could just about imagine herself 'decomposing', which is what her father had said it was called, when she asked him if what Daniel had said about the eyeholes was true. But you couldn't always believe what your father said because once, when she was little she had asked him about where she came from and he said that he had found her under the gooseberry bush. The gooseberry bush? Didn't she get wet in the rain? How long had she been there before he found her? For a while every time she passed it on her way up the garden path towards the swing she would stare at the bush in puzzlement. By now of course, she knew that people came out of their mother's stomachs, although she wasn't all that clear about how they got in there. But she was pretty sure that she could believe what her father had explained about things decomposing, because once she had found the body of a mouse at the end of the garden which had all but disappeared apart from its skeleton and a few tufts of fur. She liked the sound of the word "decompose." It seemed like a good word. It was the opposite of the word "compose", which she also liked. A composer, she had recently discovered, was somebody who listened to all the separate notes of music and wrote them down in a special order to make a song. She knew from playing her xylophone that you sometimes had to leave the right length of silence in between the notes too. There were only seven notes in the whole World, (ABCDEFG) but all the songs that were ever written came out of those few letters, although there were some 'in between' letters too that called 'flat' or 'sharp'.

Pia dawdled along the road singing softly to herself. She tried to catch the sound of her voice so that she could hear what it was about it that Mrs Abrahams hadn't liked, but she couldn't tell. Her mind turned to the song "Frere Jacques", which apart from "All Things Bright and Beautiful" was her favourite song. She thought that the composer of "Frere Jacques" must be very clever because if some children began to sing the first line, just as the other children were singing the second line, then all the notes and rhythms blended together to make a beautiful sound. Everybody knew "Frere Jacques." It was a good song and it helped you to learn French too, because it was about a little boy who fell asleep.

"Frere Jacques. Frere Jacques, Dormez-vous? Dormez-vous? Compose, composer, compose."

She said the words aloud to herself enjoying the sound of the "p's" as she reached the gate of her house. A composer was a much nicer thing than a decomposer, Pia decided. She shuddered for a moment as she thought of all the dead people in their coffins. Suddenly she thought of something strange. If a song was composed by a composer, did that mean it could be decomposed too? She imagined a piece of sheet music written by the man who wrote "Frere Jacques" who she thought most likely had a beard. But he accidentally dropped the piece of paper in the road one day on the way home from work, when he was in a rush, like when her father lost the car keys. The piece of paper containing the music would most likely get wet in the rain and turn to mush and then it would probably disappear away to nothing in the end like the mouse. She felt a bit sad as thought about it. She imagined the sound of the lovely song slowly fading away as the ink dripped off the paper, never to be heard again. But what if the composer already knew the song by heart? He'd be able to write down the song all over again and it wouldn't even matter! That cheered her up again. And he might have already sung the song to some of his friends and they might know it by heart too.

"Composer, compose, composer compose."

Pia ran up the garden path so deep in thought that she almost didn't see her brother Billy who was coming out of the back gate towards her. He was carrying a slug in his out-stretched palm for her to see so Pia leant

BORDERLINES

forward and stared at its slimy body and waving tentacles for a moment and then the two children walked around the side of the house together and put the slug back down in the vegetable patch where Billy had found it.

Pia noticed that her brother had been digging again. Billy was four now and he hardly ever spoke to anybody but he liked to dig and the garden was pock-marked with examples of his handy-work. By the wall was the hole where he had tried to dig a tunnel into next doors garage, because he wanted to know what old Mr Johnson kept in there. Next to the runner beans was an oval shaped pit, which he said was going to be a swimming pool for the worms and finally at the end of the garden behind the shed, was the largest hole of all, which lead directly to Australia.

Billy had enormous pale blue eyes and white hair and white eyelashes and their older sister Susannah had told all her friends that he was an Albino even though he wasn't. Susannah was twelve and she was and sometimes she was left in charge of her younger brothers and sister when their mother was out. Susannah had a friend was called Lucy Buzzard who was a 'bad influence.' One day, when Susannah was supposed to be looking after Pia, Lucy came round and the two girls decided that they wanted to 'go shopping'. There was a little row of shops in the village, a bakery where you could get broken biscuits, a post office, the hairdresser's, the greengrocer's and the sweetshop. First of all Susannah and Lucy shut themselves in the bedroom whispering to each other for ages and when they came out they said that they were going to the shops and that if Pia wanted to come she had to wear her purple shoulder bag. Pia didn't want to wear her purple shoulder bag. She didn't like it because it was crocheted and the strap itched her but Susannah said that she had to wear the shoulder bag, otherwise she would tell mum about when Pia wet herself and buried the knickers in the garden. They all walked down the road with Pia lagging reluctantly behind until finally they reached the sweet shop. The children went in and Susannah spent a long time choosing some penny sweets making a fuss about who would eat which ones later and finally she took them over to the till by the front door to pay. She spoke nicely to Mrs Potts who was smiling and laughing as she counted the sweets into a white paper bag and rang up the money in the till, meanwhile at the back of the shop Lucy Buzzard was picking up a handfuls of chocolate bars and sweets and was shoving them into Pia's handbag.

Pia felt the bag getting heavier and heavier as the Mars Bars, Marathons and a can of Coke were loaded in. She stood stock still,

BORDERLINES

mortified as it dangled from her shoulder, certain that Mrs Potts would see at any moment. She daren't move, the bag was bulging and rustling, her face was going crimson with shame. She stood there rooted to the spot until finally Mrs Potts said "Goodbye dearies," and Lucy pushed Pia towards the doorway glaring so hard that she didn't dare to utter a sound. Outside the shop Pia was overwhelmed by the shock of it all and began to cry. Susannah and Lucy said that she had better shut up or they would tell Mum that she had been stealing. Lucy was a definitely a bad influence. Susannah was usually kind and nice to Pia but she did bad things when Lucy was around.

Pia looked through the kitchen window to see if her mother was there, but she wasn't. Pia hoped her mother wouldn't ask her how she had got on at school that day. She felt sad that she couldn't be in the choir. It had been embarrassing when she had to stand down away from the other children. Pia walked up the garden path towards the swing as the September sunshine warmed her back. She took off her shoes and socks and ran through the cool long grass into the shade of the pear tree. A scent of honeysuckle from the hedge drifted over and she breathed it in with delight. Pia's little brother Billy followed her up the path to the swing and as she sat on its broad, wooden seat and held onto the rusty chains, he stood behind and gave her a push. Soon she was flying through the air, higher and higher, the air whooshing against her skin. She called to Billy to "mind out" just in time and he jumped aside just as her feet were about to crash into him.

Billy was always falling over. He was always cutting himself or grazing his knees or bumping his head. When he was born he had yellow jaundice and he had to go in the oxygen tent because he couldn't breathe. One day he said that he could remember being in the oxygen tent and that it had a funnel and was green. He said that the doctor who had helped his mother in the hospital had a bald spot on the top of his head and that he knew that he did have, because he had seen it from the ceiling. Pia told their mother about it and she said that the funny thing was that the oxygen tent was green and the obstetrician did have a bald patch.

Once Billy ran out in front of the milk float and was nearly run over. Then, when he was three he almost died because of a pear –drop. The car swerved when a dog ran out and the sweet slipped right down his throat. Their father pulled over and desperately thumped the little boys back, shaking him as hard as he dared but the sweet was firmly lodged. Daniel, who was eight at the time, said that that a person can only go without air

BORDERLINES

for four minutes and then their brain gets ruined. After three minutes Billy went limp and his face was blue. Pia watched as her mother ran along the pavement, calling for help, crying out for a telephone, but they were near an old factory, it was Sunday and nobody was there. Finally their father held Billy upside down by the legs with one hand and with the other he hooked his fingers right down inside the child's throat. The sweet suddenly flew out and landed on the pavement in front of them.

Pia swung higher and higher that afternoon, enjoying the sunshine and marvelling at the blue of the sky. She wondered what it would be like to go up to the sky. She knew that Heaven was up in the sky and she knew that children were christened so that if they were to die they would be able to go to Heaven, but Billy, who had nearly died three times already, had not been christened at all and so Pia felt worried for him. Her parents couldn't remember why Billy hadn't been christened. They said that it was too late now and that they would wait until he was old enough to decide for himself whether or not he wanted to be christened but Pia thought this was a bit risky under the circumstances. All the other McKenzie children had been christened. Pia was proud of her own christening because she had seen a certificate which said that it had taken place in the Church of St Mary's, which was the little chapel that lay inside the grounds of an old castle about a mile away from their home. Sometimes they would go there for a picnic. They didn't go to the services anymore because their father said it was a sham but once her mother had taken the children inside the church to say their prayers and the vicar had shown them the special book with all the names and addresses of everyone who had ever been christened there. And there was Pia's name among them.

There were no photos of the christening though. There were no photographs of Pia at all because her father had had to sell his photography equipment when she was born. There were no pictures of Billy either which was worrying because what if one day he were not to have such a lucky escape from one of his accidents?

Pia let the swing slow down to a halt and she stared into her little brother's face as he stood in a pool of light by the pear tree. She tried to remember his features by heart, the slightly bulbous nose, the floppy white fringe, the cobalt eyes, the scar on his eyebrow from when he fell off his tricycle. It would be awful if Billy didn't go to Heaven. Where would he go to instead? He always said his prayers. He always ate his dinner up and said please and he was even kind to spiders. Pia wondered if God mightn't let Billy go to Heaven after all? It didn't seem right if he wouldn't. If Billy didn't go to Heaven that meant it would just be a drive up the Crem in one of the big black cars for him. They'd put him in the oven and that would be that. Tears began to roll down Pia's cheeks at the thought of it.

"Lets go in now," said Billy feeling uneasy as his sister wept quietly on the swing. "Mum's made fairy cakes."

Pia wiped her eyes and the two children made their way back down the garden towards the house.

Callum Graham
THE HOBGOBLIN

I watch her in the glass,
Brooding,
Dark and mysterious.

The Hobgoblin dances
Across my mouth.

So difficult to fathom,
The light and shadow change her,
Amber to black,
A rich poison.

A villain of the worst kind,
She strikes
From within.

But she whispers,
Soothes me,
Hushes heavily

And once the glass is empty,
Only time will take her.

Jade Juilien
TULIPS

She has waited all winter,
to watch the red arrow heads
of her husbands' tulips shoot up from the ground,
like paint drying.

The family opposite
have kids like cockroaches,
they leak out of their house.

They never liked her gardener.

Looking at the garden path,
she longs for him now.

The way each bulb he planted,
he held like the carcass of a baby.

She liked to buy him expensive biscuits,
the ones that came in tins.

Some days she would try
and keep him inside,
he listened like an empty room

and nodded like her father
when she was a little girl,
breathing in
her fallow tulip filled years.

Slowly they open,
as if little monkeys
had come in the night
and peeled the petals open
hoping for bananas.

BORDERLINES

Her face like wax melting,
no post today,
no gifts of gas bills

and her gardener no longer visits.
Apparently her tulips
are fine.

Except today,
their cheap lipstick red colour
like squashed tomatoes
in the grass.

How pretty a tree would have been.

With muddy hands,
she rips them out of the ground.

Like a crow on a cadaver,
she eats her tulips by the dozen.

BORDERLINES

Contributors

Ina Albert
Ina Albert is co-author of *Write Your Self Well...Journal Your Self to Health*, a journal/workbook written for people suffering from illness and stress based on research demonstrating the health benefits of expressive writing. As a healthcare public relations professional, trainer, workshop facilitator and consultant, Ina has written numerous articles for healthcare publications during her 35 year career. Her work is included in *The Art of Grief* (Routledge Press) and her short stories for children and adults have appeared in various publications including *Parent Magazine*. She lives and writes in Whitefish, Montana.

Linda Albert
A lifelong member of the theatrical community, Linda has acted, directed and worked on play adaptations. Her academic essays, creative fiction, non-fiction short stories and poems have appeared in many publications, including *McCalls Magazine* and *The Wall Street Journal*. Among Linda's awards are the Olivet and Dyer-Ives Foundation Poetry Prizes. She is a recipient of the International Merit Award in *Atlanta Review*'s 2007 International Poetry Competition. Linda resides in the United States at Longboat Key, Florida with her husband. Visit her online at www.lindaalbert.net.

Jane Anderson
Jane Anderson grew up in York, leaving at the age of eighteen to join the Women's Royal Naval Service. Two children and a variety of administrative jobs later, she returned to study and is currently approaching the final year of a part-time degree in Humanities at the University of Portsmouth. This is the first time her work has been published. She has recently reduced her working hours, aiming to concentrate on her degree, and her long-term ambition is to continue with creative writing. She is married and lives in Portsmouth.

BORDERLINES

Brian Appleton
Brian Hanson Appleton was born in 1950 in Tokyo, Japan. He has a BA Degree in Anthropology from George Washington, University. He has been a professional lighting designer and manufacturer's representative for the past 28 years. He has just published his first book *Tales From The Zirzameen* about his experiences in Iran in the 1970s, and the revolution of 1979 during which he was taken hostage. His second book also non-fiction; a biography about four generations of an Assyrian family is complete and will follow in a year. He speaks Farsi, Italian, French and conversational Greek. His hobbies are writing, reading, martial arts, skiing, scuba, travelling. He has a wife, Laura, and two sons, Luke and Alex. Read more about Brian and his new book at www.zirzameen.com.

Liz Barlow
Liz is a third year Creative Writing and Media student at the University of Portsmouth. The three poems included in this anthology are taken from her dissertation portfolio, which aims to explore the female authoritative voice through Confessionalism.

Quentin Bates
With several abandoned careers behind him, Quentin Bates fell into writing for a living in an obscure branch of journalism largely by accident. After repeatedly dismissing fiction writing as a complete mug's game, the only thing to do was give it a try – hence enrolling on the Creative Writing MA at Portsmouth University where he has just completed a new crime novel set in Iceland.

Dean Borok
Dean Borok is the nephew of Nobel Prize-winning author Saul Bellow. The circumstances of his birth are recounted in the denouement of Bellow's groundbreaking novel, *The Adventures of Augie March*. After many years of living abroad, Borok returned to the U.S. and worked as an accessory designer for top Fifth Avenue fashion houses. With the advent of the Internet, Borok, who had previously disdained the politics of publishing, started to write directly to the public. He operates a Dada-ist comedy Web site at www.200motels.net.

BORDERLINES

Andrea Bowie
Andrea was brought up on a large farm but is quite scared of chickens. She likes to sit in cardboard boxes and one day, when she grows up, she would like to have a house with a gold knocker on the door and an endless supply of crumpets with marmite.

Diana Bretherick
Former criminal barrister Diana Bretherick lectures in Criminology and Criminal Justice at the University of Portsmouth. She teaches, reads and writes about crime but has not yet committed one – however there is still time... Diane is enrolled on the MA in Creative Writing at Portsmouth University and writing an historical crime novel.

Cat Coles
Cat is currently a student at the University of Portsmouth studying English and Creative Writing. She loves writing poetry and singing. She wants to be a publisher when she leaves university and publish her own anthology. She has previously been published in *2001: A Poetry Odessey*. She has also made her own album called *Bonafide and Counterfeit*.

Aby Davis
Aby is on the undergraduate Creative Writing programme entering her third year and writes critical reviews and writers profiles for Hackwriters.com. She has profiled authors Jon Grimwood and Beverley Birch this year and she likes to run away to Thailand whenever she can. She is currently writing a children's novel.

John M. Edwards
John M. Edwards is a Mayflower descendant and oil millionaire, who is part owner of America's "oldest personal holding company." He has travelled worldwide (five continents plus), getting into adventures as various as surviving a ferry sinking off the coast of Thailand to being stuck in a military coup in Fiji. His work has appeared in such magazines as *CNN Traveller, Missouri Review*, Salon.com, *Grand Tour, Islands, Escape, Richmond Review, Michigan Quarterly Review,* and *North American Review*. He recently won a NATJA (North American Travel Journalists Association) Award and a Solas Award. He is working on two future best-sellers, *Move* and *Fluid Borders*. He lives in a loft in New York City.

BORDERLINES

Anona Evans
Born in Wales, Anona obtained a BA Honours in Film Studies and Creative Arts from the University of Portsmouth. Her fiction includes elements of the gothic and fairy tales. She is now on the MA in Creative Writing at the University of Portsmouth and writing a childen's novel.

Ria Floyd-Berry
Ria is currently studying Drama and Film rather inefficiently at the University of Portsmouth. She is extremely interested in modern, political and cultural art, with a penchant for surrealism and expressionism. She is desperate to finish her degree and travel the world.

Callum Graham
Callum is a first year student studying Media and Creative Writing at Portsmouth university. He has a great a love of reading and writing, in particularly using people and the world around him as stimulus for his work. He also plays guitar and has an interest in film production.

Josephine Green
Jo is currently studying for a BA in English and Creative Writing at the University of Portsmouth. She has previously had various articles and reviews published on the international writer's online magazine Hackwriters.com. Much of her work is inspired by her travels and she recalls some of her earliest memories being from the early nineties when she lived in Sri Lanka. After finishing the days' homework she would spend afternoons at the swimming club in Colombo, surrounded by palm trees and sunshine, overlooking the Indian Ocean.

Alison Habens
Alison Habens is a senior lecturer in Creative Writing at the University of Portsmouth and the author of three novels (*Dreamhouse, Family Outing* and *Lifestory*). This short story, *The Magic of Marriage*, written for a workshop, attempts to crystalise the plot of a further novel *Pencilwood* in a thousand words so it is different in style from her usual 'postmodern' literary fiction.

BORDERLINES

Carolyn Hughes
Right now, Carolyn is obsessed with mediaeval England - bubonic plague, smoked-filled hovels, revolting peasants. She finds the whole grisly business deeply fascinating. Whether the obsession will pass once she's written her novel, only time will tell, though she thinks this is highly doubtful.

Calvin Hussey
Calvin Hussey was born and raised in Portsmouth and is currently studying Film and Creative Writing at Portsmouth University. He grew up on a diverse mixture of authors such as Hunter S. Thompson, Terry Pratchett, Philip K. Dick, and Brett Easton Ellis. Writing is a great passion of his and he continues to work in the fields of journalism and fiction. Calvin also takes a keen interest in music, promotion and production. He is currently working on an all-encompassing multimedia entertainment web industry Excess Dog, due to launch in spring 2009.

Olivia James
Olivia was born on 11 December 1972 and is currently in her fourth and final year of a BA (Hons) degree in French and European Studies at the University of Portsmouth, which is her first degree. Born and brought up in London, educated at a boarding school in Kent, she has been a secretary, waitress and TEFL teacher. After finishing her degree, she hopes to live in Paris for at least two years, to improve her French. She has previously had an article published in 2002 in the *Galactosaemia Support Group Magazine* (galactosaemia being a genetic metabolic disorder.)

Rachel Chan Suet Kay
Rachel Chan Suet Kay is a wannabe sociologist with a penchant for ending up in shorts and slippers. She has co-written a book with like-minded people on women's issues in Malaysia entitled *Young Women Speak Out*. Currently she is dabbling in the art of self-indulgence while awaiting the green light to prolong her childhood by going back to university. She wants to reiterate that she is 22, although she is not getting any younger.

BORDERLINES

Tracey Leach
Born in 1987, Tracey is the youngest of three girls to Henry and Gillian Leach. She is currently studying for a degree in English and Creative Writing at the University of Portsmouth. Tracey takes her inspiration from her immediate surroundings as well as wider influences, with a strong interest in the inter-relationships of human-kind. These are the first poems of Tracey's to be published, and are dedicated to her family whom she loves dearly.

Victor Manley
Victor Manley is currently in his third year as a student of English and Creative Arts at Portsmouth University, and next year he plans to do an M.A. in Creative Writing at Portsmouth. He is interested in both poetry and prose, particularly those novels which brush most casually past the pretentious end of the literary spectrum (i.e. Proust, Joyce, Tolstoy). He hopes one day to single-handedly reignite this country's sleeping passion for poetry, but until that day he will amuse himself by cultivating his own arrogance. His only previous publication has been on Hackwriters.com.

A.R. Marsh
Born in New York and raised in New Jersey, A.R. Marsh attended Rutgers University following a stint in the U.S. Navy. After raising his family and retiring from a long career in business, A.R. and his wife relocated to central North Carolina. Twice a Weymouth Center for the Arts & Humanities short story award winner, A.R. pursues his passion for the written word in the small town of Southern Pines.

Louise Mathewson
Louise holds a Masters degree in Pastoral Studies from Loyola University in Chicago. An author and poet, her work has appeared in numerous publications including *Wordgathering: Journal of Disability Poetry, Cup of Comfort* (Vol. 1), *Mochila Review, Boulder County Kid* and *Sasee* magazines. Louise has always loved to write about the sacred moments in everyday experiences, but today those experiences hold even deeper meaning. In February 2003 Louise emerged from a two-week coma following an auto-accident in which she suffered a traumatic brain injury. Though a struggle at first, Louise resumed writing as soon as she was able. Today she lives with her husband in Eden Prairie, Minnesota where she continues to write and recover.

BORDERLINES

E. Morice-Atkinson
November 19th 2002 was the day when something happened. She boarded a Boeing 747 in Brisbane bound for London on a one-way ticket. Armed with a pen, journal and 23 hours of solid flying time, she wrote furiously. A year later she managed to pause and look up at England, triumphantly leaving Australia as ink on the page.

Nikesh Murali
Nikesh Murali has published several collections of poetry online with international publishers. His works have been translated into seven languages and featured at international book festivals including the 29th Feria del Libro festival held in Buenos Aires. They have appeared in anthologies, journals and magazines all over the world. His poems and short stories have won and have been short listed for several major writing contests. He was nominated for the PUSHCART PRIZE in 2007 by Shalla Magazine. He was awarded the IFLAC-MCA Bilingual Club Poets for Peace award in 2006.

Sam North
Sam is the course leader of the Masters in Creative Writing at the University of Portsmouth and Director of the Borderlines project. He is the editor of www.hackwriters.com - the international writers journal and the author of several novels, notably *Another Place to Die*, *The Curse of the Nibelung – A Sherlock Holmes Mystery* and his new novel being published this June 2008 *Mean Tide*.

Linda Regan
Linda is currently studying at Portsmouth University for an Masters degree in Creative Writing. Her previous publications include two crime novels, *Behind You!* and *Passion Killers*, both published by Creme De La Crime and available on Amazon, and good book shops. She is an actress turned novelist, www.lindareganonline.co.uk.

BORDERLINES

Freya Scott
Freya is a passionate, playful, part-time feminist currently in her third metamorphic year of a scintillating English and Creative Writing degree at Portsmouth University. She plans to do an M.A. in Creative Writing next year, because it is too much hassle to move away. She founded the much revered University Creative Writing Society, and has enjoyed an erratic presidency for the last two years. Likes to love, laugh, and linger unexpectedly. In all seriousness, Freya is an impassioned writer with a predilection for all things coffee-flavoured.

Ali Shaw
Ali Shaw is the lead singer and lyricist of *The Cranes* on tour in Europe this year. She is graduating from the Masters programme in Creative Writing at the University of Portsmouth in 2008

Anita Sheard
Anita enjoys a symbiotic relationship with Cornwall where she lives with her partner, a dopey Rottweiler, a mad Terrier and 2 errant cats. She is 48 and still trying to make sense of it all... though writing helps!

Ryan Sirmons
Ryan is a dashing, young American writer, living in the UK. Writing has been his passion since learning his A, B, Cs. Finally, after several years in the navy, and three years in Europe, Ryan is ready to write the next "Great American Novel". He drives an Italian car, drinks Irish Whiskey, and summers in Michigan.

Steven Stemp
Student, Cynic, Geek. Steven has wanted to write since a very early age, and draws inspiration from - and has great admiration for - a mix of talent, from R. Scott Bakker to Douglas Adams. He is currently studying Media and Creative writing in sunny Portsmouth, with hopes of progressing to masters level. He has always seen the act of writing as being at least as important to humanity as procreation; indeed words are - in a sense – the author's children, born not of his Genes, but his Memes. Ultimately, his goal is to have a novel published before his death, not for commercial gain, but simply that even one person in the world might find inspiration in his words. Beyond that, let the dice fall where they may.

BORDERLINES

Russell Thomas
Born August 18th, 1988, in Surrey. Lived in town called Hersham - more like a village. Went to school for a bit. Wanted to be a writer. Came to University. Likes fashion and drinking. Still wants to be a writer.

Lisa Timmermann
After studying Film Studies at the University of Gloucestershire in Cheltenham, and at Concordia University in Montreal, German native Lisa R. Timmermann is currently enrolled on the MA Creative Writing programme at the University of Portsmouth and working on a mystery novel.

Rebecca Wass
Rebecca is currently in her second year at the University of Portsmouth studying English and Creative Writing. She lives near Penzance in Cornwall when not at university. When not writing she plays bass guitar, and spends her free time training to be a BSAC Ocean Diver.

Elizabeth Weaver
Elizabeth is a high school Language Arts teacher of the International Baccalaureate program by day and a full time doctoral student by night. She is in her last semester of coursework for a degree in Texts and Technology in the English Department. She is the author of a young adult coming of age novel, *Rooster* (Marshall Cavendish Publishers), which was an American Library Association Best Book for Young Adults as well as an ALA Top Ten Best Novel for Youth. She likes the challenge of writing short stories for adults.

Andrew Williams
Andrew Williams was born in London in 1965. He left school aged 15 to work for builders. Years later he returned to education and started to write. A keen musician, he played in many bands and once sang on stage with Shane McGowan. He plans to teach and continue writing.